PRAISE FOR ME(

'Meg Mundell's *The Trespassers* dis(commercially driven, punishment-focused migration system through three fine-grained human stories. Compelling writing and flinty observations make this chilling story all too believable.' – Jane Rawson

'Stylish, assured writing that rewards close reading. Mundell is a fine observer, and her descriptions are insightful and fresh. You will be held captive by this book – the story never flags. In a genre that is becoming increasingly popular, Mundell's work stands out for its literary quality.' – Graeme Simsion

'Beautifully written and absolutely gripping. I could not put *The Trespassers* down.' – Favel Parrett

'Original and compelling, *The Trespassers* is a thrilling novel with a brave and tender heart.' – Anna Krien

'A thought-provoking near-future thriller. *The Trespassers* is a riveting read.' – Jed Mercurio

'*Black Glass* is a superb debut. Meg Mundell has invented a compelling futuristic version of our urban world that is not only original but frighteningly recognisable.' – Chris Womersley

'Brooding, surreal and unsettlingly vulnerable, *Black Glass* marks the arrival of a striking new voice. A brilliant debut.' – James Bradley

'*Black Glass* is thoughtful, intelligent fiction.' – Sophie Cunningham, *Readings Monthly*

'*Things I Did for Money* is a collection of exciting and imaginative stories from one of our most innovative writers. This is a book for readers hungry for a highly original voice.' – Tony Birch

Meg Mundell is a writer and academic based in Melbourne. Her first novel, *Black Glass*, was shortlisted for two Aurealis Awards, the Barbara Jefferis Award and the Norma K. Hemming Award. She is the author of the story collection *Things I Did for Money*, and her fiction, essays and journalism have been widely published, including in *Best Australian Stories, Meanjin, The Age, The Monthly, The Guardian, The Sydney Morning Herald, The Australian Financial Review* and *Australian Book Review*. Meg is also the editor of *We Are Here: Stories of Home, Place and Belonging*, a collection of writings by people who have experienced homelessness.

THE TRESPASSERS

MEG MUNDELL

UQP

First published 2019 by University of Queensland Press
PO Box 6042, St Lucia, Queensland 4067 Australia

uqp.com.au
uqp@uqp.uq.edu.au

Cover design by Christabella Designs
Author photograph by Joanne Manariti
Typeset in Bembo Std 12/16pt by Post Pre-press Group, Brisbane
Printed in Australia by McPherson's Printing Group

The University of Queensland Press is
assisted by the Australian Government
through the Australia Council, its arts
funding and advisory body.

ISBN 978 0 7022 6255 5 (pbk)
ISBN 978 0 7022 6355 2 (pdf)
ISBN 978 0 7022 6356 9 (epub)
ISBN 978 0 7022 6357 6 (kindle)

A catalogue record for this book is available from the National Library of Australia.

University of Queensland Press uses papers that are natural, renewable
and recyclable products made from wood grown in well-managed forests.
The logging and manufacturing processes conform to the environmental
regulations of the country of origin.

For Andi and Charlie, who carry the light

Don't lie down on the sands where the hole in the sky is.
Too many people being gnawed to shreds.
Send me your voice however it comes across oceans.
Safety, safely, safe home.
– Carol Ann Duffy, 'Who Loves You'

THE
STEADFAST

1

CLEARY

Small for his age, and Irish too, Cleary was one of the last to board the ship. He stuck close to his ma as the queue shuffled along the dock between the chain-link fences. More than once he found himself pinned against the mesh, strangers' bodies pressed in tight around him: manky coats, a wide backside, a woman's perfumed hip. Beyond the fence the wharf dropped away to the river below. And everywhere, mixed with the dank scent of river water, the smell of other people.

There were kids in the crowd, the young ones clutching a soft toy or a parent's hand, the older ones shifting their backpacks and yawning. Painted on the ship's hull was a red star, and an unfamiliar word: *Steadfast*. Overhead a forest of masts and sails soared into an overcast sky, but the vessel itself seemed too narrow to hold all these people. Cleary recalled a magic trick he'd once seen in a Dublin train station, a traveller pulling an endless string of scarves from his mouth – but here the flow ran backwards. Could this skinny ship really swallow them all?

Space was tight, and the rules were strict. Suitcases stowed below, each passenger was allowed a single piece of hand luggage: essential items only, portable memories, treasures small enough to pocket. Only one toy per child, and no devices – they were banned. You could bring an old-style watch or closed console, but no tabs or linkups, nothing that hooked into the stream. This was for privacy's sake, his ma had said, to stop the snoops from gossiping. This morning the guards had scanned everyone, kids included, and seized two devices from their mortified owners, smashed them to bits on the cobbles while everyone pretended not to notice.

The English were boarding first. On the gangway a heavy-set man in an Arsenal tracksuit stumbled, dropping to one knee. Below on the dock the waiting Scots and Irish raised their arms in what looked like a cheer of encouragement, but probably was not. As the man tried to regain his feet he lurched against a woman dressed in black, knocking something from her grasp: a white box flew out over the rail, lost to the river below, and people peered down to see what had landed in the water. The woman in mourning gear pressed a hand to her cheek, like a person with bad toothache.

Cleary had become an expert watcher. He spotted an object down there in the murky water, now floating free of its box: a fancy cake, like the ones in shop windows, a pale mound topped with pink swirls. It listed sideways; the sea gave one rude belch, and the cake vanished, leaving a few sad bubbles in its wake. Nobody was laughing now. People turned away, as if embarrassed by its fate, and the woman in black stood motionless on the gangway until her husband took her arm and led her gently onto the ship.

The Scots were next to cross. As they shuffled through the last turnstile they waved back at their loved ones on the dock. From this distance, with the masks, you couldn't read their expressions, let alone their lips, but the ones left behind had a lost look. They dabbed their eyes, or hugged each other, or stood very upright, as if to prove that saying goodbye was nothing to make a fuss about. Further back, behind a line of police, a handful of protesters waved placards. Cleary strained to read the block letters: *Ship rats! Deserters! Travel makes trouble! Close all borders!*

This city they were leaving was not home. Beyond the barricades and old brick buildings rose Liverpool, a place they'd only seen in passing. Getting here had taken ages. All those appointments back in Dublin, the endless questions, his ma surrendering their data: gene profiles, health records, head reports. They'd jogged on a treadmill, been poked with needles, had their eyesight and hearing checked (he'd failed that one, of course, but his ma had argued their way through, shown his apt tests and references). They'd touched their toes, puffed hard into a tube, had their irises scanned, worn monitors for weeks. And these past few days at the depot, more tests and meds: mouth swabs, skin scrapes, pills to swallow, a nasty jab that left him feeling faint. They'd coughed into bags, pissed into containers. They'd even shat in one – that hadn't been easy.

Now, finally, they were off. As the last of the crowd trickled aboard the ship, Cleary felt a great tiredness sweep over him and pictured the cabin where they'd sleep. A round porthole, soft beds, a vidscreen. A table set for two, plates piled with roast meat – the real stuff, made from actual cows – plus spuds and gravy. And for afters, fancy cake, just like the one that sank. A rare treat, proper cake. He planned to have three pieces.

His ma tugged his arm. They cleared the final turnstile and there was the gangway, sloping up to the ship. She stepped onto it right foot first, for good luck, and Cleary did likewise. They crossed the strip of grey-green water onto the deck. A silver-haired man with rosy cheeks saluted them, gold braid on his cuffs and shoulders, and Cleary returned the salute. The captain, he must be.

The deck smelt of salt and wet rope, and here the mood had shifted. Passengers emerging from below had a distracted air, and those who'd jostled to board now stood at the rail, gazing landward, as if they wanted to cross back over. As if they'd changed their minds, or left something important ashore.

Now the dock was almost empty – just a scatter of police and workmen, and the people who'd been left behind. The gap between ship and dock was too wide to jump, the water beneath them a broad moat, the gunwale like the parapet of a castle. As the drawbridge was reeled in, Cleary gave his subjects below a kingly wave. A few strangers waved back, and some raised their heads as if calling out, masked messages he couldn't guess at from this distance.

As workmen swung the last of the cargo aboard, a flurry passed along the deck: vibrations, heads turning, fingers pointing. Craning his neck, Cleary tracked the fuss to its source. Splashed down the side of the dock, invisible from dry land, ran a violent slash of red; tall as a house and shining wet, the crimson bolt streaked down into the waterline.

Blood: some huge sea monster slaughtered here, thrashing itself senseless against the dock before sinking to the bottom to die.

Fear jellied his muscles. His mind filled with footage of the serpent, some diabolical creature of the deep, blood erupting from its mouth. His granda had told him about these monsters: huge mutants that patrolled the pitch-black reaches of the ocean floor, their genes scrambled by generations of toxic spills and sickened prey. Granda saw one once, out past Skibbereen: scared the bejesus out of him. The old man had rolled his eyes back in their sockets, acting out a monster driven mad by hate and hunger. A creature like that: it could creep up behind you, burst out of the water and snatch you off the deck, crack your spine with a single crunch.

Cleary's ma shook him, breaking the spell. She mimed a sweeping motion, then pulled her mask aside to mouth some words. He concentrated on her lips: *Pain ... it's pain!* What did she mean? She swiped an imaginary object back and forth, and he twigged: *Paint*, she was saying. *It's paint, sweetheart – just paint.* She slipped her mask back into place, glanced around to check no-one had seen.

Just paint being shipped off to some far-off factory or port: a load of spilt paint.

He took long breaths, as she'd taught him. Sensed his heart slowing down. These episodes of fright were sharply felt, but never lasted long; the crack soon mended, the world restored, by his mother's steady presence.

Crewmen were unmooring the ship now, tossing thick ropes across the gap, and tugboats nudged in close to tow them out into the harbour. And just like that, they were off – at sea. Or floating down the river, anyway.

He'd planned to feel a bit mournful at this point but instead felt a buzzing in his chest, anticipation cut with the afterglow of fright. He couldn't shake the image of that monster, a slippery mass of muscle rearing up to fix its mutant stare on him. One snap of those jaws and he'd be gone. Better keep his eyes peeled.

No-one had come to wave them off. The trip across to England was too expensive, the curfew rules too strict. The night their ferry left Dublin his gran and granda had been invisible in the crowd. His ma had cried, though she'd tried to hide it. Leaning against her legs he felt her sobs gradually ebb away as Dublin's lights shrank to pinpoints then vanished into the drizzle and darkness. *It's not forever, my love*, his gran had jotted in her spidery hand. *You'll be back home before you know it, when you're a bit taller.*

Now they slid past rusted ships, old cranes pointing up at nothing. Once clear of Liverpool they'd sail out past Holyhead, skim the Irish Sea, then head down through St George's Channel and on past Ireland, get one last glimpse of home if the weather would let them. Cleary saw his granda's finger tracing a line across the old globe on his desk, out through the Celtic Sea and on into a wide expanse of faded blue. When they reached the open water they'd be allowed to take off their masks.

How did the captain know which way to sail? Were there rocks in this channel, lurking beneath the floating rubbish? Cleary had always hoped to find a message in a bottle, but there were too many bottles here, like a layer of scum on soup, and no way to check what any of them held.

They were passing Holyhead when the deck boomed and reverberated beneath his feet. All around him people waved their arms, or blocked their ears, or clutched at each other, or just stood there staring landward as the ship's guns fired out a last farewell.

BILLIE

Billie flinched as gunfire split the air, covered her ears against the racket. Some ritual of departure, she guessed; shooting blanks, but loud enough to burst your eardrums. In the aftermath a hush descended and people gathered along the rail to watch England disappear.

She tracked the land's slow retreat, the churn of grey water unrolling in their wake. The ship skimmed through floating debris, clearing a temporary trail that vanished as the rubbish reconverged, like a zipper gliding shut. Seagulls wobbled overhead, filling the air with rusty screeches, and a sharp wind whipped her hair around.

People were clustered across the deck, the tribes already seeking each other out, a subtle sorting of accents and allegiances. Soon there'd be nothing but saltwater on every side, nine long and lurching weeks of it, with a ship full of anxious strangers for company. Sixty-odd days before they reached their destination, a far-off place that shimmered indistinctly in her mind: a blur of images and clips, promises and rumours.

A container ship swept past, heading into port, its rust-streaked hull towering high as a cliff. Two seamen in high-vis vests stood on the bridge, their faces bare, and a few passengers waved up at them. But there was no response, just a moving wall of rust and those two immobile figures staring down.

'Cheer up, ya grumpy bastards!' yelled an English voice behind her. 'It's not so bloody grim up north.' There was laughter, half-hearted jeers, the passengers united against this sullen giant.

Their own vessel's crew stepped around their human cargo, immersed in a world of sweat and grunt, the verbal shorthand of their work. Billie read this as reserve, rather than hostility. But top brass were another story. Back at the depot she'd been processed by the first mate, a pallid specimen with an acerbic manner and a voice to match: Cutler. All spotless uniform and murky innuendo, the kind of guy who had a hard-on for his own epaulettes. She'd dealt with the interrogation as civilly as she could.

'So, Glasgow,' he'd begun. 'Going downhill fast. People getting desperate. No work, no food.' His knuckled hands ugly paperweights, pinning her docs to the desk.

'Same story everywhere,' she'd answered. 'All the big cities have gone to the dogs.'

He ignored this. 'Spent some time up there myself, a few years back. Grim place in the winter. Still, has its charms.' He surveyed Billie in a way she did not like. She sat very still. 'And you can hold a tune, I'm told?' he asked, peering at his screen.

There'd been some music at the depot, harmless stuff, nothing political: old ballads from home, heather and myrtle, warbling blackbirds, some Burns. A singalong to make the wait go faster. Some fellow Scots had packed a fiddle and guitar – no wind instruments allowed, bagpipes now dubbed 'bugpipes' by a germ-spooked world – and an older guy had invited her to sing with them. How he'd picked her as a singer was anyone's guess. They'd shared their whiskey too, generous slugs in lukewarm tea, but kept the noise low, finished well before lights-out. No sense in drawing undue attention to yourself.

So what did this bampot want? Her papers were in order, nothing left to chance. He must be bluffing. 'I've sung in choirs since I was a wean,' she offered.

He'd raised his eyebrows. 'Ah. That must have come in handy at the hospital. Remind me why you left that job again?' An abrupt shift.

Don't blink. 'Lay-offs,' she said. 'It's all there in my profile.'

'But sickness ... that's Scotland's main growth industry, isn't it? Why would your hospitals be ditching staff?' He was enjoying himself.

She'd kept her voice level. 'All the big hospitals had lay-offs. Mostly HCAs – health care assistants, they call us, like nurses' aides. Austerity measures.' In fact the lay-offs had been minimal, but the justification rang true. The outbreak had decimated the Scots economy. Treasury knew lives could not always be saved, but money could. The bug had a talent for metamorphosis, unleashing a rolling pandemic that mutated as it spread, and anti-virals were useless against the newer strains. Staff called quarantine the death wards.

'Well,' said the first mate, 'I hope growing cabbages beats wiping arses for a living.' Then added, mock polite: 'No offence.'

She stole a glance at the ceiling. No doubt this was being recorded. His needling could be a tactic, a test to weed out hotheads and troublemakers. Trying to push her buttons, but too ignorant to know their true location. She'd worked the death wards. In that place, shit was the least of your worries.

'Right,' he'd announced, evidently tiring of his game. 'You check all the boxes medically, and nothing major shows up legal-wise. No *serious* black marks ...'

Billie fixed her eyes on his uniform pocket, the Red Star logo, as he signed her off. No point in getting upset. Keeping your gob shut was a fair price for a fresh start.

It had been a lonely six months. Her exit from work was not easily explained, and that silence had proven fatal for several friendships. She'd thought they were a tight group, the death-wards crew – persona non grata to the general public, sharing the dry humour of exile. Disconcerting, how easily she'd fallen from their ranks.

A mistake. That's what had landed her amongst this shipload of strangers, all seeking to leave bad luck and poor choices far behind them.

Now she was one of them – squinting up into the sails, stepping cautiously on the shifting deck. Parents and kids, childless couples, solitary specimens like herself, all with the unmistakable whiff of poverty, the mended clothes and bad teeth, the weary expressions. That hard-won look. Most had been settled for generations in the homelands they were leaving; amongst the pale-skinned majority were darker gradients, proof of forebears who'd made similar journeys. All of them now tracking in the long-dissolved wake of migrants who'd braved this route centuries ago, for a similar mess of reasons. They shared an air of quiet defiance, a readiness to trade hopelessness for mere uncertainty; a faith that given the chance, they would do better somewhere new.

Another fresh shipment of muscle, fit and ready for work.

The vetting process had been rigorous but not unforgiving: sound health, basic literacy, reasonable physical fitness. No elderly or ex-crims, no bad debts or transmissible diseases. Otherwise you were fair game – welcome to apply. The ads promised regular wages, cheap medical care, onsite schools. Given the dire prospects at home, people were flocking to sign up.

For all the talk of *assisted passage* and *mutual economic benefits*, the slick persuasive ads from rival shippers eager to cash in, they all knew what BIM was: an indentured labour scheme. Balanced Industries Migration, a term dreamt up by spooked politicians and embraced by venture merchants who knew the value of live cargo, a healthy human body delivered cheaply to the right buyers. International handshakes, old ties and new treaties. Imports and exports, relative needs, holds full of grain exchanged for unskilled labour. Shipments guaranteed bug-free, propelled across the globe by wind power, no need to waste a drop of precious fuel. Deals swung by the former motherland, now crippled by disease, caught short with mouths to feed and nothing to put in them.

But Billie had other hopes. Given the choice, who'd spend three years slaving away in a food factory to nourish some foreign population? The pay was generous and the job secure, a reassurance her homeland could no longer hope to match. But she'd heard the rumours: if you could slip free of your contract, this new country offered better options. Forget working the land, the whispers went: others were busy plundering it, and opportunities lay in wait on the fringes of all that manic excavation.

The Third Boom, they were calling it. An army of overpaid mine workers and cashed-up executives keen for after-hours entertainment that went beyond the skin trade, booze and grey-market meds. An economy as bright-eyed as the former UK's was bedridden. Cash to burn: enough to send a decent chunk back home and set her own future on a brighter course. *Mineral wealth*: the phrase had a lovely chime to it, a sparkling metallic note, like a bell hit with a jeweller's hammer. She'd better keep her own instrument in working order.

Through her mask Billie hummed a run of notes, searching for a song. Nothing too gloomy, not with all these hopeful people crowded around her. As the dull light of England rang back off a stony sea, she sang under her breath, a sea-shanty invented line by line: a mermaid, tired of wrecked ships and drowned sailors, lost souls wailing in the night, sets her sights on a change of fortune. On sunshine and calm waters. A ticket up and out, into the light.

TOM

Confiscate their gadgets and people have no idea what to do with their hands. As England receded into the distance, I noticed tell-tale flickers of device withdrawal manifesting all over the ship. Fingers wiggling, pockets being patted, wrists rubbed, but coming up empty every time. No stream to divert our attention, no digital selves to act out. All we had now was each other: face to face, unfiltered.

At first glance the *Steadfast* looked sound enough: sleek and scrubbed, evidently seaworthy. But below decks things weren't quite as I'd imagined. Space was in short supply, a bare-bones set-up with minimal creature comforts and scant natural light. Two passenger saloons with screens and games, a few basic alpha-wave pods: that was the sum of the communal rec-space. With three-hundred-plus passengers on board, legroom was limited.

My bunk was down on C deck, in one of the single-men's dorms. Our bodies stacked in berths that hardly left you space to sit upright. Almost morgue-like, the way they'd shelved us, and the 'privacy curtain' bore an unfortunate resemblance to a body bag.

Down here, as I rightly suspected, things would soon begin to stink. Two loos and four wash cubes for the sixty-odd men in our dorm, and no real way to enforce the hygiene orders: *Daily Full-body Swabs ... Mandatory San Procedures ... Penalties Apply ...* The showers spat out filtered seawater – *DO NOT DRINK!* thundered the sign. A vomiting stick-man drove the message home.

But we'd be fed and housed. And I'd have stable work.

The crew already seemed to know who I was; Captain Lewis, our silver-haired skipper, offered a practised smile, and that first day one sailor addressed me directly. He was aiming a strange pistol overhead, the officer beside him pointing up into the rigging.

For a moment I thought an unlucky seagull was about to be dispatched. Then I spotted the drone, a black dot hovering above. The crewman downed it with a single shot, and the machine fell into the sea. The officer gave a mock salute, and his subordinate caught my eye. Almost painfully handsome: green eyes and creamy skin, shaved head, mid-twenties. Absolutely drop-dead.

'I'm a crack shot, Teach,' he said in a broad Scots accent. 'Let me know if those rug-rats give you any trouble.'

The kids, I thought with a twinge of dread: fifty souls, all mine for six long hours a day.

Wild lot, from what I'd seen at the depot: a gang of Scots kids tearing around, shrieking their heads off. Two undersized Irish boys scrapping on the stairs. The English kids no better off – all state schooled, all dirt poor. No toffs amongst them. I hoped my accent wouldn't count against me.

Free schooling was part of the package: all projections doomed these kids to a lifetime of manual labour, but they'd be educated for the duration of their parents' contracts. Thanks to trade treaties, we'd be spending a lot of time together. My goal was twofold: to do my best by them, and to make it out the other side in one piece.

Our classroom was on B deck, amidships (that naval lingo rolling readily off my tongue). I'd run two sessions, one either side of lunch.

Teaching – the profession had such a worthy ring to it, at first. But by the time I'd signed my contract with Red Star, reality had knocked off that rosy glow. Poor career choice, it turns out, if you're cursed with an anxious streak and a score that relegates you to the roughest schools. Hacked tests, vandalised gear, objects hurled at your head. Apprentice thugs, lost causes, kids loaded to the gills on Calmex and Paxotrin. Kids so dirt poor they had to sneak lunch out of the bins. Kids who'd given up hope, or never had it in the first place.

Even the smart ones, what could you promise them? The times offered scarce room for optimism: curfews and closures, slashed budgets, so many jobs dead in the water. The light at the end of the tunnel was permanently on the blink, the wiring shot, the whole structure crumbling.

Meanwhile the plague tolls ticked steadily upward, city by city, the length and breadth of our formerly united former kingdom, from Brighton to Inverness, Cork to Londonderry. The home stream was awash with it: travel bans and curfews, airports virtually deserted, unrest in quarantine centres, gloomy soundbites from epidemiologists.

Those poor kids. No wonder their parents pinned their hopes on some remote landmass on the far side of the planet. Lured by clips of kangaroos and blue skies, beach picnics and rolling surf, white teeth chomping into fruit. All aboard for the live human trade! How obedient we were.

Zipped up in my bunk that first night, I tried to slow my scrolling thoughts. Hopping vocations was a tempting idea. I'd heard talk of contractual loopholes, extended visas for off-base assignments, a series of savvy sideways steps. But into what, I wondered?

We were barely out of the channel, and already I had the jitters. I considered a nightcap to soothe my nerves, then thought better of it. Best to wait it out, try to ration my stash. I'd met the chief medic – Doctor Kellahan, Brummie guy. If he wasn't open to friending, I planned to give his subordinate a shot: Owen Price, a weedy young Welshman. If the shark-shit hit the fan, I'd need a reliable supply.

An unwelcome thought kept looping through my head: *Please don't let us sink.*

Then Dad's voice would butt in: *Old Catastrophe Tom, eh – always finding something to fret about.*

After several sleepless hours, I gave in: allowed myself a single solitary tab, just to take the edge off. Worries dissolving, I slid gratefully into oblivion.

2

CLEARY

Cleary had spotted the man on their first day at sea: head bald as an egg, a thickset fighter's body and a gaze that hung on longer than was polite. He loitered near a hatchway, scrutinising his fellow passengers with cold eyes, as if he was putting a price on them. Reading the man as trouble, Cleary avoided him.

He watched the sailors going about their mysterious work, heaving on ropes and cranking winches, gesturing up into the rigging. The crew were a whiskery, hard-bitten lot: their faces had a blasted look, even the youngest sporting a permanent squint.

Once England disappeared, his ma's spirits had picked up. She'd become her lively self again, eyes bright above her mask as she chatted with a group of women. It had hurt him to see her cry, to witness her grief at leaving Gran and Granda behind. But now she'd come right. She turned to Cleary, indicated the women, tapped her chin and signed an L-shape beneath it: *Dublin*.

They were up on deck, nothing but water on every side, when the all-clear signal came. The crowd paused as one, heads raised. Then off came the masks. People took great gulps of air; teenagers pinged their masks away like slingshots, laughed as the wind rolled them around the deck. One man stomped his flat, making a joke of it, and a gang of kids began flinging theirs overboard, until a crewman reprimanded them.

Cleary pulled off his mask. Free of that barrier the world sharpened into focus – cold air on his cheeks, the wind tickling his teeth, language returning to the faces around him. He stuck his tongue out into the wind. He could taste the sea.

~

A few nights later, when the screens in the saloon showed Spain nudging into view, Cleary and his ma queued for dinner in the mess-room. The space seemed moulded from a single block of plastic – walls and floor, tables and benches all rendered in a wan industrial grey. Footprints wavered across the food-streaked floor. Crew slopped dinner into their trays: a lumpy yellow stew that reminded Cleary of puke, a blob of mash, and chewy brown strips meant to resemble meat.

They joined their usual table, the people mostly Irish, so he'd gathered. A red-haired woman greeted them with a wave. The yellow muck tasted better than it looked, and he'd soon scoffed down half of it.

Sensing eyes upon him, he saw the bald-headed man had taken the seat opposite. The man leant in close, his breath a rank mix of fake meat and sour gums, and repeated his question slowly, like he was talking to an idiot: *Where's – yer – da?* His words reached Cleary as a faint hum of nonsense, bees buzzing in a jar, but he recognised their shape. He gave the man his best death-stare, screwed up his nose and drew back beyond range of that rancid breath.

'Dead,' his ma had already replied; Cleary knew her response by heart.

The bald man mouthed some false sympathy at her, then fixed on Cleary to deliver his next jab. He knew this one by heart too: an insult disguised as a question.

He felt his ma tense up, saw their fellow diners clock her sharp reply, alert to trouble. *He's not touched, just hard of hearing. Bet he's got double your IQ.* These words, or some variation. Cleary knew the sentiment backwards. His ma had a fierce side, would eat the face off anyone who bothered him.

The bald man shoved up from the table and stalked away. Heads were shaken, consolations offered, the malice smoothed over and dismissed. Focusing on their mouths, Cleary made out the words *gobshite* and *header*, and the red-haired woman patted his ma's hand. Then the ship rolled, sending cutlery skating, and people laughed, or feigned fear, clutching after their knives and forks. Cleary concentrated on his jerky, chewing the tough strips into something worth swallowing.

Soon he realised he was under scrutiny again. A few seats down a boy his own age, a freckled kid with a mischievous face, was mimicking him, stuffing food into his gob and chewing with exaggerated frenzy, like a starving squirrel. Before Cleary could shoot him the finger, the boy dropped his slagging and offered a complicit grin. Cleary responded with his best mental face – eyes crossed, teeth bucked out – and the kid laughed in delight.

Their game was cut short when the boy's ma cuffed him around the ear and shot Cleary a look: *stop acting the maggot.* Subdued, the boys finished their food in a pantomime of prim obedience, chewing like a couple of Holy Joes while sneaking glances at each other. All through the remainder of the meal Cleary felt the presence of his silent accomplice.

After dinner his ma issued her usual cautions, pointed out the clocks, and set him free to explore for an hour. *I'm going for a kip,* she signed. Their cabin had been a disappointment – not a bedroom at all but a crowded family dorm, row upon row of bunks, each berth sealed off like a black cocoon. It was gloomy and cramped down there, the air already stale.

Up on deck the air was just the opposite, so painfully cold and clear it stung your eyeballs. The wind crammed into your chest, a mineral tang that scoured your throat and fizzed your blood. Gripping the rail, Cleary felt the ship shudder with effort as she carved her way ahead, a live creature straining against the great blind push of wind and water, while high above the sails cupped fat bulges of air.

The restless sea stretched right to the horizon. The ocean was a mysterious thing, too gigantic to get your head around. How did the ship stick to that curved body of water, glide all the way around the globe? What stopped the ocean from pouring away in a planet-sized waterfall, whales and ships and sharks all tumbling off into outer space? Gravity, that was what. He half remembered the shape of the word, its triangular play of syllables, before sound had deserted him. Gravity: an invisible glue, pins clinging to a magnet. The magic trick that held you to the planet's surface.

Someone sidled up to him: the kid from dinner. *Howya*, he said, or something similar, and Cleary nodded. He didn't trust his voice, not with strangers. He'd seen the stares, could picture the sniggers; better to stay silent than make a bags of it.

The boy had fine features, snaggled teeth, a smattering of freckles across his nose. Focusing on the kid's lips he made out the word *deadly* but missed the rest, realised he couldn't bluff it. Would have to run the risk.

'What's your name?' Cleary spoke, shaping his words with care.

'Declan,' answered the boy.

Cleary repeated the name aloud, then voiced his own. This was a risk he rarely took: some kids could be unkind. But this boy didn't flinch.

Then Cleary pulled out the notebook and pen his ma made him carry, the explanation already written out in his own neat hand, a single sentence. Declan read it, then grinned. *Grand,* he said. He pointed out a couple huddled on a bench. After some confusion – Cleary couldn't work out what the boy was asking him to do – Declan commandeered the pen, scribbled a question. His spelling was cat, but the writing was clear: *You can spie for us! Whats ur man there saying?*

Cleary watched the couple. She had a puss on her, and the man was gesturing in a pleading way. The argument was complicated, something about money; lip-reading was hard work, and he struggled to make out more than a few words. *Boring,* he scribbled. *He's after getting plastered again.* Declan nodded. He sized Cleary up, as if weighing a decision. Then his expression opened into a smile. He jerked his head, an invitation: *Come on then.*

BILLIE

She emerged into a jagged wind, the sky serrated by clouds. Found a spot at the rail and rolled a cigarette by touch, surveying the swells. Let the smoke rip from her mouth and vanish over the side.

Walking was an old habit, but Billie was used to having Glasgow's maze of streets and back lanes at her disposal, its parks and shortcuts; a city you could roam for months without repeating the same loop. At first the *Steadfast* had felt almost roomy – until you realised you were trapped, with no opportunity for exit. Then the ship began to make its confines felt.

She was trying to learn the vessel's thoroughfares, its snakes-and-ladders labyrinth of passageways and stairs, pacing out long figure-eights through the guts and arteries of the ship. But all that roaming left her feeling both cooped up and hopelessly lost. She'd cross her own path repeatedly, her efforts to compile a mental map foiled by identical passageways and multiple levels. The ship's true size eluded her, much of it closed off to passengers by heavy doors and forbidding signs. Electronic wristbands granted the crew entry to restricted zones: staff quarters, the supplies kiosk, the bridge, nooks where obscure maritime paraphernalia was stowed. *Authorised Personnel Only.*

Not that she'd enjoyed free rein of Glasgow these past few years. It wasn't the humming city she'd fallen for in her early twenties – a place full of grit and promise, game for anything. Poverty and crime had spawned a rash of no-go zones, and a thriving black market for pepper spray. But the real lines were drawn by the rolling curfews, the plague paranoia that crouched over the stricken city like a fog.

Glasgow's native smells – diesel and Lorne sausage, damp moss and the briny stink of the Clyde – now drowned out by the chemical reek of decon. You'd turn some familiar corner and come up against a cordon, plague vans lumbering past with blackened windows, soldiers in hazmats waving you back. Her hospital ID had once granted her some leeway, but since she'd been fired there was no getting around that tape.

Walking was a private pursuit, a chance to wander the world alone, lost in the rhythm of your own steps. But a crowded ship stole away that solitary appeal. You kept passing the same people – couples nestled in alcoves, kids playing tag, families huddled before game-screens. A pair of crew members on cleaning duty who'd exchange a knowing smirk, diagnosing you on sight, a case study in cabin fever.

When the ship began to hem her in, she made for the foredeck and turned her attention outward, taking solace in that limitless arc of air and water. As land receded, the lacework of floating rubbish had thinned out to lone flotillas, while the sea morphed from dishwater grey to a bright inky blue. A world all sky and weather, a rolling vista punctuated occasionally by a distant cargo ship, the milky blur of a jellyfish swarm. A view both monotonous and ever-changing.

She squinted into the wind: a ship was materialising from the distance, making straight for them. As it drew closer a crowd gathered to watch. A Spanish fishing vessel, by the looks of it, green hull streaked with rust, the name *Sombra Nocturna* picked out in white paint. On the *Steadfast*, crew converged along the rail, gesturing across to the Spanish sailors.

The Spanish ship drew alongside, close enough to make out the smiles of the crew, and the two vessels rode the swells in unison, dipping and rising like dolphins. Kids waved to the Spanish sailors, and they waved back. A *Steadfast* officer began bellowing orders,

24

and his crew shot lines out over the gunwale, connecting the two ships. Slowly they winched a wooden crate across from the fishing vessel. Once the crate was safely deposited on the *Steadfast*'s deck, two sailors heaved it aloft, staggering under the weight, and carried it below decks.

As the mooring lines were reeled in, the Spanish ship sent out a farewell blast over its PA. Billie knew the melody, an old bossa nova tune: 'The Girl from Ipanema'. People cheered as the two ships drew apart, the Spanish sailors shimmying to the music, hamming it up for the kids.

When the horizon had consumed the fishing vessel, Billie rolled another ciggie. She was burning through tobacco at an alarming rate. *Ship at sea*: the term failed to capture the full absurdity of their situation, the blind foolish faith of human beings. A herd of land mammals crammed into this flimsy capsule, lost in a great expanse of liquid emptiness. A speck afloat on a vast, forbidding ocean. Did your head in, if you were mad enough to dwell on it.

Billie flicked her lighter: dead. Cursing, she set off for the kiosk on the foredeck. The crewman on duty grinned, revealing a gold incisor, and slid a red lighter across the counter.

'Keep it,' he said. 'I collect 'em. Might be yours, for all I know.'

She thanked him, sparked the wheel and drew deep.

'Heard you singing,' offered the crewman. 'Back at the depot. That's some voice. Don't overdo the smokes.'

She ducked her head, awkward in the face of praise. 'Just roughens the edges. Makes it easier to hit the low notes.'

The man laughed, gold tooth gleaming in his sun-tanned face. 'Ah, the things we tell ourselves.'

Back at the rail she sidestepped a queasy passenger, a patchwork of mediplasts stuck to his neck, gulping air as he fought to quell the nausea. Billie was grateful she didn't get seasick. Her dad's vocation had saved her from that particular hell. Out in his old boat she'd adjusted to the constant sway, but these ocean swells were an entirely different beast – less a rocking motion than a violent bodily displacement, snatching you metres through space in an eye-blink.

Earlier she'd passed a woman slumped in a passageway, a greenish pallor to her skin, pupils blown out to the size of grapes. 'You need to up the dose a bit,' Billie had advised. 'That should take the edge off.' Too ill to speak, the woman had groped her way along the passageway towards sick bay.

Rules were posted everywhere, their barking tone ensuring no-one mistook this for a pleasure cruise. No smoking indoors or below decks. No alcohol outside the two designated bars, rudimentary boxes that opened at noon and closed at midnight. No fraternising in the dorms at night. Rules for mealtime procedures and water rationing, returning used cutlery and storing personal effects; a rubbish regime, a laundry roster, strict hygiene protocols for sanning your hands and washing your body. The orders posted in the loo came dangerously close to telling you how to wipe your arse.

It wore you down, all that hectoring, and fresh air was a welcome antidote. As long as you set your sights ahead, avoided staring down the ship's wake. That was a recipe for melancholy and nostalgia, sentiments sure to muddle your head.

Billie's final visit home had stirred feelings of that sort. The landscape she'd grown up in had forgotten her; life rolled on, not registering her absence. Stripped of its childhood enchantments, her parents' small fishing village had become a place of sagging houses and paint-flaked boats, of poverty and scraped-together pride, governed by set routines and a wariness of outsiders.

Her parents seldom asked about her life in the city, a place they mistrusted and feared. The daily rituals of survival consumed all their attention: her mother tending the garden and bottling preserves, her dad trawling the tides and lugging his catch home to the smokehouse, selling whatever they didn't eat. And Jamie – twenty-five and still a child, delighting in the antics of the chickens, entranced by a caterpillar or a coloured leaf, his chores defining the simple shape of his life. Thinking of them, left behind, sparked a guilt-tinged tenderness.

Enough. She'd speak home once she reached land, send them a cut of her wages. Get her mother's teeth fixed, pay some bills. And remember to say the words out loud. They knew she loved them, but reminders never hurt.

'Will you be coming back?' her mother had asked, skiddling in the sink while Billie dried the dishes.

'Mam! I'm going for the work, not for eternity. We'll talk every week.'

No further word about her leaving. Her mother just said to stick the kettle on, and take a biscuit, anyone would think they had a scarecrow visiting. Her parents had said little on the subject, but she sensed their dismay – their only daughter disappearing to the far side of the globe. A decision that had its critics. Not just the germophobe nutters who wanted to ban all travel, all migration, as if that was any kind of solution, but a deeper sentiment: the mutterings about traitors deserting the homeland in its time of need, abandoning dear old Scotland to its Dark Days.

As for Billie, she'd had a gutful of scrubbing floors and toilets for dirt rates, scoring the occasional gig in some backstreet dive for a pittance, all to barely make the rent on a bedsit with a single power-point and one cold tap. Sick of scraping by on toast and hot Bovril, the odd charity food parcel, bootleg tobacco and paint-stripper booze.

When she'd lost her hospital job, a part of her had been thankful – you didn't admit to trauma, not if you wanted to stay employed, but all that death and suffering left its mark. The relief had been short-lived: despite the clean reference, a solid wage had proven elusive. She'd tried Gartnavel and Royal Alexandra, but evidently neither was hiring. She even interviewed for an outfit that tracked quarantine violators, but was soon reduced to casual shifts of grunt work, cleaning office blocks downtown. She wasn't fool enough to be sucked in completely by the BIM recruitment ads, their eternally blue skies and beaming workers. But she'd endured her fill of dark days. Sunlight, at least, would be a blessing.

'Wet out there,' said a voice. Edinburgh accent, that upward inflection: the older Scot she'd sung with at the depot, the fiddler who'd shared his whiskey. Built short and solid, his bristled face creased into well-worn smile lines, the grey eyes sharp and canny, pale as ash. 'Robbie's the name.'

Reminding her before she had to ask, nodding as she offered her own again.

'Got a niece called Billie, coming up for twelve,' he said. 'Mona's missing her already, keeps forgetting there's no outbound comms. Stupid rule, I'd argue, but ours is not to etcetera.' He pulled out a tobacco pouch, rolled a smoke and offered Billie the bundle. She hesitated, force of habit, then took it: remembered they were clear, a bug-free zone.

'Has your wife been seasick?' Billie recalled an older woman: olive skin, white hair pulled back in a bun, singing along to the music. A gentle demeanour, at least one missing tooth.

'She's had a spell,' Robbie said. 'But it's passing. Rotten thing.'

'It's a misery,' Billie agreed. 'We're lucky to escape it.' The wind tore their smoke away. The tobacco was strong and malty, like pipe-smokers' stuff.

'Do miss being in touch with home,' he said. 'They say it's down to germs, the ban – devices being grubby.'

'Aye, right. They also told us it was for privacy, to keep the howlers at bay.'

Robbie snorted. 'Privacy! Avoid bad publicity, more like. Pics of the food, then clips of people having a boak over the side.'

It wasn't just Red Star: all the shippers had the no-devices rule. Billie had always leant towards the dry end of the spectrum, but she missed it too, the daily chatter of the outside world, the babble of the stream. Her family's faces.

'At least they let us smoke. Some don't.'

'True,' he granted. 'And they're not so nosy, this lot. Willing to turn a blind eye to a vice or two.' He peered up into the overcast sky, the sun a muffled white glare. 'Wouldn't know the whereabouts of the yardarm, would you?'

Billie searched her memory for nautical terms, came up blank. 'Wouldn't recognise one if it bit me on the arse,' she admitted.

'Well, I'd say the sun's just over it. Fancy a bevvy? My shout. There's a few of us been meeting for a post-noon medicinal.'

She weighed up her customary caution with strangers. Judged the man harmless, recalled that musically they'd been an effortless click. Noon had safely come and gone.

'Why not. Just one or three.'

'Good lass,' he said, flicking away his butt. 'Proceed this way.' He set off on bandy cockatoo legs at a surprisingly quick pace.

'Hang on,' she called, 'isn't the bar down that end?'

Robbie turned, gave a corny wink. 'Shhh,' he said in an exaggerated whisper. 'Got ourselves a private boozer.' He beckoned, casting shifty glances at a couple who were plainly listening in. 'Scots only. Birds of a feather. Crew privileges.' Tapped the side of his nose like some movie gangster. She hesitated.

'Flock together,' he instructed, scuttling off. 'Follow me, Songbird.'

TOM

Despite my paranoia, our lessons got off to a decent start. The kids were not the menaces I'd feared. A mixed lot, but no obvious bad eggs.

We had close to full attendance that first day, thanks to the diligent crewmen who combed the ship, rounding up anyone underage and marching them into class. Seasickness kept a few in bed at first, but there was a zero-tolerance policy on truancy – a contractual obligation, according to Delaney, the cheerful old sailor in charge of the muster (so chosen, I suspect, for his resemblance to Santa Claus). A tight ship, as the saying goes.

One poor kid vomited on the floor and was escorted off to sick bay. A crewman mopped up the mess and sprayed air freshener everywhere, managing to squirt himself in the eye in the process, swearing like the proverbial – 'Bastard fucken *cunt* of a thing!' – much to the kids' delight.

Finding ourselves on unfamiliar ground – no ground at all, in fact – we bonded as a group with relative ease. I hoped it might knock the edge off any potential troublemakers, that sense of being all at sea. Yes, the maritime clichés were coming thick and fast.

'Remember,' I told the kids, 'we're all in the same boat.' Groan. Crossed my fingers we'd avoid a mutiny.

Resources were primitive, although management preferred the term 'analogue': an old vidscreen, a limited clip library, an antiquated whiteboard. The kids cawed in disbelief when I handed out exercise books and pens. 'No linked devices,' I reminded them. 'We're going unplugged. Like time travel. Pretend we're back in the twentieth century.'

They played along: 'Hey, Teach, Teach! Wossiss fing, some kinda laser?' said one of the English kids, waving a pen.

On that first day an air of goodwill pervaded the room: it was an adventure, having classes inside a rolling ship, and the old-school gear was part of the novelty. The age range posed a challenge, so I'd split them into two groups, youngsters in the morning session. Eased in with the usual routine – ice-breakers, rollcall, matching names to faces – then ran some aptitude tests disguised as quizzes. Divided them into subgroups, ostensibly by age, adjusting up or down for ability.

Their handwriting was a mess, especially the English kids, who'd grown up almost entirely onscreen. As expected, literacy and numeracy were low across the board. Had their families not been borderline destitute, those kids would never have been on that vessel.

Nor would I, but for the crashes. Family money only cushions you while it lasts.

A few bright sparks had clearly hoovered up whatever education they'd been offered. You soon learnt not to rely on appearances: the snot-nosed kid with perfect grammar, the dull-eyed maths whiz, the silent girl who churned out five articulate paragraphs in as many minutes. One deaf kid too, as per my briefing notes, although you wouldn't pick it. Reluctant to speak, but could lip-read a bit, and smart as a whip. Had the most beautiful handwriting, verging on calligraphy.

Alliances would soon form along the usual lines, I knew: nationality, blood, skin-tone and ethnicity, football team. And religion, especially the Irish kids; anyone raised to think that Jesus was the only game in town. I always discouraged segregation, but kids pick up that clique stuff early, that stick-to-your-own-kind

31

dogma that flourishes in fearful times. Drummed in from birth, it masquerades as natural.

Lessons were to be largely practical, as per my contract – lit and num, comp and prac, basic skills to equip them for a low-skilled future. But secretly, I hoped I might do more: get them thinking, exercise their imaginations. Draw out their individual talents, perhaps even hint at a less mediocre life.

Then doubt would strike: who was I kidding? I had an outdated screen, a bloody whiteboard and a middling track record. I wasn't some gifted mentor to the juvenile underclass. And this lot were consigned to a career of digging up potatoes.

A familiar cycle, this: where did my responsibility end, and my ego begin? How much difference could one low-ranked teacher make? Then again, the job had its bright spots: when you saw that light blink on, that internal spark fire up; when a kid asked a clever question, wrote a poem, volunteered some unexpected insight. Then hope would creep back in: could my fits of doubt simply be nerves? Perhaps I *was* meant to be a teacher?

Round and around it spun, the hamster wheel of indecision.

When the classroom emptied I locked the door, stretched out on the sofa and told myself everything was going to be fine. Surely I was due some downtime, a reward for surviving the first day unscathed. Not an all-out cranial holiday – just a mini-excursion.

I'd spotted him again yesterday: that handsome young crewman. Lean but strong-looking, clean-shaven, his features distinct amongst a sea of beards and stubble. Uniforms … there's something to be said for them.

Passing in the passageway we'd made eye contact just a split-second too long.

He stopped. 'You're the teacher.'

I held out my hand. 'Tom Garnett.'

No mistaking that clasp: a fraction too firm, a reluctance to break hold. In place of his name he offered a sly smile. 'Off-duty at the moment, though, aren't you?'

Worth a daydream, I thought now, conjuring him up: a two-hundred-milligram occasion, with a cheeky chaser of Somatriptol. A mental aperitif, a few hours of bliss before the dinner siren went.

Lights dimmed, blinds lowered, I closed my eyes and gave myself up to the rocking motion of the ship.

Ah. Yes. That was better.

So much better.

Limbs dissolving, colours melting. That delicious alchemy of blood and pharms, that welcome reservoir of inner calm ...

Neurotic git, I chided myself. *All will be well.*

Then: a knock at the door.

Rising unsteadily, I opened it to find my handsome daydream manifesting in the doorway. I stood there blinking, not sure if he was flesh or apparition.

'You busy?' he asked. I shook my head.

Keeping his voice low, his eye contact steady, he laid it out without a trace of shyness: he knew somewhere we could go. After sketching a map on the door with his finger, he tapped our invisible destination. Observed my face as I repeated his directions.

'Wait five minutes,' he said. 'Then follow.'

Heart pounding, I wound my way through the ship to the designated door: *Housekeeping.* The passageway empty, I knocked.

Practically a broom cupboard: mops clanking and cleaning products sloshing, the scent of clean towels and guest soap. The light was dim, but we could see each other well enough.

'Look at you,' I said, admiring his sleek outline, the clean-jawed symmetry of his face, offset by that slanted smile. A picture ripe for endorsement. 'You need an agent. You're wasted on this sailor stuff.'

He took my hand and placed it around his wrist, encircling the cabled bracelet etched into his fair skin. 'Do you ever shut up?' he asked, pressing close.

And so I did.

3

CLEARY

Woken by his bladder, Cleary lay there, absorbing the ship's pitch and roll, a movement that had begun to infiltrate his dreams. He peered down at the bunk below: his ma just a dark shape breathing there, oblivious.

Not only did he need to pee, but he was thirsty too. He groped for his water bottle: empty. You weren't allowed to fill your own, because of bugs, and you mustn't drink the water from the washroom taps – there was a big red sign with a shouting stick-man, and his ma had mimed vomiting – so he'd have to get a refill from the kiosk. He bundled on warm layers and crept down the ladder in a way he hoped was silent.

The bog stank, and he held his breath while he peed, watching the yellow swirl vanish down the bowl. Where did it go – straight out into the ocean? He imagined his pee drifting in the cold water, the yellow cloud briefly enveloping a passing fish, a fleeting warmth softening the ocean's chill. Could a fish smell piss? Did fish even have noses?

Dim lights lined the walkway of the sleeping dorm. Cleary trod the centre of the aisle, balancing against the sway, playing with the motion of the ship. In the gloomy corridor he paused to read the signs, orient himself within the maze, then set off in what he hoped was the right direction.

A tall figure was heading towards him down the corridor: a uniformed crewman wrapped up against the cold, face framed by the hood of his windcheater. As he drew close, the man locked eyes with Cleary. His black beard was damp with rain, and there were dark spatters of muck on his coat. A deep-set gaze, mouth a hard line, slight stoop about the shoulders. Across one chalk-white cheek, from nostril to temple, ran a lurid streak of red, like the aftermath of a nosebleed. The man seemed mildly stunned, as if he'd just woken up.

Cleary hugged the wall to let him pass, but the bearded man shot him a sharp look and ducked into a doorway. Passing the entrance Cleary caught a waft of feral air, dank with the smell of sleeping men – *Men's Dorm B, Male Passengers Only*. Maybe sailors got seasick too; the man looked like he'd just had a puke.

The passageway all his again, Cleary cruised the swells hands-free, an indoor surfer joyriding in pyjamas. Past the women's dorm, a ripe whiff of sweat and perfume, then the smell of baking bread floating from the kitchen. He climbed the companionway and threw his weight against the door.

No rain out here, to his surprise, but the fresh air never lost its shock, biting cold and clean, nipping his lungs awake. Still dark, but a pale hint of dawn leaking in at the horizon, while overhead the stars flickered in a bottomless stretch of remnant night. Near the front of the ship crewmen were backlit against the wheelhouse, and he saw glimpses of other night workers: a torch clicked absent-mindedly on and off; the glow of a cigarette swung out in some explanatory arc. A whole other life out here, a secret society that came alive when the rest of the world was lost to sleep.

He headed for the kiosk, a bright beacon on the foredeck. Walking like a sailor, feet wide for balance, joints loose to absorb the passing swells. He directed a seamanlike nod at the darkly rolling landscape out beyond the rail.

The kiosk was ablaze with light, but the serving hatch was locked. Through the window he saw shelved supplies, a swipe-pad and a fire hydrant. Against the wall sat squat tanks of drinking water, the contents sloshing in perfect unison. One tank was open at the top, its cap jouncing on a little leash, gushes of water shooting up like a whale's spout.

Where was the shopman? Now he really was thirsty. Cleary rapped his knuckles on the window, waited. Banged again, harder.

No-one in sight, no way to fill his bottle. How stupid to be half dying of thirst in the middle of a big wet ocean full of stuff you couldn't drink.

He stood on tiptoe, peering into the tiny room. On the floor was a slab of navy blue material, the same colour as the crew's uniform. Face pressed to the glass, he could just make out a black boot, flopped over at the ankle. Then realised what he was seeing: a leg, a person's leg. Someone was lying flat out on the floor.

Cleary hammered on the window, but the leg's owner did not stir. Skiver, he thought, sneaking a kip on the job. Or maybe the man was drunk, passed out from pouring whiskey down his neck. He dragged a crate over to the window and climbed up for a better view.

That's when he saw it: a bright red mess, streaked across the floor in sticky rivulets. A puddle had gathered in one corner, beneath the water tanks. The liquid made a long black stain where it had soaked into the fabric of the uniform.

Cleary's heart lurched as he realised what he was seeing: a man's body, lying in a pool of blood.

He fled down the gangway, making for the wheelhouse, the crewmen now visible in the dawn light spilling across the sky, bathing the world in a sickly amber glow.

Men spun around, startled, as Cleary flailed towards them, vaguely aware that his mouth was stretched wide open and some strange inhuman noise was pouring out.

BILLIE

Waking to the wail of a Hoover centimetres from her head, Billie scowled up at the crewman wielding the machine.

'Godsake,' she said over the racket. 'Do you have to do this bit now?'

The man hitched up his backpack and vroomed away, disrupting another dozer nearby.

She was curled up on a settee in the fore saloon. Since the disturbing news, sleep had proven elusive, her bunk taking on an increasingly coffin-like aspect with every hour spent in its dim confines. Earplugs helped to block the noise, but lately there were smells to deal with too, intimate and horribly mingled, wafting through the dorm whenever someone emptied their bowels, peeled off their socks or spilt their stomach into a sickbag – or, as she had once witnessed, into a sleeping neighbour's shoes.

Her dorm-mates rummaged, or snored, or dropped things, or discussed the whereabouts of missing toothpaste at unnecessary volumes. And now, after lights-out, they formed anxious clusters, the whispers taking on a newly fearful sibilance. There was no peace to be had down there. Nobody could sleep.

She'd wait a few more nights before resorting to pills. Instead she tried to walk herself to sleep, pacing her circuits of the ship, passing other insomniacs: bleary night owls hunched over backgammon screens, fidgety loners twitching from stream withdrawal, solitary smokers on the foredeck. And the guards, now posted in doorways and corners, alert and quick-eyed, missing nothing. The scrutiny was palpable, but for once she didn't resent it.

A fog of anxiety hung over the ship. People watched each other, alert for any hint of threat – a careless word or false smile. Reverting to their clans, gathering like moths in well-lit areas. Parents kept their kids within reach, spoke in bright tones to hide their fears.

Billie tried not to catch the floating paranoia, but insomnia had sunk its hooks into her all the same. Around four this morning she'd succumbed, and her stomach now told her she'd missed breakfast. The kiosk was still shut, but water, rocklike biscuits and weak coffee were now laid out in the mess-room at all hours.

The mess was empty, but a kitchenhand waved a knife over his shoulder. 'Juliette and them are out back,' he said. 'Go through if you want.'

Billie poured a slow coffee. Thanks to Robbie's introductions she'd spent several evenings in the galley storeroom with the cook and her gang. With forty-odd crew making this regular run, they got sick of the same old faces. On every trip, it transpired, they'd pick out a couple of passengers – or 'parasites', as the crew called their human cargo – to invite into their circle, fresh blood to beat the boredom. This time she and Robbie fit the bill. The music helped, no doubt, but Robbie also had some deal going with the cook, the details of which were vague and likely illegal.

Billie had enjoyed their company, but overdoing it might be unwise. Weeks of sea-bound limbo lay ahead, and privacy was scarce in this floating rabbit warren. Dodging an unwelcome acquaintance would be awkward. She'd never been a huge joiner, and those years at the hospital had dimmed her talent for chitchat. Once people found out you worked the death wards, they didn't ask you round for dinner.

Still, solitude turned sour in big doses, and their company had its benefits: fresh bread hot from the oven; fly booze, poured free or sold dirt cheap, shared with people who swore you sang like an angel. No, that never hurt.

She ducked down the passage and knocked on the hatch. It flung open to frame Robbie's whiskered face, clearly the worse for wear.

'Songbird!' he cried, exhaling a gust of flammable air. 'Climb in, hen. We're swapping some theories.'

In a cramped corner of the storeroom, perched on upturned buckets, were three others: the plump cook, Juliette, a fellow Weegie; Scoot, a handsome young deckhand from Aberdeen, who rarely spoke but had trounced them all at cards last time; and the chief steward, a tall, sallow-faced man called Marshall, who knew all the verses of 'Skye Boat Song' by heart.

Billie was welcomed, a drink poured, a seat found. As fellow Scots, and musos, she and Robbie had been deemed honorary members of this group – the Stocktakers, Marshall called them. 'Not because we pinch the stock, mind,' he'd said. 'Just 'cause we like to keep an eye on things.'

'Management's on panic stations,' said Juliette. 'Mind we don't flash that around.' She pointed at Scoot, who was sloshing liquid from unmarked bottle to mug, revealing a rope tattoo etched into the white skin of his wrist.

'Still say it was a revenge thing,' said Marshall. 'That Davy fella was sleekit. Maybe he had it coming?'

Juliette spoke sharply: 'That's pure shady, Marshall. The man got his throat cut the other night. Chibbed in the neck. Who deserves that?'

Marshall raised his hands. 'Just saying he wasn't a saint. Lazy, too. Got caught sleeping on the job more than once.'

'Never heard a bad word about Davy Whelan,' said Juliette. 'Bought me a pint more than once. Wasn't he a pal of yours, Scoot?'

The Aberdeen sailor shrugged, stared down into his drink.

Rumours were already gathering like blowflies as people traded scraps of information – overheard, gleaned or invented. Most theories pinned the violence on a crew member: who else could have entered the kiosk, unless the dead man swiped them in himself? But now Marshall was wondering if the culprit could be a passenger, some nutter who'd talked his way in. A robbery gone bad.

'Nothing caught on camera,' said Juliette. 'Spoke to the fella on watch that night.'

'Kiosk camera's broken,' said Marshall. 'Half the cams on this ship are on the blink.' The chief steward oversaw the stock flows, Billie recalled. His grasp of what could safely be skimmed relied on inside knowledge, familiarity with the security regime and its loopholes. This hideaway, where they now sat drinking stolen booze, had not been chosen by accident. A chalk-line on the floor marked the border of the blind spot.

Robbie leant forward. 'A killer in our midst,' he said in a theatrical whisper. 'Someone quick and brutal, with a temper. A bajin.'

A heavy swell tipped the room, cans clanking and cooking oil slapping wetly in its barrels.

Marshall broke the hush. 'Bad weather coming.'

'I can't get a wink,' said Billie. 'My whole dorm's spooked.'

Scoot held out the bottle, but she declined, stomach too empty to tolerate the caustic bootleg.

'Didn't see you at breakfast,' said Juliette. She produced a slab of spanakopita. 'My mum's recipe. Get some scran down you before you disappear.'

Billie listened as she chewed. They kept circling back to the murder, sifting the possibilities: a bad debt or swindle, some festering grudge. Drug deal gone sour, fight over a woman. Or – Robbie's gleeful suggestion – a lovers' tiff, one randy seaman jilted by another. That theory rubbished by Juliette, who'd seen the victim snogging a girl in port a while back.

'Some of 'em swing both ways, those Scouser bastards,' Robbie insisted.

Marshall snorted. 'Stay up late picturing that scenario, did you?'

'They say Davy had a kid back home,' said Juliette. 'Little boy. Lives down Bristol way, with his mum.' A hush fell, the child a half-glimpsed presence.

Scoot stood, threw back his drink and nodded at the floor. 'That's me,' he said, and was out the hatch and gone in three long steps, their farewells trailing after him.

'Moody lad,' said Juliette. 'Got questioned yesterday. He was just coming off nightshift when that wean found the body.'

Senior brass were working through the crew, she said, interrogating anyone with a link to the dead man: cabinmates and friends, anyone who'd worked that shift, entered that room, gone near the crime scene after sundown.

'Got the third degree myself,' said Marshall, affronted. 'Had to scare up a list of every swipe logged that shift, across all of Stores. All kiosk transactions. Took me bloody hours.' Passengers would be next, he said. Cutler fancied himself a cop, swore he'd find the bastard who did it.

'Cutler?' said Juliette. 'Fucking bawbag. Cannot stand the man.'

'Those ex-navy bastards are the worst,' Marshall agreed. 'Half of them discharged for being wrong in the head. Sadists and sickos. Probably one of them who malkied that fella.'

'Not a passenger, then?' said Robbie, a bit tersely.

'Top brass are mostly ex-navy,' said Juliette. 'Love their uniforms, that lot. Law unto themselves, and Cutler's the worst of them.'

A face sprang to Billie's mind: the first mate, her sour interrogator. That was Cutler alright, the others confirmed: flawless uniform, caustic tongue. Nasty piece of work.

'I've got lunch to prep,' said Juliette, rising to her feet. 'See you tonight, at Limpet's?' The bar ran a happy hour, and Billie had peeked in once: the room heaving with people, the one place passengers and crew seemed to mingle relatively freely. The odd low-ranked uniform, but not an epaulette in sight.

Robbie pressed her to come, join him in a song or two. 'Payment in tobacco and drinks,' he promised. 'Got a deal going with the bar manager.'

'Don't be a fearie,' said Juliette. 'We'll all be there.'

The ship's confines made Billie cautious, reluctant to stand out in such a finite mix of people. But her voice had opened doors over the years. Singing was a liberating act, one that somehow bought her grace. A way to piece the world together, if only for an hour or two. Turning down an audience seemed a waste.

'Aye, alright,' she said. 'But there better not be any hecklers.'

Robbie gave a sodden cheer. 'Anyone heckles, we'll chib 'em!' A silence fell. Juliette swiped the moonshine from his hand.

'You're half plastered already,' she said. 'Sober up and eat a decent lunch, or you'll never last the distance.' Chastened, Robbie surrendered his mug.

They exited the hatchway into the smell of frying onions. Billie said her farewells, then struck off alone. She had thoughts to think, fresh air to breathe, information to walk off. She headed out into the rising wind, already planning her route.

TOM

Two days after Davy Whelan bled to death, management summoned me from lunch. I'd heard the gossip, but wasn't sure what to believe. We'd struck a patch of foul weather – huge seas, tearing winds, a miserable lashing rain – and the whole ship felt queasy, on edge. Abandoning my plate, I followed a lackey down the wildly lurching passageways to meet with the deputy kingpin, a sour man called Cutler, and his officious sidekick.

At first I thought – or was led to believe – that I'd be briefed on what had befallen that poor crewman. To start with, Cutler certainly gave that impression. He conveyed the awful facts, advised that an investigation was underway. My own role, he said – casually citing a clause from my contract – was to support management's efforts: help contain the situation, protect the wellbeing of the minors in our charge. Translation: relay the official version of events.

An accident, I was to tell the kids. The sailor had been using a dangerous piece of machinery. He'd cut himself on a sharp blade, and there'd been nobody nearby to help. Very sad, but just a freak accident. The poor man had been careless.

'What kind of machine?' I asked, aiming to be helpful. Seeing the heat rise in Cutler's face, I quickly added: 'These kids are smart, they'll ask questions. What should I tell them?'

Placated, he considered. 'Some kind of slicing machine. For opening boxes.'

Something with a big sharp blade. Perhaps the safety cover was left off. A cautionary tale. My task was to disseminate this story to the kids and parents, if they asked (and they did). Quash all other versions, assure them all was well, then move on to less distressing topics.

'Absolutely,' I gabbled. 'Excellent proactive strategy, I'm completely on board.' (Another maritime clanger: I winced, but they didn't seem to notice.)

Then our chat abruptly changed direction. Where was I in the early hours of Wednesday morning, between three a.m. and dawn?

'Asleep,' I said without hesitation.

Cutler was observing me closely now.

'Asleep where?' asked the other officer.

'After dinner I usually head to the classroom to prepare the next day's lesson. Sometimes I'll nod off and sleep the night there.' Tuesday night being a case in point. 'It's quiet, the sofa's comfy, nobody's snoring. Unlike the dorm. Which, to be honest, doesn't smell great.' I was rambling, but they seemed satisfied. As if this just confirmed what they already knew: I hadn't slept in my bunk that night.

Stewart, from Aberdeen. At first, my handsome sailor had been reluctant to tell me his name. Had tried to fob me off with a nickname, but I'd coaxed the real one out of him. Told him I liked privacy as much as the next man, but anonymity did nothing for me. Not up close.

How did these officers know my bed was empty that night? Cameras? Some temp-sensing system that registers an absent body after lights-out, or human monitors – info gleaned from my fellow passengers? But who might have noticed my absence? I'd ziplocked my bunk, so it wouldn't have been obvious.

I had nothing to hide, not really – I *had* slept in the schoolroom that night. But scrutiny has an insidious effect: forces you to scroll back anxiously, replay all those unguarded moments, alert for anything you've said or done or thought that could be held against you. Thought crimes! Old Orwell in action. Enough to drive a man to medication. Which wasn't ideal, given my own dwindling supplies.

Released from Cutler's clutches, I staggered back to the schoolroom for the afternoon lesson, trying not to dwell on our predicament: a stick of driftwood battered by a hostile ocean, the elements against us, land nowhere in sight. The floor tilting at crazy angles, I turned my dazed Calmex smile on the children, concealing my nerves, pretending this was some kind of fun-ride. Avoided certain words: *Overboard. Wreck. Sink.*

On the morning of the killing, the deaf boy, Cleary Sullivan, had missed rollcall. He'd shown up with his mother at the tail end of class, pale and glassy-eyed, and plonked down beside his friend. His mum beckoned me into the passageway to break the news.

Horrific thing for any child to see. Especially a sensitive kid with a vivid imagination.

I promised to look out for her son, keep him engaged in lessons, occupy his mind. There was a former priest on board, I began, but his mother interrupted: 'That fella's Catholic.'

No surprise that Cate was protective. Cleary had been deaf three years, a legacy of some super-flu that almost killed him. She'd had him on the deaf school wait list (despite, she noted, that also being Catholic), but it was a hopelessly long list. Dublin had ground to a near-halt under the curfews, stream access was patchy, and virtual ed was straining at the seams.

Cate had encouraged his writing and drawing, helped maintain his friendships, spent countless hours practising lip-reading together. They began learning sign language too, she explained, but stopped when they got BIM approval: doesn't translate overseas, apparently. Instead, they'd coined their own language: a mix of gestures and facial expressions, official and invented signs. With home far behind them, the future a wild guess, and no Deaf community waiting to embrace them, mother and son were obviously close. No certainties ahead, just the hope that Cate's new salary might buy her child his hearing back.

The boy struck me as a keen observer, so I lent him my binoculars: a bid to distract him, direct his attention outward, beyond the confines of the ship. *They're meant to be waterproof,* I wrote in his notebook, *but try not to drop them overboard.* This raised a smile and a neatly penned: *Thanks, Teach!*

After relaying the official verdict on the 'accident', to lift the mood I set the kids a creative exercise: imagine a perfect world. Design it any way you like. Write about a day in this world, making yourself the main character. Fifteen minutes: *go.*

Three stories stood out. Lucy, a shy tween, read hers aloud: humankind lived up in the clouds, weightless and free, far above the earth. Gravity had no place in her Utopia: the sky people floated, without effort, wherever they pleased. Homes were mounds of cumulus, beds soft puffs of vapour, and everyone had birds for pets. No rulers, no crime, no wars. People spent their days creating elaborate cloud sculptures, to be illuminated by brilliant sunsets. The room listened intently. No-one asked what happened on cloudless days, or why humanity had abandoned solid ground.

Declan – nine or ten, a monkey-faced Irish kid, cheeky in a harmless way – dreamt up a very different paradise. If Lucy's genre was magic realism, Declan's was sci-fi action thriller. In his world Declan had the godlike power to make anyone obey his commands. Happily he was a benign dictator: he acquired a ferocious dinosaur to do his bidding, and they spent their days exploring volcanoes, feasting on cakes and stealing gold from pirates.

Bloodshed featured in just one tale: Troy, bolshy English kid, not yet twelve but built like a solid sixteen. His world was a machine-gun splatterfest, the plot lifted from some mindless digi-game.

Written to shock, I supposed, or get attention. Or perhaps simply a bid to mirror the recent violence, respond to a perceived threat – a way to process the gruesome rumours?

~

Overnight the sky cleared to a glorious washed blue, the wind died down to nothing. Passengers surfaced from below to sun themselves, sprawled out on the deck like lizards, all bare flesh and hairy shins, getting under the crew's feet. One group attempted tai chi, a bid to ward off device withdrawal, their graceful slow-mo ballet lent a drunken air by the occasional big swell.

Sunshine is such an underestimated pick-me-up. But as the rays shot down through the rigging, an angry blush crept across the paler specimens. The smart passengers reapplied sunscreen, sought shade or retreated below. But others seemed content to let their flesh cook. Cancer: king of the bad side-effects. So easy to forget that gorgeous light and warmth has a deadly side.

We soon found ourselves becalmed, the *Steadfast* languishing on glassy seas. When a breath of wind at last appeared, our progress was slowed again, this time by a massing of strange organisms. For days we laboured through the milky soup of a jellyfish bloom – millions of alien blobs crowding the water like malignant cells, their tentacles strung with debris, dragging at the hull.

It was eerie enough, being slowed by these boneless creatures. But while we languished in their clutches, the sea offered up a far more grisly apparition.

A woman's scream rang out – loud, urgent. People flocked to the rail, pointing, and like a sheep I followed. Saw it floating there, just below us, close to the hull of the ship: a human body, bloated and monstrous, tangled in with the jellyfish and rubbish, its rotted eyeholes open to the sky. Chunks missing from its torso, the skin mottled greenish black, coming away in sheets. Too late I turned away, the image already imprinted.

Crewmen ordered us back, and Captain Lewis hurried to the rail, straightening his cap, as if he'd been caught napping. He stared down, then faced his officers, his even features sagging slightly, disgust not quite concealed.

'No,' I heard him say. 'Absolutely not. Just photograph it. We need to be making way.'

The crew ordered us below decks until nightfall. Conversation at dinner was stilted, the obvious topics deemed unfit to broach, with people eating and children within earshot. I swallowed several precious doses before sleep came that night.

By morning the wind had picked up and we broke free of the jellied sludge, making up lost time, crossing the warm belt of the equator and heading south towards Cape Horn. Progress, delays, speed, direction – all was out of our hands. Being a passenger, I was learning, is an act of trust.

Big screens in the saloons tracked our progress. Rendered in pixels the ship resembled a bath toy, the Atlantic a harmless puddle – a neat digital taming act, designed to reassure. A wise move: a map that depicted our true predicament, an insignificant twig at the mercy of that vast indifferent ocean, would have had the whole ship gobbling Calmex by the box.

My own med supply waning, I'd exchanged a few strategic words with Kellahan, the ship's senior doctor. He struck me as a dry sort – polite enough, but not giving much away. My private-school accent did me no favours in that setting: I was just another migrant contractor, indentured labour like the rest, whereas Kellahan, working-class to his Afro-Caribbean boots, enjoyed a far senior rank. Status flipped by circumstance, the old rules reversed. And why not?

That evening, during dinner, a platoon of crewmen searched the men's dorms unannounced, combing through everything – lockers, clothes, bedding. Ransacking our personal effects.

Hours passed before I realised what was missing. Before I went digging in the lining of my luggage, seeking out those magical packets. A panicked scrabble of disbelief, the truth slowly dawning: my entire supply, gone.

4

CLEARY

The first time they'd tried to question him about the dead sailor, he'd gotten so flustered that his ma had cut the meeting short. But he knew that wouldn't be the end of it.

Sure enough, a few days later, they sent for him again. From the moment he entered the captain's rooms he willed himself not to look directly at the man guarding the door, not even a glance. That looming presence: at once he recognised the height, the slight stoop, that blur of hair half-covering his face. *Blackbeard*.

Captain Lewis had a kind face, but you could see the fright in him. With his ma acting as go-between, Cleary answered question after question, signing to her and scribbling words in his notebook. The captain sitting very straight and proper, the serious men in smart uniforms. And that bearded crewman guarding the door, watching and listening to everything. Writing out his answers, Cleary kept the man on the edge of his vision.

Did you see anyone near the kiosk that night?

No, he wrote.

He pictured the bearded man standing before the washroom mirror, examining that tell-tale streak of blood across his white cheek. Recalling the boy he'd just passed in the hallway. A boy he would forever recognise.

Breathe in, he told himself. *Breathe out. Look at the captain.*

Cleary knew the sailor in the kiosk was dead but wasn't sure how he'd been killed: what kind of wound could make a person's blood pour out like that. Not until this morning, when he'd seen Declan miming the attack with a group of kids: someone had crept up behind the man and slit his throat.

This news had filled Cleary with fresh horror. This was his secret fear, the one that had haunted him ever since his world had fallen silent: someone sneaking up behind him. An unseen, unheard attacker.

Stumbling down the corridor that night, Blackbeard had had a darkness coming off him, like someone who'd woken from a nightmare to find it was all true. Now Cleary felt that darkness taking on an almost physical force, the man's stare transmitting an unspoken threat. From the corner of his eye, he sensed the man's gaze shift from Cleary to his mother. His ma: the killer was staring at his ma. Cleary tried to focus on the captain, his jacket's shiny brass buttons, the gold embroidery on his cap.

Did you see anything else that night? asked the captain. *Anything you want to tell us about?*

No, wrote Cleary. He made the letters big, the word impossible to miss.

At last his ma called a halt and took him up top for some fresh air. He stole glances back, checking the man wasn't following them.

They walked in step, her hand resting on the back of his neck. Ever since that night she'd kept him close, touching his hair or shooting him quick smiles, passing a fork or clean socks before he could think to reach for them. She still let him run off to play with Declan after school, but made him promise to meet her in the saloon before dinner. And she'd set new rules: stick with the other kids, don't wander off alone, stay clear of the crew's areas, and no more roaming the ship after dark. Not ever. If he needed to pee – if he needed *anything* at night – he was to wake her. *Understand? Promise me, Cleary. Cross your heart.*

Blackbeard: he'd gotten the name from something Declan said. *Pirates,* his pal had mimed, slashing the air with an imaginary sword. *It was pirates killed your man.* Pirates in disguise, dressed up like normal sailors.

At night, after the dorm lights went off, Cleary was all in bits. He couldn't banish the sight: water sloshing in the tanks, light fizzing off the kiosk walls. The man's body lying in that slick pool of blackish red. The picture kept returning, leaving him weak and queasy, like that sickening swoop in your guts when a big wave snatched the floor from under you.

For comfort, he'd been creeping into his mother's bed, curling up against her like a puppy until sleep finally washed over him. But from now on, he decided, he'd stay in his own bunk. He was too big to get caught sleeping with his ma.

~

After school the next day Cleary joined a game of hide-and-seek. He'd found the perfect hiding spot, inside one of the orange lifeboats suspended over the gunwale. Too perfect, perhaps – he'd been hunched up in there for ages. The air was cooling, the wind turning sharp, a light rain misting the deck.

He had a knack for tucking himself into small gaps, keeping still for long stretches. His hiding places always offered a clear view of his pursuers. Best to see them coming: less of a shock, that way, when they pounced.

Cleary checked the spyhole. Huddled together, their hair and faces damp with drizzle, the children were tiring now, would soon give up the search.

The lifeboat scooted above the waves, a bird shadowing the

mothership. Canvas flapped, revealing an overcast sky, an ashen ceiling pressing down upon the sea. Under a seat he'd found a first-aid kit packed with tourniquets and tape, aspirin and seasickness tablets, coloured sticking plasters and a waterproof first-aid card. Cleary knew the bleeding section off by heart: *Elevate the legs. Apply firm pressure to the wound. Use your hands if nothing else is available.*

He pocketed a handful of sticking plasters. Stuck discreetly to walls, at eye level for an almost-ten-year-old boy, they might help him navigate the ship's tangled warren of corridors: green for safe routes, red for risky areas.

Out on deck Cleary could see the children were trailing away, heading below to continue their hunt, or perhaps abandon it. Declan brought up the rear, swinging a length of hose, a weapon for beheading any pirates they encountered. Cleary watched his friend go, half willing him to backtrack and discover him. But the kids vanished through a hatch into the belly of the ship.

A cramp twinged in his leg. The light was fading, the deck almost empty, just the odd sailor going about his work. His ma would be wondering where he was.

From here he couldn't see the kiosk, the crewman now guarding the door. Declan had pushed him to revisit the scene, inspect the deck for clues or bloody footprints. Not wanting to seem cowardly, Cleary had gone along with it, but was relieved when they'd been shooed away.

Bright red, the blood had been, pooling on the floor so slick and rich and wrong. It had been an omen, that first day back on the dock – that scarlet streak trailing down into the water, like the dying gush of some huge sea creature. Monsters could be lurking below him right now, squirming through the sea-floor muck, hunting for flesh.

He shivered. Was he safe here, dangling like bait above the waves?

Maybe not. He abandoned his hiding spot and dropped to the deck, wincing as pins and needles sparked through one leg. Staggering on his bocky limb, he almost collided with a couple rounding the corner, their cigarettes trailing sparks into the wind. He hobbled away, making for the warmth and shelter below decks.

Near the hatch loomed a tall figure, facing the sea, head concealed beneath the hood of a raincoat. The man turned as he approached, and Cleary's heart jerked like a hooked fish. Eyes fixed on his quarry, Blackbeard tipped his head back and slashed an invisible knife across the white skin of his own throat.

Cleary stumbled for the hatchway, aware of that shadow in his peripheral vision, like a shark seen from the corner of a diver's mask. He yanked the door open and felt its weight bang home behind him, shutting out the man and the rain and the coming dark.

BILLIE

She was becoming a regular at Limpet's now, her bar tab paid in song, Robbie playing along on fiddle. Tonight's set had gone down well, but two drinks away from closing time a ruckus broke out at a nearby table. Billie turned to see a passenger swaying on his feet, hands cupped to his face, blood leaking between his fingers.

'What the fuck?' Pure disbelief. An Irish voice, brown eyes full of injury.

A crew member glared back, primed for trouble. The room was hushed.

'Never say those words at sea,' said the crewman. 'If you parasites don't know that, you don't belong in here.'

Tabling his drink, Marshall stepped forward: 'And don't go whining to brass,' he warned the bleeding man. 'Not unless you want more of that.'

The crew swayed as one, all focused on the offender. The injured passenger threw a bewildered glance around the room, then let his friend lead him away.

Robbie exchanged a look with Billie. They were drinking with Juliette and Len, a sailor pal of hers, a wiry man adorned from neck to knuckles with blurred tattoos. Crew outnumbered passengers in here by five to one.

'What was that about?' Billie asked.

'Shush,' warned Juliette.

Their drinking partner spoke in a low voice. 'Certain words, it's bad luck to say them at sea. Only way to put things right is to spill blood. Punch on the nose does the trick.'

Billie kept her voice down too. 'Certain words?'

Len nodded. 'Example: a common expression for wishing a person good fortune.'

'Don't say it!' Robbie hissed in her ear.

She waved him away. 'I'm not daft.' Addressed the sailor: 'Why not? In case it has the opposite effect?'

'Correct. And you never refer to someone, let's say ... perishing in a particular way. A wet way, if you catch my drift.'

'Got you. What else?'

The tattooed sailor took a swallow of beer. 'There's a notorious number – everyone knows it. That's out too. We say "twelve plus one" instead.' And yes, he confirmed: however lovely the voice, singing the forbidden words was just as bad.

Billie scanned her memory for lyrics: just the other night, in this very room, she'd sung 'The Daemon Lover', that old song where the ship sank in the last line. Mentally she scratched it from her repertoire.

Their drinking companion had been at sea all his life, and had the wind-battered squint to prove it. These rituals were second nature for seamen, he said. But on this journey the crew were especially jumpy, alert to omens of all kinds. Good ones were in scant supply.

'Some say this whole trip's cursed,' said Juliette.

An easy rowdiness had reclaimed the room, the tension dissolved, as if the blow had never happened. A burst of laughter, drinks poured down gullets.

'What about the sickness?' Robbie asked. 'Can that be spoken about?'

A rumour was doing the rounds that despite all the elaborate precautions, the vigorous superscreen they'd all endured, disease had somehow followed them aboard. Several passengers were said to be confined below with an unspecified malady. Some people had resumed wearing masks, but there'd been no official announcement, so Billie had dismissed this as the usual germophobe nonsense, a paranoid overreaction to what was likely just an upset stomach.

But now the tattooed seaman told another story: two of those sick passengers were dead. Buried covertly at sea, their loved ones confined below decks for monitoring. Three more ill passengers were locked up in sick bay. No-one but the doctor and his deputy was allowed in that room, and they donned masks and gloves before coming within spitting distance of the door.

This made no sense to Billie. They'd been at sea almost three weeks. The superscreen had guaranteed them clean, zero risk, and they'd been dosed up on immune-boosters before departure. How could a bug have come aboard? An image flashed across her mind: an empty bunk in her dorm. The berth vacant several nights now, the woman who'd slept there gone. She'd assumed an onboard romance.

'This is all for a fact?' asked Robbie. 'It's not just blather?'

'Horse's mouth,' said Len. 'My mate had to kit up and swab the passageway outside sick bay – walls, doors, bloody ceiling. Highly contagious, they're saying.'

Brass were working hard to keep it under wraps, said Juliette, but were plainly shitting themselves. The crew's outbound comms were in lockdown, their mail now vetted before sending. Any mention of illness or trouble on board and the message would be dumped, the sender fined and locked up. Whatever this sickness was, brass were desperate to keep a lid on it.

Robbie frowned. 'Right, no devices. But why block the staff's outbounds?'

'Bad for business if this got out,' said Juliette. 'Hurt the company name.'

'Big money in these routes,' said Len. 'Competition's fierce. You lot are valuable cargo.' Then he leant in, his presence suddenly heavier. 'But you didn't hear any of this from me. Right?'

'Mum's the word,' said Robbie. 'Loose lips ...' He trailed off, that ready grin nowhere in evidence.

'How does it manifest?' asked Billie. The tattooed man looked blank. 'The sick ones – what are their symptoms?'

Len hadn't got that close, and didn't plan to. Bad omens had been racking up, he said. They'd departed on a Thursday – Thor's day, the thunder god – which was just asking for trouble. Brass had cited orders from on high, but this ill-chosen date had made the crew uneasy. Some were alarmed to see so many bereaved passengers boarding in black mourning garb. Others had remarked on the high number of redheads amongst the human cargo, which also boded ill.

'No getting round that one,' said Juliette. 'Scots and Irish blood's riddled with the red gene. Did you see the dock when we left? Gingers everywhere.'

And then there was the ship's name. '*Steadfast?*' said Robbie. 'Sounds solid. Reliable.'

'Yeah,' said Len. 'But that's not her original name. When Red Star bought her she was the *Albatross.*' The huge seabirds were once a lucky omen, he explained, and killing one was said to bring misfortune. But that portent had shifted with the times. Now, with the species nudging up against extinction, the bird had lost its lucky connotations.

'Couldn't get crew to sign on,' said the sailor. 'Company had to change her name.'

'Bloody tragic,' put in Juliette. 'What idiot names a ship after a bird that's going extinct?'

'But she's not the *Albatross* now,' said Billie. 'Surely that's no black mark.' Then, hesitant, 'Do you believe all that stuff?' Her seafaring dad had always rubbished these superstitions.

'Course not,' replied the sailor, studying his hands, the skin inked with swallows, stars and dice, a compass rose. Juliette remained silent.

The rabble swelled as people drained glasses and ordered last drinks. Billie saw wet mouths on glass rims, wristbands swiping credit screens, the barman dragging a dirty rag across the counter. Envisaged all that wasn't visible: saliva traces, microbes, lungfuls of used air filtered through damp human interiors, infusing system after system. The atmosphere felt close, over-breathed.

'What about that murderer, then?' asked Robbie brightly, angling for a shift in mood. 'Nabbed the bastard, haven't they?'

A bulletin had aired a few days back, Captain Lewis' smooth voice issuing from unseen speakers. Identified and detained, he'd said.

'That's what they want you to think,' said Len.

But the crime was solved, Robbie insisted: the culprit captured, the death declared an accident. A fight that got out of hand, some argument over black trading.

'A fight with who?' asked Len. 'The brig's empty. No killer locked away down there.' He changed the subject, and soon excused himself.

As the drinkers trailed out into the night, Billie spotted an image on a screen above the bar. A smiling sailor, the Red Star logo on his cap, a gleam of gold tooth giving his grin a rakish air. *Davy Whelan*, read the text. Then a span of dates. Billie took a sharp breath: she knew that face. Squeezed the red cigarette lighter in her pocket, the one he'd slid across the counter to her. Did a quick calculation: he'd been thirty-three, just five years older than her. *Rest in peace, old mate*, she read.

~

Sleep that night was fitful, marred by uneasy dreams. Stretchers hurtled down long white passageways, and at her feet coloured lines snaked off in the direction of the death wards.

Next morning she made for a private spot, a guano-spattered alcove she'd discovered, open to the air and just big enough for one. Tucked behind some loud machine, the clamour of its motor loud enough to mask her voice from passers-by, it was the perfect place to run through scales, to practise old songs or make up new ones.

Sun warmed her skin. A container ship ploughed across the middle distance and seabirds flapped in the rigging above, seeking a solid perch to rest their wings.

Fear would solve nothing: cautious vigilance was the best defence. San thoroughly and often, hands off your face, beware of body fluids, avoid second-hand air. Be alert for any sign of illness: the person dishing your dinner or replenishing cutlery. A cough, a sniffle, the telling flush of fever. Vomiting – well, that was no useful clue out here.

She'd left her mask in her bunk. The few passengers now wearing them again were drawing attention, facing demands about what they knew, even outright anger at the idea such measures might be warranted. A stomach bug, it had to be. Fear tended to skew talk towards disaster. As for the rumoured deaths, perhaps there'd been a heart attack, an aneurysm. Some buried physical fault not picked up by the superscreens.

Soon they'd round the Cape of Good Hope, then head south towards the Roaring Forties. The vessel moved with the inbuilt urge of a migratory bird. Not an albatross: some common seabird, light-boned but hardy, built to go the distance. She tracked the lonely bulk of the container ship, its grafted-on sails – no elegance there, just pure function, an old vessel retrofitted for maximum fuel efficiency, its container stacks a monument to the needs and wants of far-off populations. In rough weather those metal boxes could tumble into the sea, wallowing just below the surface, a booby trap awaiting some hapless ship.

Lost buckets were a common sight. The flotsam was a parade of clues, evidence of remote mishaps, and Billie passed the time by speculating on its origins: an algae-ridden mattress, dumped on some Spanish beach when a relationship soured. A basketball, bobbing like an oversized orange, kicked off an Angolan pier by kids too young to dive in and retrieve it; a plastic washing-basket, tossed from a Brazilian balcony by a drunken maid. Fence palings and broken tents, wrecked kites and lost shoes: human souvenirs torn loose by floods and hurricanes.

Your eyes played tricks on you out here, the whole vista lending itself to hallucinations.

Billie took a full breath and sent a run of notes into the wind, a rising chain of melody that filled her chest and vibrated through her blood, her very cells alive with it. Her voice drowned out the static: the yammering machine, the slap of wind, the white noise of her thoughts. Her single gift and talent, it rang from deep inside her body and flew out to meet the vastness of the sea.

TOM

One balmy Saturday morning I was up on the main deck, trying to soothe my scrambled neurons with an ancient paperback I'd found in the saloon, when shouts rang out – a male voice, raised in clear distress.

A commotion down the deck, a glimpse of flailing arms. When I arrived the crowd was swelling, but standing well clear. Against the rail, his back to the sea, was a man in his early thirties – Liverpool accent, British Bangladeshi guy – swinging what appeared to be a broomstick. He looked possessed: eyes like black holes, hair wild, sweat streaming off him. Voice hoarse, a broken half-scream: 'Get back! Don't let it touch me!'

Crew were trying to calm the distressed man: it's alright, mate, take it easy. Put that down, you'll hurt yourself.

But the passenger was past listening or reason. Kept screaming, in that pitiful rasp: 'No no no, don't let it near me!' Slashing the air like he was fighting an invisible dragon: 'Get it away from me!'

When the delusional man began to clamber over the ship's rail, a group of crewmen leapt forward and tackled him to the deck.

He thrashed and bellowed, voice cracking mid-scream, a terrible sound: 'Noooooo! Get away from me!'

Flung aside, his weapon landed at my feet, and I wedged it safely out of the way beneath a bench. A pointless act, but I felt embarrassed for doing nothing to help.

Crewmen herded us away. Looking back at the deranged passenger, now pinned beneath half a tonne of seafaring muscle, I recognised the man on the top of the pile: my beautiful sailor, the man whose skin now occupied my daydreams. Body braced, features half obscured, but still recognisable.

That's when I first noticed it. At the time I dismissed it as protocol, a routine measure for handling unspecified insanity at close quarters: the crew struggling with the crazed passenger were all wearing masks and gloves.

Later, over lunch, one of the dads remarked that at least this awful incident cleared up a mystery: the crazy fella, well, surely, he was the murderer. I bit my tongue, resisted asking: the same murderer who's locked up somewhere in the bowels of the ship? There's no end to the creative explanations that will flourish in a vacuum.

Fronting my class the next day – unmedicated, nerves a-jitter, my membranes raw – I fielded a question from eight-year-old Tamila: 'Teach, are bad people allowed on ships? Murderers and that?'

'There are no bad people on this ship,' I said, taking care to face the deaf boy, speak slowly, catch his eye. In big letters I wrote on the board: *This is a safe place. You're all safe here.*

Mia, eleven, raised a hesitant hand: 'But what about the crazy man? The one who tried to drown himself?'

'He's not a bad person,' I replied. 'Just muddled up. Maybe he stayed out in the sun too long without a hat. Now, who can tell me what the equator is?'

Talk travelled fast, and I wished I'd gotten out in front of it, not improvised some half-baked tale of sunstroke. But what should I have said? The old euphemisms for mental breakdown were too foreboding: unwell, sick, ill. There were already rumours on that front. I just prayed that's all they were – groundless rumours.

People had noticed: the masks, the gloves, the empty bunks.

Since Davy Whelan's violent death, parents had been seeking

me out for private chats, asking about emotional containment and support measures, anxious for news, checking their kids were in safe hands.

Now a new strand of disquiet was surfacing: were the stories true? Had sickness come aboard?

5

CLEARY

Floating out his bedroom window, Cleary paddled a slow breaststroke over the Pearse Street flats, skimming the lichen-mottled roofs. He soared over the washing lines, the car park and basketball court, across Hanover Street where a burning car belched acrid smoke, and on towards the green-black sleekness of the Liffey.

But when he reached the river he began to doubt his powers, his ability to stay aloft and steer. Dead ahead loomed the rigging of the boat restaurant, waiting to ensnare him. Helpless, drifting, he willed himself higher, but it was no use. The web slowly reeled him in.

He woke with a jerk and lay in his bunk, trying to quell a lingering dread as the ship rolled gently beneath him. The cabin lights were on and people were stirring, heading off to breakfast.

In the bunk below, his ma's curtain was shut tight. Strange: normally she left it open for him. He unzipped it, but as the light spilt in she turned her back. Her bedcovers lay twisted at her feet and the air in her compartment had a sour smell. He shook her bare leg, but she raised one hand and waved him away, her face sunk in the pillow.

Need more sleep, she signed. *You go on without me.*

Setting off in slippers and pyjama pants, he found Declan finishing breakfast with his parents in the mess-room. Cleary accepted two scoops of porridge, made himself a mug of sugary tea, which he wasn't strictly allowed, and took a seat beside his friend. Declan's mum had a good gawk at his pyjama pants and gave a thin smile, just to show she didn't like the cut of him, so he got busy constructing an angry face with raisins on the surface of his porridge, Declan squirming in appreciation. As he left with his parents Declan shot Cleary a grin: *See you in class.*

Returning to the dorm with a jam sandwich for his ma, he found her bunk zipped tight again, but now the lock was activated too. He sniffed, checking for her scent, her presence, but could tell the sealed-up space was empty. He drummed his palms on the taut fabric, feeling an involuntary sound escape his throat. A woman poked her head out of a nearby bunk, face rumpled with sleep, a finger pressed to her lips.

He made an effort to calm himself. In the shower, that's where she'd be. Or the jacks. No need to be a baby about it.

A hand touched his arm: the red-haired lady, Fiona. She knelt down, her smile not quite reaching her eyes, said Cleary's name, then held his shoulders and spoke in an exaggerated way, so it was impossible to make out the words. She waited for some sign he'd understood. But Cleary froze, distress zinging through his blood. Something was badly wrong.

With the woman stood a girl from Cleary's class. She handed her mother a pen and a piece of card, and Fiona wrote: *Morning, Cleary. Your ma's with the doctor. Don't worry, she's just a bit seasick. You're to stay with us tonight.* He stared at the message until the woman plucked it from his fingers, wrote on the back and returned it with a bright smile: *School now. Erin will go with you. Best change out of those PJs!* She clapped her hands, like this was a game.

He climbed into his bunk, knowing full well he was being lied to. His ma would never leave him like this: she'd have waited, no matter how sick she felt. She knew how much he needed her, how worried he got. No: someone had taken her.

Blackbeard. Could he have done this? Cleary dressed quickly, and as he descended the ladder his legs felt rubbery. Dazed, he followed the girl, Erin, through the ship, stumbling like a sleepwalker, his mind locked onto a single thought: *Lost your sea legs. Lost your sea legs.*

Another boy had taken Cleary's regular seat next to Declan, a heavy kid who'd once tripped him in the hallway. Declan made an apologetic face and rolled his eyes towards the interloper.

Teach was showing a nature vid, writing words up on the board: *Foraging, Migration, Safety in numbers.* Cleary's thoughts were all tangled. Up on the screen fish hovered in the shadowy ocean depths, a great writhing ball of silver bodies, flashing in unison as light caught their scales. Back and forth they shivered, one undulating mass, a body without a head, lost in the inky water. Teach seemed to find this strange dance beautiful, but to Cleary it resembled panic. Kids turned to stare, and he realised he must be making a sound. He tried to steady himself.

Onscreen a barrage of seabirds broke the water's surface one by one. Beaks sharp as arrows, they plunged into the knot of fish, the silver mass quivering and bulging in mutations of fright. *Shoaling*, wrote Teach. *Schooling. Predators.* Cleary clung to his desk as if it was a raft.

Could he fake illness, hurl on the floor? Get sent to sick bay, try to find her? But his body felt heavy, stuck to his chair. His thoughts skittered off in all directions, and beneath his confusion pulsed a low throb of dread.

A man entered the classroom: the old sailor with the white Santa beard, the one who rounded up the mitchers and brought them into class. He gave the children a jolly wave, then drew the teacher aside. The class began to fidget as the men huddled together.

When Teach turned back to them his expression was gentle, his movements deliberate. He held his palms out, a soothing motion.

He kept repeating a phrase as the sailor opened a bag, took out a white tube-shaped object, tore off its plastic wrapper.

Teach waved to catch Cleary's attention, then spoke his name. *Nothing to worry about,* he wrote on the board as the crewman walked down the aisle, handing out a familiar white shape to every kid.

A long moment of dismay as, one by one, the signals blinked out. Then Cleary lost the words his teacher was saying, lost all of them. Gone: the world retreating one step back, as if the air itself was thickening, a forcefield pushing him away from other people. Mouths concealed, speech erased, words buried by white masks.

BILLIE

The man stopped Billie as she left the dining hall after lunch. She saw the blue uniform first, the Red Star logo on the pocket. When the sailor touched her arm a jolt of panic went through her. She had feared this might be coming. It took a second to place him: Len, the heavily tattooed crewman they'd drunk with in the bar, the superstitious guy. Expression blank, he gave no sign of recognising her.

'Billie Galloway?' he asked as the lunch crowd trailed past them. She nodded: no point in denying her own name.

'Come with me,' he said. 'Management wants you.'

He was already walking away, so she followed at a discreet distance, trying to act like they weren't together. Denials and counter-accusations raced through her mind: no, she had no idea what they were talking about. What infraction? Hadn't she passed all the security checks? This was ridiculous, outrageous, a mistake.

The tattooed sailor kept glancing back to check she was following. They went down several narrow passageways before he swiped a security panel, shoved against a heavy door, held it open as he waited for her to catch up. *Authorised Personnel Only*, said a sign.

Billie stopped. 'What's this about?' she said. The cool tone deliberate, no sign of nerves.

Len blew an impatient breath. 'Don't ask me, I'm just following orders. Rounding up the troops.'

'For what? Where are we going?'

He wasn't a big man, mid-fifties maybe, but he was wiry. If need be, she might be able to fell him with a well-aimed kick. She tried to read his eyes, could spot no recognition there, nor any obvious threat. But this didn't feel right.

'They'll explain. I'm not to say anything, just fetch you lot.' Len seemed annoyed, like she was wasting his time. Through the doorway she glimpsed a flight of stairs leading down to god knew where.

She planted her feet. 'What's going on?'

'Jesus Christ,' he said, exasperated. 'You want me to tell them you won't come? Because none of us has a choice here. Let's go. Brass will explain.'

They followed a maze of passages to a grubby door marked *Equipment*. It opened onto some kind of storeroom, full of people, fifteen or so passengers seated on rows of plastic chairs, as many crew standing around the walls. There were ropes and plastic bins stacked in the corners, notices stuck to the walls, a roster scrawled on a board.

Up the front Billie saw the first mate, Cutler, sitting with two offsiders, the trio holding court behind a table draped with a British flag. Heads turned as Billie and the crewman entered, the passengers wearing apprehensive looks, the crew bored or grim. She found a seat near the back, out of Cutler's sightline.

Mostly women, the assembled passengers, and most her age or older. Some were murmuring to each other, indignant, but others stared fixedly ahead, their faces fearful or defensive. The air was charged with tension, as if the crowd was braced for trouble, accusations set to fly. Billie spotted Marshall up the back, scanning the room in anxious leaps. Catching sight of her, the chief steward quickly looked away. She felt a new prickle of unease.

When the last arrivals locked the door behind them, the room fell quiet. Cutler took the floor, threw back his epaulettes and addressed the room in a tone charged with a cold authority.

'You are here under strict legal confidentiality,' he told them. 'Nothing said in this room today will be repeated outside these walls. We will provide an official story before you leave, and that is the explanation you will use to respond to any enquiries – from your fellow passengers, your family, your loved ones. Anyone.' He glared around for emphasis. Snagged Billie's gaze, held it.

'This ship is now under Maritime Emergency Law. I will assume that this situation is, quite understandably, outside the experience of most of you here, so let me explain what that means.' A theatrical turn, hands clasped behind his back. More targeted glaring, like a prison warden scanning would-be escapees.

Billie got the sense Cutler had dirt on everyone in this room, was privy to information both private and compromising. But this, of course, was the intended effect. All bluff, she told herself. Just bully tactics.

'Our captain's word is now law,' the first mate continued. 'My word, and that of my officers, is now law. I have the power to deputise crew members, and their word, too, is to be regarded as law. All passengers will obey instructions, without question, or face immediate imprisonment, followed by rigorous prosecution dryside. The charges will relate to treason, and will carry a maximum penalty of nine years' imprisonment.'

The only motion in the room was the gentle synchronised sway of bodies, moving in mute obedience to the ocean swells.

'You may be aware that we have an outbreak of serious, potentially deadly illness on board.'

Billie took this in, the implications dawning: this was not about her, not about her past. Or not entirely.

An outbreak, he continued, of an unspecified and evidently highly contagious disease. Despite exhaustive screening measures, despite thorough bio-vetting of every person permitted to board this ship. Despite the company sparing no expense, no effort, to implement the most rigorous world-class bio-scans, designed to rule out the faintest possibility of infectious disease coming aboard. The superscreening protocols devised by international experts and guaranteed foolproof by governments on both sides.

'Personally,' he spat, 'that strikes me as distinctly suspect. But I will leave that particular investigation to the forensics team that now awaits us dryside.'

This speech was not all bluff, Billie saw. The bitten-off words, the rigid posture, the air of contained rage: the man was genuinely angry. Fearful too, perhaps, although he hid it well if so.

'You are here' – another calculated pause as Cutler surveyed individual faces – 'because you have been selected to be part of the emergency response. Let me emphasise something: this is not optional. Not voluntary. Under the legal framework now governing this vessel, you do not have a choice.'

Now there was movement in the room. Bodies shifting, brief snatches of eye contact. A woman in a headscarf raised her arm. The first mate ignored her, continued speaking.

'There will be an opportunity for questions before you are permitted to leave,' he said. 'For now, your role is to listen. This situation could not be more serious. At this stage we don't know exactly what we're dealing with. But Captain Lewis has issued orders: this disease must be contained, at any cost. Losses must be minimised. The sick must be immediately isolated and nursed, to the best of our abilities, to maximise survival rates.'

Billie felt something inside her drop. *Please, no. Not this.*

The death toll, Cutler went on, now stood at four. Eight others had been identified as ill and isolated below decks in a provisional sick bay, a hastily converted section of the hold. The ship was not ideally equipped to deal with an outbreak of disease: given all the precautions that had been taken, nothing like this could have been envisaged. A work detail was currently fitting extra sick-room beds and building an antechamber, to be used for decontamination purposes.

He picked up a device from the table, flicked through screens. 'The passengers in this room have been identified as possessing skills related to medicine, hygiene or personal service industries. Shortly I'll hand over to the ship's doctor, who will outline rostering arrangements, care regimens, and isolation and decontamination procedures.'

The wards. The death wards, all over again.

But first, Cutler continued, he wanted to assure them of three things. It was imperative that they themselves did not fall ill, or contaminate other passengers. They would work under strict quarantine and decontamination protocols, to be outlined shortly. A blonde woman next to Billie sank her head into her palms.

'Second, under Maritime Emergency Law, you will be compensated for your work through payment of extraordinary wages. These are generous rates – over-generous, perhaps, but that particular decision is out of my hands. A small stipend will be paid weekly, and the remainder logged and paid out to you in full on arrival dryside.'

Billie sat there, numb, as she listened to the rest of Cutler's spiel, a series of threats, warnings and ultimatums. They were duty-bound to ward off speculation and panic amongst the passengers, and legally compelled to disclose nothing of what had occurred in this room, besides the officially sanctioned version. The pay rate he outlined was a surprise – almost five times what she'd earnt back home, before being unceremoniously sacked. She focused on that figure, tried to keep images of the death wards at bay.

A crew member manoeuvred a board into view. Billie saw columns of names, rows of neat capital letters. Spotted her own name at the top of the last row. Shift teams: a hospital roster. People shuffled, those near the back craning to read the board, and Cutler held up one hand, a command for stillness. Arms were waving now, but he ignored them.

'I promise you this: should anyone here breach these conditions – or disobey orders in any way – they will find themselves spending a long and very unpleasant stretch of time inside a maximum-security prison.'

Failure to cooperate would mean prosecution, jail, ruin: the room was silent as he let this sink in. Then he motioned a short black man forward. Grey-haired, dressed in a white lab coat, his glasses slipping down his nose, he gripped a folder and looked distinctly anxious.

'I'll now hand over to the ship's head doctor, Jim Kellahan, for a medical briefing. Questions will follow. Then you'll be fitted with wristbands that allow access to the controlled zone.' Cutler resumed his seat, and Billie saw a scarcely perceptible wince cross his face. The man deflating slightly in that moment.

The doctor stepped forward, opened his mouth to speak, but was interrupted by a sharp screech, the sound of a chair abruptly shoved back. Then a male voice from the back of the room: 'Fuck this.' A man was on his feet, weaving between the chairs. White guy, early thirties, dark curly hair. English. 'Fuck this,' he said again, louder, making for the door.

A solid crewman blocked his way, took a grip on his arm. 'Steady, mate,' he said, a warning. 'Nobody's leaving.'

The curly-haired man examined the meaty hand clamped to his bicep, then appealed to his fellow passengers. 'They can't do this,' he said to the room, casting around for backup. He addressed the first mate. 'You can't force us to do this.'

'Sit down,' said Cutler. He remained seated but removed his cap, set it on the table beside him. His hair stuck up on one side, and fatigue was evident in his whole bearing. He spoke with weary impatience, the anger gone. 'The criminal charges I mentioned are a promise, not an empty threat. The jails where we're headed are nasty places. We can lock you up right now, if you'd prefer, but it would be much smarter to cooperate.'

The passenger threw a final pleading glance around the room. 'Let go of my arm,' he said quietly, and the crewman did.

As the objector sank into a chair, Billie tried to send him a look of solidarity, but his head was down, shoulders hunched in defeat.

The doctor took this as his cue, drew himself up to his full five-foot-nothing, and delivered the room a watery smile. 'Now then,' he said in a bright voice, Brummie accent. He gestured at an anaemic-looking young guy skulking behind him, also dressed in medical whites. 'This is Doctor Owen Price, my deputy. Let's run through how we're going to tackle this.'

TOM

From bad to worse, that was the unmistakable direction. While I was chewing my nails over the remote possibility of shipwreck, a much more insidious horror had been brewing in our midst.

I'd barely begun our morning class when a messenger pulled me out, announced that school was cancelled for the day, and hustled me off to an urgent meeting in the captain's quarters, with a handful of senior staff – Captain Lewis, the doc and his deputy, officers, managers in charge of various sections.

Evidently my rank had climbed a few notches, but the change was far from welcome.

The captain's face was grave, no trace of his professional twinkle. He left it to Cutler to deliver most of the bad news.

Four dead so far, Cutler announced bluntly, and more than twice that number sick.

The head doctor chipped in, reported that details were scarce: they didn't know what the sickness was, or how it was spread, but clearly it was both lethal and highly contagious. We all had to be vigilant for signs of illness, fever, confusion in fellow passengers or crew – and, he added, in ourselves.

The sick had been isolated, their clothing and bedding burnt. The dead were on ice down in the hold, awaiting the pathologists and virologists once we reached dry land. All scheduled stop-offs in foreign ports were cancelled. Both governments had been informed. We would be held in quarantine when we arrived at our destination.

Fear was palpable in that cramped room. Beneath it ran a frantic subcurrent, a tally being conducted in every head: who coughed in my vicinity, used the wash cube before me? Who leant too close, whose stale air did I inhale? How clean was that doorknob, the breakfast cutlery, my own hand? What did I touch? *Who* did I touch?

Disbelief and shock were plain on people's faces. All those tests and protocols and scans, all those assurances: they'd promised we'd be safe. A sterile zone, guaranteed risk-free.

When Doctor Kellahan finished his grim summary, Captain Lewis took the floor. 'Tomorrow there will be a mass decon up on the main deck.' He made it sound routine, but the details were unsettling: every soul on board herded into makeshift cubicles, stripped to the skin, and foamed to within an inch of our lives. All chemmed in one fell swoop, including the captain and his officers, a show of solidarity to head off any accusations of unequal treatment. Crew would be on hand to assist, Cutler added. Unrest, perhaps even resistance, was anticipated.

'We must all play our part,' said Captain Lewis, regarding each of us in turn. 'Follow the containment protocols strictly. Enforce the rules, report any breaches.' He adjusted his mask. 'But morale is also crucial. The passengers will take their cue from us. Be stringent, but aim to carry on as usual. We need vigilance, not hysteria.'

The message was clear: we must toe the sanctioned line, placate a shipload of frightened people, defuse anxiety before it bloomed into full-blown panic.

Just being in that stuffy room, with its sharp undercurrent of fear, made me feel faint.

'What are the symptoms, exactly? How does the illness manifest?' An intense dark-haired Scotswoman, addressing the captain, no kow-towing. A passenger, but not intimidated by the company.

Captain Lewis deferred to the head doctor, who recited an alarming list: headache, nausea, aches and pains, high fever, vomiting and diarrhoea, coughing and wheezing, rash, blood nose, possible delirium and hallucinations.

I recalled that crazed man slashing the air with his broomstick, fighting off an invisible enemy.

The Scotswoman fired out more questions, then outlined a series of steps that should be put in place. Clearly she knew this territory well. When Cutler tried to interrupt her, she spoke over him; the captain held up a hand, silencing his offsider, granting her leave to continue as he scribbled notes.

'Do we have PPE on board?' the woman asked. An awkward silence followed. 'Personal Protective Equipment,' she enunciated.

The answer, it seemed, was no. At this news, the Scotswoman swore under her breath.

They kept us there three hours, planning the response. The captain's announcement, made over the PA during lunch, was couched in tones so reassuring that at first it drew scant reaction. People continued to chew their food, murmur banalities, clink cutlery. Laughter rang out, then was abruptly cut off by an elbow.

There were shushing noises as the message landed. Forks were lowered, heads raised.

'It is important that we all remain calm,' Captain Lewis was saying, his voice low and steady. 'My staff have the situation in hand. But from this point on, when a crew member asks you to do something, that should be taken as an order.'

Eyes drifted to those of us already wearing masks: me, the kitchen staff, the crew guarding the exits. Frightened glances: what did we know?

As the facts sank in, a pulse of dark energy swept through the mess-room. A collective intake of air, a stifled sob. Crew members walked the rows, dispensing masks, my handsome sailor amongst them. He caught my eye – just briefly. We'd planned another rendezvous, but that seemed unlikely now.

Crew commenced a ferocious regime of scrubbing and swabbing, the chemical reek of bleach and decon drifting through the passageways. A delegation of passengers was soon demanding an audience with the captain.

My brain fuzzed by anxiety, I struggled to sleep that night. I felt raw, frayed, emotionally threadbare. Had to keep reminding myself to breathe.

The whole ship was now officially a crime scene. There were rumours the outbreak had been deliberately induced. 'Been done before,' I'd heard a crewman mutter as we left the captain's rooms. 'Rabbit fever. Malpox, Chimera 9. All those airports.' The last round of attacks, the final straw before they shut down Heathrow, was blamed on biovigilantes – anti-migrant hate groups, raving nationalists hell-bent on closing all borders in both directions. But why target us? A single ship, a harmless herd of labourers? It made no sense.

Surely now, I thought, there'd be no shame in approaching Doctor Kellahan – or trying my luck with Owen Price, his deputy? Explaining how my medications had been stolen, assuring them I'd always stuck to the prescribed dosage.

Classes were suspended until further notice. I worried about the children: how frightening this would be for them. What might lie ahead for them, for all of us. Surrounded by that alien tract of ocean, more than a month from land, caged in with an invisible killer.

Staring into the darkness I felt weak, jittery, unprepared. And fearful, knowing that fear was now the logical response.

6

CLEARY

Night had fallen hours ago, but he must be patient. He'd only get one chance. Crouched shivering behind a pile of ropes, he watched the door that led to the sick room, the crewman now guarding it. *Danger: No Admittance.*

When a bundled figure approached, wheeling a trolley wreathed in hazard tape, the guard scanned their wristband and stood aside to let them pass. The door cracked open, light spilling out across the deck.

Cleary picked his moment: the guard holding the door wide, his attention elsewhere, as the trolley lumbered through. He dashed forward, shoved past the trolley, went flying down a ramp and along a corridor, making for the door at the far end: *STOP! Biohazard – Restricted Area – Do Not Enter.*

But the door was locked. Fists pounding on metal, he opened his mouth and screamed for his mother.

Hauled away roughly, his arms pinned to his sides, Cleary kicked and struggled in vain. His captors dumped him in a wash cube and turned the cold water on full blast. A masked figure sprayed him with decon foam, the chemicals stinging his eyes. They left him there, soaking wet and sobbing, for what seemed like hours. Then someone pulled him to his feet, dried him roughly with a towel and fitted a mask over his face.

He had no memory of making his way up to the foredeck. No idea how long he stood here, hands clamped to the rail, damp clothes clinging to his skin, the wind chilling his flesh right through like refrigerated meat, as the sky grew light and the sea transformed from black to brilliant blue. Hypnotised by that great mass of water heaving away in every treacherous direction, swallowing up distance and time.

Vaguely aware of a human presence, a warm hand thawing his frozen one. An oversized coat wrapped around him.

Then he spotted it: a distant object, white against the sapphire waves. At first he thought it was a sail, but it sat strangely for a ship. It had a solemn air, like a mountain poking its snow-capped peak above the swells.

He raised his arm and pointed out to sea. Turned in wonder to the woman crouched beside him, her dark hair whipping around her head like tentacles. She followed his finger, her eyes widening as she saw it too: an iceberg.

People gathered to watch it drifting past. Huddled together for warmth, Cleary and the woman stood transfixed as the huge chunk of ice rode the swells with a tired sort of majesty, as if in no hurry to reach its destination. Its exact size was hard to gauge, but it looked as big as an office block. Its blue-white bulk had finely sheared edges and swooping curves, like a mound of meringue sculpted by a sharp knife. Broken off from its moorings, it wandered the ocean like a lost thing.

They tracked the iceberg as it slowly shrank into the distance. When it had gone the crew seemed subdued. The wind had died down, and the seabirds had settled in the rigging. Like some alien king, a floating omen from another realm, the iceberg had left stillness in its wake.

Numb with exhaustion, Cleary turned to the woman and raised

his arms in an automatic gesture. As she lifted him, he wrapped his limbs around her and burrowed his freezing face into her neck. Carrying him across the lurching deck, she stopped to speak to someone. As they moved off again, Cleary looked back over the woman's shoulder.

There, watching them depart, stood Blackbeard. Cleary hid his eyes and held on tight.

The woman carried him around corners and down stairs, and laid him on a bed. She posed a mute question – pointing at him, then tapping her chest and lifting both hands, eyebrows raised – but the gestures meant nothing, were not part of the language he and his mother shared.

So cold, his bones chilled to the core. The woman felt his forehead, checked his pulse, brought him a heatpack and a cup of hot soup. Then sanned her hands and gestured for him to remove his clothes. Briskly she rubbed his skin down with a scented cream that drew the warmth back into his blood. As the chill receded Cleary closed his eyes. Gave himself up to the spreading heat, the safe pressure of her hands.

Thawed out, he scoffed a chocolate bar as the woman watched. No smile, but her eyes were kind. He recognised her now: the long dark hair and upright walk, pale and skinny, but strong looking. These past few days, watching from his hiding spot, he'd seen her come and go, the door that led to the sick room admitting her as if by magic. A hazier memory, too: back at the depot, the woman's mouth moving as people swayed and clapped all around her. A faint patter and hum reaching his ears.

Now she placed her cheek against her hands: *Time to sleep.* She tucked the blanket over Cleary, lay down beside him, killed the light and turned away. Her body fell still immediately, like she'd dropped straight off a ledge into the depths of sleep.

Sobs broke out of him, deep involuntary shudders. At once the woman rolled over and held him close in the dark. She was thinner than his ma, and smelt different – almost boyish; shampoo and pepper, mixed with a smoky chemical scent.

A buzz began to emanate from her body: words patterned into music, her fingers tapping out a gentle rhythm on Cleary's chest, over his heart. She was singing to him. Lulled by the hum of her voice – a felt vibration, faintly audible, like the purring of a cat – he soon sank into sleep, her solid warmth beside him.

~

That afternoon Cleary woke alone. In his shoe was a note: he should go back to the family dorm, it said, stay close to his parents. And keep his mask on. *Take care*, she'd signed off. No name.

He made straight for his ma's bunk, hoping to find her there – unsteady and pale, but out of danger, on the mend. Instead he found a big yellow 'X' taped across the sealed bed. *Biohazard*, read the black letters. *Do not cross.*

He could not bear to stay here in the family dorm – Fiona's forced smiles fooling no-one, the other parents snatching nervous glances, hustling their kids away, Declan not even allowed to talk to him. Cleary shoved some things into a rucksack and set off.

At his knock the schoolroom door cracked open. School was cancelled, but he'd seen Teach hovering, his hair and clothes rumpled, as if he'd been napping in there. Teach pulled on a pair of gloves, made Cleary do the same, then sanned two pens and started scribbling in Cleary's notebook.

The info was not new: his ma was sick, she had to rest. She was in safe hands, the doctors were looking after her, but the bug was contagious. Cleary must stay away. Teach was sorry – sorry he didn't have more info, or better news.

New rules, Teach wrote next. Cleary recognised the plague drill from back home: mask on, san your hands. Don't touch your eyes, nose, mouth. Don't get too close to other people. Wave the screens, no contact. Avoid touching doorknobs, handrails, taps. Guard your water bottle, be careful at mealtimes: fresh gloves, clean cutlery, mask back on the second you finish eating. Wear gloves in the loo and bin them after. Cover any cuts and scratches. And if you notice anyone looking unwell – coughing or sneezing, sweating, vomiting – stay well away, and tell one of the crew immediately. Did he understand all that?

Be brave, Cleary, wrote Teach. *You're not alone.* But Cleary knew this wasn't true. He had never felt so alone in his whole life.

There was one person he felt safe with. One person who had access to his mother.

Cleary took up the pen: *Can you take me to the singing lady?*

Skinny, long black hair? wrote Teach. He frowned, as if she was bad news. Then he nodded. He'd walk Cleary to her dorm but he couldn't promise anything. Then a warning: *She looks after the sick people, Cleary. Keep your distance, it's not safe.*

Lining the women's dorm were rows of identical bunks, all numbered, but no clue to which was hers. A glimpse of light or movement through a gap in a curtain, a stray sock abandoned on the floor, but nothing to mark out a specific human presence. Waking up today he'd been so fuzzy-headed, he hadn't thought to leave a trail of sticking plasters.

Cleary settled against the wall to wait. Hours passed. Women entered and left, but none of them were her. He ate the snacks Teach had given him, but didn't dare leave his post to pee.

All night he kept vigil inside the doorway, praying that the woman would come back.

BILLIE

Addled from lack of sleep, she surfaced from the hellhole of the sick room into a hazy half-light. Wondered for a second: was it dawn or dusk? Her shifts were all over the place. Black coffee: she caught a sharp whiff as a guard screwed the top off his thermos. Morning, then. Her stomach was hollow, calling for breakfast.

It still clung to her: the sick-room horror, the stink of shit and sweat and fear. The ship medics regularly left her in charge now, and her co-workers were struggling: overwhelmed and inexperienced, shaken by the onslaught, all that suffering up close.

Billie trudged back to her dorm with a stash of warm bread rolls. Unzipping her bunkbed, she felt a light touch on her arm. She spun around.

The boy's eyes were puffy, his features smudged by fatigue. Had he waited here all night for her? For several long seconds they stood, swaying in unison, like weeds in a breeze. Then Billie lifted the bag of food, mimed eating: an invitation. They sat cross-legged on her bunk to devour the rolls, then shook the crumbs out and curled up together without a word.

Halfway through last night's shift, she'd worked out whose child he was. One of her patients: Cate. Struggling to lift her fever-racked body out of bed, straining towards the sick-room door, the woman had kept repeating a name: 'Cleary … Cleary … Where's my boy? My little one? Cleary …' A single mum, so Kellahan had said.

Now the child beside her was asleep, his breathing deep and regular. Billie hadn't chosen this; back home she'd worked the adult wards, had no experience with kids. After the previous night's shift she'd been having a quiet smoke when an officer marched up to her.

'Move that deaf kid inside,' the man had ordered, pointing to a small figure on the foredeck. 'I don't give a fuck how you do it, just get him below and keep him there.'

'Not my job,' she'd said, too dog-tired to watch her mouth. 'Find someone else.'

'Your job,' spat the officer, 'is whatever I say it is. Get the little bastard under cover, or there's a cell dryside with your name on it.'

Arguing had been pointless. This man could dock wages for non-compliance. Crew saw the nurses as scabs – fearful of contamination, unwilling to do the dirty work themselves, but still jealous of the pay.

The boy had stood frozen at the rail, a pale ghost locked in a solitary stare-down with the open sea. The temperature was close to zero and he wasn't even wearing a coat. His hands were tinged blue and she'd detected a tremor in those thin shoulders. Hypothermia couldn't be far off.

Peeling off one glove, she'd covered his icy hand with her own. Felt warmth seep from her flesh into his, a slow exchange of body-heat.

Holding the boy close as the iceberg drifted past them, an old memory had surfaced: her little brother, soaking wet and whimpering, dumped by a wave on Achmelvich Beach. Billie hugging him: *Shush now, dinny greet* …

As she'd carried the child below decks, Marshall had appeared, demanded to know what she was doing. 'Following orders,' she'd said, pushing past him. But those orders hadn't extended to playing mother.

Now, lying in her bunk, listening to the boy's steady breathing, she realised she couldn't turn him away. He'd chosen her, and that was the end of it. Nestling close to the small stranger, Billie shut her eyes and waited for sleep to come.

~

Protocol banned talk of death in front of patients. The night they lost their fifth person, Billie and the head doctor transferred the body to the antechamber off the sick room, where the body bag lay in wait. Carried the man out unceremoniously, as if he was asleep, so as not to raise alarm.

They swabbed down the body bag, then watched two cleaners lug it out the door. The dead man's name was Toby. Father of two, from Luton. Tattooed across his upper arm, in elegant scrolled font, the names of his wife and children.

'What are the chances this thing's airborne?' Kellahan asked as a doffer helped remove their gear. Stationed overseas these past few years, the doctor had limited pandemic experience.

'You know I can't answer that,' replied Billie. 'We have to assume the worst.'

The doctor held out his arms as their doffer removed the makeshift gown. 'Guesswork has no place in medicine, I know. But what's your best guess?'

Billie peeled off her gloves. 'From the pattern so far, I'd say body fluids,' she said. 'But no way I'm going in there without a respirator.'

Kellahan swore under his breath. 'Four respirators. No lab, no autoclave. No viral profile. We're low on basics – IV fluids, pain meds. And these bloody rubbish bags for aprons.' They'd been forced to improvise the PPE: shower caps, safety goggles, flimsy coveralls and smelly rubber boots requisitioned from the crew.

Billie stepped into a tray of decon, began levering off her boots. 'I'd like some decent wellies, at least. These ones stink of sailors' feet.'

They busied themselves with the intricacies of the doffing process, not quite automatic yet for either of them, not in this slapped-together setting.

'If that airdrop's not approved soon …' Kellahan trailed off.

'You can shower first,' she said. 'Don't worry, I won't peek.'

~

When the government airdrop finally landed, Billie felt an almost physical rush of relief on tearing open the boxes. Pure treasure: fresh meds; proper PPE in various sizes – respirators and masks, overalls and gowns, long gloves and shoe covers. But no news on what this sickness was. The drone was not permitted to take biosamples back.

Included was a fresh consignment of body bags: two dozen black cadaver pouches, with a long zip and a label to write the person's name. She unpacked the new gear with Kellahan and Owen. The deputy was a young Welshman with a fragile ego. Fresh out of locum training at a tiny rural practice, he had no hospital experience.

'All this decon fluid,' said Owen, kicking a crate. 'Where are we meant to store it?'

'We'll need it,' said Billie. 'We're not being vigilant enough. We need to tighten our fomite protocols.' Owen gave her a blank look.

'I don't think *that's* the main problem,' he said in a haughty voice.

She regarded him coolly. 'You do know what fomites are, right? Dirty surfaces, chief. Med school 101.'

'Okay,' Kellahan broke in. 'Let's stay focused here.'

Who knew how long the virus could survive on any surface? The bug was an unknown quantity. It sent her cold, the whispers that the outbreak might have been a deliberate act – the idea that, thanks to some unfathomable brand of malice, she had to watch people slipping through her hands, their dignity stripped away, shitting and ranting down that treacherous slope to nothingness.

It couldn't be true. But how could this have happened? The biofilters had been guaranteed foolproof, and deadly pathogens didn't just drop out of the sky. She'd discussed this privately with Kellahan, but only in passing. Hands full, they had no time for anything beyond the urgent and immediate. No energy to dwell on the unthinkable.

'We're on our own,' Cutler had said in a rare bout of frankness. 'There'll be an inquiry in quarantine, once we reach land – for those of us still alive at that point. Until then we have to manage this ourselves, as best we can.'

The relief of the new gear was short-lived: the deaths continued. The night they lost their sixth patient, Billie and the head doctor sat slumped in the limbo-land of the decon room.

'I won't be hung out to dry for this,' said Kellahan, out of nowhere. 'Right from the start I told them our backup protocols were borderline, too low-tech to cope if anything went wrong. They cited the zero-risk rating, told me system oversight wasn't my job. They had *in-house advisers* for that.'

The first flash of anger she'd witnessed from him. Too weary for tact, she replied carelessly: 'Hope you got that quote archived.'

Kellahan peered at her over his glasses. 'They'll try to shift the blame. You wait. And it won't just be me.'

'How could they possibly blame us?' Her voice rising.

'They're a crooked lot, this corporation,' he said. 'Bunch of hard knocks. We'll need to back each other: you, me, Owen. Once we get there – *if* we get there – you two can forget your bickering. We'll need to present a united front.'

TOM

Strung out and shaky, I rapped on the deputy medic's door. I'd already tried Doctor Kellahan, the more personable option, but my knock had gone unanswered.

The cabin door swung open on a scowling Owen Price, dressing-gown revealing a bony chest. Hair rumpled, sour expression. It was late afternoon, but I'd obviously woken him. He regarded me in sullen silence.

'Owen,' I began, 'I'm so sorry.' A thousand apologies, and so on. I explained my predicament: anxiety amplified by current crisis, medications filched by unknown opportunist, buzzing thoughts and rampant insomnia, and now the shakes, which were a clear sign of withdrawal. I held out one trembling hand to demonstrate, recited the list of medications I normally took on a daily basis.

'It's all on my file,' I assured him. 'My meds regime, diagnosis, doses.'

'Meds are locked down,' he muttered. 'I'm not rostered on till six.' Acne speckled his jaw; he looked young for a doctor. He drew back, as if to end the conversation.

'Thing is,' I gabbled, 'I've got the jitters pretty bad. Is there any chance—'

'Meet me outside the clinic,' he snapped. 'Just before six, I won't wait.' And he shut the door in my face.

Listless and weak, I retreated to the empty classroom. I locked the door, shut the blinds, dimmed the lights and collapsed on the sofa. Tried to distract myself with pleasant daydreams: called to mind Stewart's lovely face, the crush of his arms wrapped tight around my chest.

But my brain kept flitting away, thoughts scattering like mercury. The room felt hot and stuffy and a headache had begun pulsing in my skull. With a peculiar detachment, I noticed my teeth were chattering.

My thoughts began to take strange turns. Puzzled by the sensation of movement, I struggled to remind myself where I was: on a ship, riding the ocean swells. Eyes closed, I saw deep-sea creatures drifting in the black: noxious jellyfish, their stingers aglow; monster fish with huge blank eyes and undershot jaws. Toxic creatures, leaking death.

I was shivering, chills racing over my skin. Waves of heat, then freezing cold. Skull shaken like a snowdome. Music reached me, faint at first. I thought I heard children's voices, sweet and high, singing a faraway song. A melody I recognised.

Fast falls the eventide … Come not in terrors, as the King of Kings. But kind and good, with healing in thy … healing in thy wings …

The hymn we'd sung at Grandma's service. Mum's shoulders shaking in the pew beside me, Dad clasping both her small hands in his large one. Rosa in her black funeral dress, mascara all down her face. My parents, my sister. Oceans away, unreachable.

The children's voices swelled, the choir drawing closer. Now I could hear their footsteps scuffling outside the schoolroom door, could pick out individual voices from the harmony.

Before delirium swept me away entirely, I had a moment of clarity: this wasn't drug withdrawal. I was running a fever.

Then static fuzzed my thoughts. I heard the children again – or thought I did. Giggles and whispers outside the schoolroom door.

Don't come in! I shouted. *Stay outside, it's not safe!*

I knew one child had already fallen ill: Mia, our resident spelling whiz, a quiet girl with a ready smile and an adoring younger brother who shadowed her everywhere. I'd watched in horror as her unconscious form was lifted from the deck and carted away, crewmen holding back her sobbing mother.

Stay out! I ranted, terrified I would contaminate them all. *I'm sick! Don't come in here!*

Had I locked the door? I must keep the children away, protect them from the danger I now harboured.

A parade of cartoon objects marched across my vision: pens, cups and cutlery, taps and handrails, soap and shavers. An old paperback, a backgammon screen, the sweat-slicked broom handle brandished by that crazed passenger – the object I'd blithely picked up and moved out of harm's way. Mia's red sunhat, dropped on the deck. All those things I'd touched.

A loud crash as the door splintered inward on its hinges. Then everything went black.

7

CLEARY

Each day Cleary taped a new note to the ceiling above his bunkbed. The second he woke, her words were there waiting for him. At night he read them over and over, the lines burning like embers in the dark long after lights-out.

Your ma says she loves you. Also: make sure you follow all the san rules. She's feeling a bit better today.

Your ma says you're her brave boy. Don't forget to brush your teeth. She's sorry she can't see you just yet. She says not to worry.

They had been moved in here a few days ago. A small room, six double bunks, all women: the nurses. There was strain in their eyes, a weary tension in the set of their shoulders, and Cleary tried to soften himself in their presence – looking away as they undressed, stepping softly while they slept, trying not to stare or get underfoot. The bunks in this new cabin had no curtains and his mattress smelt of man-sweat, but he felt safe in here. A pink scarf was tacked over the porthole and a breeze filled the room with flickering light.

Billie was asleep in the bed below, hair splayed across the pillow in dark tangles. Gone most nights, busy caring for his ma and the other sick ones, she often went to bed at dawn and slept until afternoon. The other nurses' comings and goings did not rouse him, but when Billie returned to the cabin he always woke, however briefly. She'd find one of his feet through the blanket, give it a squeeze. Then the ship would rock him back to sleep. In the morning there'd be another note tucked inside one of his runners.

Today's note, penned in Billie's scratchy handwriting: *Your ma says you're her darling rascal.* He read the words over and over. Sure, that was how his ma talked. But had she ever called him that exact name? Had these messages truly come from her?

His yearning for his mother was constant, an ache that flowed through him like blood. Before this, they'd never spent a single night apart. When he closed his eyes, there she was: calm and solid, always ready with a hug, quick to offer praise or reassurance. Reading his moods and guessing his thoughts. The warm scent of her skin, like spiced milk, a smell you could fall asleep to. The smell of safety, home, protection. Being separated from her, knowing she was sick and alone, was a kind of torture.

The fear, when it came, struck without warning, a sharp blow to the throat: what if his mother died? What if she was already dead, killed by the bug – or by a knife, slashed across her neck as she slept? Heart slamming, chest pulsing with the force of it. He'd try to slow his breathing, wait for the wave of panic to pass. He'd even tried praying, but you never knew if you'd got the wording right, if anyone was even listening. Most of his prayers went straight to her: *Please get better. Please be well again. Please come back to me.* She must be alive. He'd kept Blackbeard's secret. And Billie saw her every day.

His ma was a strong person, said Billie, but she was very sick. A bad dose. He might not be reunited with her until after they reached land.

The memory of his own illness was hazy: too weak to walk, limbs gone boneless, Granda carrying him up to bed. Vomiting all over his favourite pyjamas, the ones with the rocket ships. Dropping off for a few minutes, then waking to find a whole day and night had passed.

Gran pressing a cool wet cloth to his face; his ma stroking his hair, sleeping on the floor beside his bed. No memory of being taken to hospital, just waking up there, conscious of something missing. At first he'd thought it was the sheer white stillness of the place, the lack of colour and activity. Then the slow realisation: people's mouths were moving but no sound was coming out. Pure silence.

He'd regained some hearing in the aftermath, but not enough to be useful: just faint echoes, rudimentary sketches. Shadow-noise, remote and muffled, like an afterthought. *We'll get it back one day*, his ma had written. *Find a fancy doctor.* But he knew that would cost money, and he'd learnt to get by without it: had taught himself the art of watching, of reading people's faces and eyes; how they held their bodies, moved their hands. The signals they gave off without realising it.

Cleary dressed himself, put on his mask. Pocketed her last note, looped Teach's binoculars around his neck.

He cracked the door open: coast clear. Outside the nurses' cabin ran a long dim passage that seemed to pass right through the guts of the ship. The light down here was reddish, like the inside of a whale, filtered from hatches far above, and locked doors led off to unknown rooms. Feet wide for balance he trod the centre of the passage, not touching the handrails. Swiped the lock with his wristband and shouldered the door open.

Moving around the ship, he kept an eye out for his navigation aids: the green sticking plasters marked safe routes to familiar areas. The red ones were warnings, signalled zones to avoid: crew-only sections, blind spots, lonely passages that culminated in dead ends.

His wristband gave him access to this new part of the ship: the nurses' cabin, the adjoining jacks and washroom, the small kitchenette where they ate, no need to brave the mess-room. But it held no power over other doors. Not the one that led down to the sick room, now manned by two guards, alert for small boys hovering nearby. He wouldn't get near her again.

Outside, the sky hung down like the belly of some huge dead fish. Cleary surveyed the upper decks: no sign of Blackbeard. The man could be anywhere. Beyond Cleary's cabin walls, the sanctuary of the nurses' area, nowhere was safe. His watchfulness was now dialled up to maximum: he kept his back to walls, more alert than ever to the threat of someone sneaking up behind him; tuned in to faint vibrations, the tremor of approaching boots; constantly scanned for figures in his peripheral vision; remained on guard, always ready to flee or melt soundlessly away.

It wore him out: always checking over his shoulder, always tensed to run or fight.

Billie would not be up for hours. Later they'd eat together, come up top to watch the clouds. But he couldn't follow her everywhere: what if she got sick of him? The other kids no longer roamed freely around the ship. Their parents kept them within reach, whole families dissolving like ghosts if Cleary got too close. Declan always waved, but they were furtive waves, and waving did not tell you very much.

Witnessing this, Billie had tried to explain it away – *It's not you, they're all just scared of getting sick* – but their withdrawal left him feeling stranded and exposed. Reminded him of other times, other people who had turned away: lost friendships, failed conversations, kids who feared that silence might be catching. But here, isolation carried a far greater risk: it was hard to make yourself invisible without the sheltering presence of a crowd. Now he loitered on the edge of family groups, close but not too close, a lost moon orbiting some indifferent star.

He found a gap in the rail and lifted his binoculars to survey the restless ocean. Bright as blue ink, the sea was now, not a scrap of rubbish to be seen, no other vessels within sight. Seabirds jostled in the rigging. A smaller bird, a juvenile with speckled plumage and a crooked leg, was being harassed by a gaggle of adults. Sidling away from their beaks, the young bird lost its footing and slipped off the perch.

A feather zigzagged down to the deck, and Cleary ran to retrieve it. A beautiful white curve, delicate but strong – a knife for slicing air. A good-luck charm, still warm from the bird's body. He'd keep it for his ma.

A blow: an object slamming into his leg.

A football lolled at his feet. Across the deck stood a kid from his class, face expectant. Cleary and the boy punted the ball back and forth, building up a rhythm on the tilting deck, until a sailor darted forward to poach it off them. The man dribbled the football away, grinning at the boys, then shot it down the deck with a playful kick. The ball stopped short, trapped beneath a heavy boot.

Blackbeard teetered, stork-like, one boot planted on the football, balancing against the swell, surveying the boys in turn as he steadied his weight against the leather. Then, with a slow smile, he fired the ball straight down the main deck at Cleary, who stood frozen, powerless to move.

The ball struck him hard in the chest, knocked the air from his lungs. As the other boy scampered to retrieve it, Cleary broke from his daze and stumbled off in the opposite direction, the pressure of the man's gaze heavy on his back.

~

Taking refuge in the crowded passenger saloon, he waited for his breath to slow, his blood to stop pounding. Surely Blackbeard could not hurt him with people all around. But what would happen if the man caught him alone? How easy would it be to slash his throat, to pick him up bodily and throw him into the sea? He must never let his guard down, not for a second.

Trapped in the sick room, his ma knew nothing of this danger. Cleary prayed she would be safe down there, protected by Billie and the other nurses until they all reached land. Prayed that Blackbeard could not reach her, could not pass beyond that heavy metal door.

A screen on the wall tracked the ship's slow course. Last week Madagascar had dropped off the edge of the picture, leaving them suspended in a wide stretch of blue. But now a new shape was entering the frame, a blunt red wedge intruding from the right. Cleary waved his hand before the image, swiping at the air. It was fiddly, the program's calibration clumsy, and it took him a full minute to zoom out to the wider view.

People gathered to watch him tinker, keeping a safe distance. A woman pulled her daughter close, arms clasped across the girl's chest, as the image settled into clarity: a small white blip edging towards a large red mass. Australia. *Time to destination: 13 days, 4 hours, 21 min.*

You could see the seconds blinking down, witness a whole hour vanish if you stood there long enough. Cleary turned away. He knew exactly how much longer this would take: a new note every day, his mother's words, recorded in Billie's handwriting. Thirteen more notes.

BILLIE

She bent over her patient. Pale and semi-conscious, still hooked up to a drip, the woman had stopped vomiting, but remained weak and barely responsive. Not out of danger yet, by any means. No more or less important than any other patient, this one, but a stark reminder of the cost if all their efforts failed.

Billie spoke softly, used the woman's name. 'Cate, let's check your pulse and blood pressure. Then I'll give you a wash down.' She doubted Cate could hear her, but Billie always talked to her patients, conscious or not, sought to treat them as responsive on some level. To remind them, and herself, that she was not dealing with mere meat, that they could still return from wherever they had retreated to. Her voice a thread, however faint, a line back out if only they could grasp it.

Cate's head was still sheathed in plastic wrap, a bid to contain the mess and keep infectious droplets from lodging in her hair. Billie checked her pulse: fast and weak, shock a risk. She adjusted the IV flow rate and began setting up the oxygen. The wash could wait.

'Hey, Cate,' she said, close to the woman's ear. 'Cleary's not had a shower in three days, the little grotbag. Says he doesn't have to. That true?'

The woman stirred — a frown, a murmur — but did not surface.

'Don't worry,' Billie whispered. 'I'm looking after him, I promise.'

Twelve people now seriously ill, crammed into this narrow room on rough-hewn beds, languishing in various states of consciousness. Cold air gusted in the open porthole but the smell was vile, took her straight back to the death wards. Near the wall lay their first child patient, fading in and out of consciousness, her body fighting an internal war: Mia, eleven years old. When Billie first saw that small figure laid out on the bed, a jet of fear shot through her. Someone's sick child, now in her hands.

'Can I give him more pseudopiate? He reckons it's not working.' Lauren, as always, a feckless English rose, asking yet another question to which the answer should be obvious. Occupied with changing an IV bag, Billie tried not to show her irritation with the girl.

'Tom can hear you loud and clear, Lauren. Check his chart. When was his last dose?'

She watched Lauren examine the chart and prep another dose of pain meds for the teacher. The blonde nurse, Holly, came close to rolling her eyes. Most of the nurses – and that's what they were now, designated if not qualified – had the drill down pat, were more or less coping. But Lauren seemed unable to retain simple information, prone to fretting over trivial things – and, more worrying, being lax about the crucial stuff.

As if on cue, Billie caught the girl dropping a shit-smeared rag in a corner of the room.

'Lauren!' she snapped. 'What the fuck are you doing?'

The girl turned, gloved hands aloft.

'The rag,' said Billie, trying to keep her voice calm. 'Biohazard. Category A infectious waste. Double-bagged, sealed up, immediate disposal – remember?'

Lauren offered no reply, just bent to tear off a plastic bag. Billie observed her, unsure how much further to press it. Decided the stakes were too high to tiptoe around the bleeding obvious.

'Please,' she said. 'This is basic stuff, disease-containment protocol. You know what happens if we don't stick to it.'

'Sorry,' said Lauren. 'I was going to pick it up in just a sec.'

Billie felt anger rise. 'Just a sec won't cut it, Lauren. You're putting us all at risk. You know the protocols. Follow them.' She didn't add an 'or' – or what? *No death talk in front of patients.* Remove the nurse from duties? They'd all jump at the chance. Imprisonment, as Cutler had promised? That wasn't Billie's verdict to deliver. She'd already drummed home the message: carelessness kills. If that didn't register with this girl, she couldn't imagine what would.

The male nurse on duty was stealing looks at Lauren too: Ruben, the guy who'd tried to resist being press-ganged into service. A former evacuation assistant, he'd turned out to be one of her most reliable workers, a steady and competent presence with a talent for soothing agitated patients. Lauren drove him mad as well.

Billie surveyed the row of bodies under sheets. A rare lull, most of the patients dozing. Holly was pressing a cool cloth to the child's forehead while Ruben did the rounds with fluids, propped up woozy heads and held drink straws to lips, urging each person on by name – *Just a sip, Sarah, come on, love; one more, last one* – as if coaching reluctant charges through a gym session.

Handwritten charts were taped above each bed. Billie scanned the names, the meds and dosages, the scribbled vital signs. So many blank spaces, so much information missing. Caught off guard, their recording systems primitive. She could hardly read her own handwriting, let alone the others' scrawls.

Whatever this virus was, it had an ugly profile. Picked up by the twice-daily fever scans, new patients were placed in an observation room in the slim hope they were febrile for some harmless reason. The next stage – soaring temperatures, nausea, joint pain, cracking headaches – saw them admitted to this makeshift clinic, where the vomiting and diarrhoea soon began, followed by respiratory distress, nosebleeds and a creeping rash.

The fever was difficult to manage, scarcely responding to standard doses of analgesics or antipyretics, and as it climbed, the patients became confused, agitated, delirious. Some needed to be restrained and sedated. Thank god there was just the one child sick so far. No medics either, despite Lauren's best efforts.

Billie adjusted Cate's oxygen, then stepped aside for the cleaner, one of the swaddled figures who kept a regular vigil, removing waste, wiping surfaces, swabbing up spills. To cover the clock Kellahan had rostered his shifts around hers and Owen's, putting each in charge for an eight-hour stretch. The doctor's reliance on Billie made her uneasy. With scant equipment, untrained staff and no real knowledge of this virus, the responsibility was risky and unwelcome. Mistakes would inevitably be made, and blame would surely follow.

Jim Kellahan was a decent man, but their plight had exposed his medical limits. He'd done time as a navy medic, and before that he'd been a public GP in Birmingham. But all that was pre-pandemic: his incident experience was close to zero. Billie's own background meant she'd been assigned to crash-course everyone in containment protocols: hand hygiene, PPE donning and doffing, waste disposal, decon. Kellahan deferred to her on that front, but she'd had several run-ins with Owen, who clearly resented her borrowed authority.

Mia's hands were cold. Billie laid another blanket over the girl, rubbed her back and sang to her softly for a while, before turning her attention to her other patients. Her goal was to keep them out of the bodybags that lay waiting in storage; from the company of the dead, laid out unceremoniously in a refrigerated section of the hold. But with no proper set-up or diagnostics, she could offer no more than supportive care: manage symptoms, control pain, ease anxiety. Analgesics, pseudopiates, fluids, salbutamol, oxygen, anti-emetics. Mop up the shit and spew, plug the nosebleeds. And try to stop the bug from spreading.

Land was two weeks away, mortality creeping higher. The

patients next door in recovery had stabilised, but their progress was not guaranteed, and all remained potential vectors.

'Billie? He's yanked his cannula out again.' Ruben, bent over the patient who'd come in last night: Scoot, the young deckhand from Aberdeen, part of the Stocktakers' crew.

On arrival he'd been in no state to recognise her: his fever nudging forty, guts in spasm, cognition skewiff. 'I didn't take it, Ma!' he kept shouting at the ceiling. 'I didn't take it, I swear!' They'd finally got his fever down, but he remained listless and confused, throwing off his blanket one minute and racked by shivers the next. Clocking off last night, she'd left Scoot in Owen's care. Bruises now mottled the tender flesh of his inner arm: the junior medic's clumsy handiwork.

'Grab us a blue one,' she said, donning new gloves. 'And some tape.' She touched the patient's hand, checked the official name written on his chart. 'Stewart, can you hear me? Scoot? Try to lie still, mate, I'll pop your IV back in. Just a wee sting. Hold on to Ruben's hand.'

Scoot whimpered as the needle punctured his vein. As Billie flushed the saline through there was a rap at the door and Kellahan entered, all gowned up. She'd lost track of time. She briefed the doctor, advised keeping a close watch on the girl, Scoot, Cate. Passing the woman's bed, Billie gave her arm a gentle squeeze: unnecessary contact, a minor breach of protocol.

As Billie stepped into the decon tray she began compiling some lines in her head, the makings of a story. The kid would be waiting for her.

~

Sleep was proving elusive. As the death toll rose management had closed both bars, but Robbie had promised to procure her some fly rum to take the edge off. He hesitated when Billie asked to tag along, but she was too tired to wonder why.

Marshall intercepted them in the passageway just off the galley. 'I'm not selling to her,' he said, stone cold. It took Billie a second to realise who he meant.

'Come on, man,' said Robbie, as if they'd already had this conversation. 'She's doing the dirty work, caring for the sick ones. She's one of us.'

'Us?' said Marshall, rearing back. '*One of us* is already at death's door, thanks to this scab. How do you think Scoot got sick?' He narrowed his eyes at Billie. 'We never should have let you in,' he said, pure venom in his voice.

Robbie tried to apologise for Marshall: said the chief steward was losing it, had gone radge, been ranting about terrorists and anti-migrant cults; Juliette had found him crying the other day, actually sobbing out loud behind the wheelhouse. But Billie waved his words away. The whole ship had been torn asunder by the sickness; emotions were raw, and weak alliances had no chance of holding. Juliette herself oversaw the patients' meals, liaised with Billie on that front. But whenever their paths crossed, the cook was clearly on edge: a brief greeting, minimal talk, then a hasty retreat.

Contaminated: that's how the nurses were seen. Carriers, vectors, shunned by both passengers and crew. It stemmed from fear, but the hostility was hard to stomach, and the nurses were now bunked and fed in a separate area of the ship. One blessing of this new arrangement: it gave you some respite from the families of the sick, whose desperate pleas for hope, for information, were neither escapable nor bearable. The task of family liaison had fallen to Owen and one of the senior officers. Billie didn't envy them.

She had her own job on that front. It was more than enough.

~

106

Clocking on that night, Billie heard a racket through the ante-chamber wall: someone was screaming for a priest.

'When did that start?' she asked Owen, who was doffing out.

'Fifteen minutes, off and on,' he said, stepping into the decon tray. 'You'd better give him a shot. He's upsetting the others.'

Typical Owen: issuing instructions for a task he could have done himself.

'Thanks for the tip, Einstein,' she said, taping her gloves. 'We'd be lost without you.'

Scoot was thrashing around as two nurses struggled to hold him on the bed. His fever was back with a vengeance. She cursed Owen beneath her breath: he had no business leaving a patient in this state.

'Steady, mate,' Ruben was saying, the strain showing. 'Take it easy, Stewart.'

'He's too strong,' said Holly. 'Can't hold him much longer.'

Scoot's skin was flushed, the cords in his neck taut as rope. He threw his head back and roared: 'Father Hendricks! Get me Father Hendricks!' A bright line of blood trickled from his nose.

Billie took over from Holly, leant her full weight on the patient, spoke firmly. Restraining him was not ideal, but god knew what he'd do if he broke loose in this cramped room.

Patients were stirring. The sick child lay rigid, staring at the ceiling.

'Stewart – Scoot. Can you hear me? It's Nurse Galloway. Settle now. We've got you.' One of his arms broke free and flailed wildly, his fist smacking against the side of Ruben's head.

'Fuck,' snapped Ruben. 'Where's the guard? We need some muscle in here.'

'Bless me, Father!' sobbed Scoot. 'It wasn't me. Not the holy water! It wasn't me, I swear.' A long, shattered scream tore from his throat.

The man's distress was spreading through the sick room, leaping from person to person. Mia whimpered, and a woman's voice called out: 'Help him! Do something!'

'It's okay, Mia,' Billie called. 'We'll be there in a sec, my love.' She pressed her bodyweight down on Scoot, turning her face aside, inches from his spittle and blood.

'Prep me a shot of Haloperidol. Five migs,' she ordered Holly. 'And grab some long bandages.'

Trussed to the bed, his arms now strapped down tight, Scoot cursed and pleaded, screamed for his mother, a priest, a doctor. When Billie jabbed the needle into his thigh and shot the plunger home, the fight quickly went out of him.

'Christ,' said Ruben, prodding his bruised ear. 'Remind me why I took this job.'

'Better get some ice on that,' said Billie. 'But check on Mia first.'

Scoot lay flattened, his face gone slack, body drained of tension. Billie freed his arms and checked his vital signs.

'You okay? Here, have a sip.' She held his head, but Scoot turned away, refused to drink. She caught a mumble, asked him to speak up.

'Poison,' he croaked. She raised her eyebrows at Ruben, who was tending to Mia.

'Paranoid,' said Ruben. 'And dehydrated. He won't drink. We need to get a drip in him asap.'

Scoot's head was lolling. 'Poison money. Bastard took it. Get the priest.'

'There's a lapsed clergyman on board,' said Holly. 'Catholic guy. But no idea where you'd find him.'

They were already short-staffed, Ruben's shift technically over, his replacement nowhere in evidence. And Billie knew that overhearing last rites would hardly calm the other patients.

She took Scoot's hand. 'Stewart? You're going to recover from this, I swear. You don't need a priest. But you must drink.'

His speech was slurring, consciousness fading out in a slow series of blinks. 'No,' he said. 'There's something in the water. Holy water. Devil water.'

'Shhh. Just rest now.' She pressed a damp cloth to his forehead.

'They know where my mam lives.' Fighting to keep his eyes open. 'They know her address. Please don't tell.'

Delirious patients said all kinds of things: spoke in tongues, got angry over nothing, confessed to past misdeeds, real or imagined; conversed with absent people, fought monsters nobody else could see. Talked all kinds of nonsense. But sometimes, in her experience, there was a grain of truth in what they said.

'Scoot,' she whispered. 'Stewart?'

But he now lay motionless, unreachable.

TOM

I awoke on a sweaty mattress in an unfamiliar room: a girlie pic stuck to the wall, a porthole revealing a blue circle of sky, trolleys stacked with medical gear. A row of beds lined the narrow space, eight people laid out flat, sleeping or resting. The smell of disinfectant hung thick in the air.

A figure appeared, dressed in full protective gear, only the eyes visible. 'Welcome back,' she said. 'You made it through. You're in the recovery room.' A Scots accent, her voice vaguely familiar.

Weak and dizzy, I struggled to prop myself upright. My limbs were jelly, and a dull ache emanated from my bones, as if I'd been bashed with concrete gloves.

'Drink this,' said the woman, holding a straw to my lips. 'You've got some catching up to do.'

I pushed the sheet aside, examined myself. Barely recognised this gaunt apparition: pyjamas hanging off my bones, knees sharp, belly hollow, arms gone thin and stringy. Skin marked with purple punctures, IV bruises blooming dark as Rorschach blots. Sitting upright was an effort. A deep weariness pressed me back into the mattress.

'It was touch and go back there,' said the Scots nurse. 'We weren't sure you'd make it.'

I peered at the other patients, half of them asleep or dozing, recognised a few wan faces. Questions swam into my woozy brain. 'The girl ... Mia ...'

The nurse lowered her voice. 'Next door,' she said. 'She's not out of the woods yet.'

'Tell her I'm waiting for her. Tell her I'll see her soon. Will you?'

'Shhh,' said the nurse. 'Rest now. Save your energy.'

~

We slept a lot, we convalescents. The staff who tended to us, who brought our food and cleaned the room and monitored our progress, all wore full protective clothing. We still posed a risk.

Each day they checked our vital signs, made notes. The head nurse, Billie, kept the room in order and the patients calm. I recognised her now: the dark-haired Scot from that first crisis meeting. Recalled that wiry intensity, her firing off questions with a cool authority, despite the looming sense of panic in the room. The woman Cleary had sought out when his mother was struck down.

Every few days they'd carry in a new survivor from the sick room next door. Sound leaked through the thin wall, an audible reminder of the hell we'd left behind: the low murmur of nurses punctuated by moans and retching noises, the occasional shout or scream.

A hefty crewman watched over us around the clock. Stationed in a chair beside the door, eyes shifting nervously above his mask, keeping his distance, not happy to be in our midst. Or perhaps it was several crew, all big men of interchangeable build. A *carer*, the nurses called him, a hint of sarcasm in their voices. Not a guard, although that's clearly what he was.

We were too weak and frail to pose any threat. But one night I was woken by a racket from next door. A woman screaming. A series of heavy thuds, then someone staggering down the passageway outside, fists pounding on a metal door. Our guard rushed from the room, yelling into his radio for help. The sounds of a struggle, a nurse speaking sharply: 'Hold her still!' More thumps and bangs, a dragging sound. Then silence.

I'd lost eleven days in that sick room, a black hole speckled by weird pinpricks of memory. Bright lights, pain, time warping. Blood on the sheets, voices fading in and out. I remembered vomiting into a white bucket, over and over, my body empty but unable to stop. Hyperreal dreams – strange writhing beasts, armies of machines, women with plastic bags around their heads. Someone screaming, raving nonsense. Me?

Then a slow surfacing, like crawling out of a mineshaft, back up into the light. Propped up in bed, sucking salty-sweet liquid through a straw. Then being half carried into this new room, hobbling like an old man, supported by a nurse on either side.

Ten of us were soon crammed into the narrow recovery ward, a hastily converted sailors' cabin. Conversation, for the most part, was conducted at a whisper. We were fragile, oversensitive to noise and light. Aware, too, that not everyone had made it through alive.

Against the far wall lay a man whose wife had died back in that hellhole. Every night we heard his muffled sobs. The Irishman in the next bed would try to comfort him, offer hushed words: 'I'm so sorry for your trouble, it's too terrible. I'm here if you need to talk.' A nurse would appear with a rattling bottle, and the man's sobs would taper off to silence.

Two beds down from me lay Max, the man who'd tried to throw himself overboard. No longer crazed by fever, he was a cheerful presence, always ready with a joke or a kind word. My mind kept drifting back to that struggle: Max pinned to the deck beneath a blur of sailors, Stewart on top of the pile. Me retrieving the sweat-slicked broomstick, placing it safely out of harm's way. Contagion taking place below the threshold of awareness, a series of invisible invasions: the virus a deadly trespasser, crossing cell boundaries, seeking out new hosts. Who could say when or how it had made the leap?

When I saw a nurse enter cradling a small figure in her arms, I felt a surge of relief. When Mia woke up, I wobbled over for a visit. I praised the girl for her bravery, urged her to eat, said her parents would want to see some colour in her cheeks when we got out of there. Eyes wide in her pale face, Mia asked when that would be.

'Soon,' was all I could offer. 'Now you scoff down that soup and get some rest.'

No other children had fallen ill, and for that I was profoundly grateful. But I knew some had lost a parent, an uncle or an aunt. And it wasn't over yet.

When I asked about the deaf boy, Billie shushed me. 'He's fine,' she whispered. 'Hold still, let's check your blood pressure.' Jerked her head, shot me a cautionary frown.

I peered down the row of beds at a sleeping form, the new patient they'd brought in overnight. Of course: stupid of me to speak so carelessly.

The moment she woke, Cate demanded news of her son. The junior doctor, Owen, tried to fob her off, spoke sternly, but Cate cut him short, called him a waste of space.

'Get that Scotswoman in here!' she yelled. 'I need to get a message to my boy.'

Summoned to her bedside, Billie spoke softly, calmed her down. As I drifted off I heard Cate dictating a message to her son, the nurse repeating the words aloud, committing them to memory: *To the moon and back ...*

Billie often sang young Mia to sleep, the pure bell of her voice washing over the room, a soothing incantation returning us to the protective dreamscapes of childhood. Folk songs, ballads and lullabies. *Honey is sweet and so is he. Hush a bye birdie, my pretty little dove. Ally bally bee.* As she bathed a patient, collected our dishes or changed our sheets, she'd sometimes hum a wordless tune beneath her breath, a drift of melody sweet as oxygen. We clung to her voice as if it had the power to transport us, take us away to somewhere better.

My own family, I was painfully aware, had no idea if I was alive or dead. Perhaps had no clue at all about this whole disaster. A twinge of guilt: at my farewell drinks Rosa had begged me not to leave, said Mum and Dad were getting on, they needed me. I'd ruffled my sister's hair and bought her another gin and tonic, told her I'd be back before she knew it.

Outbound comms were still banned, the nurses told us. A bid (I thought, but did not say) to contain the scale of the inevitable shitstorm once we reached dry land.

As our strength returned, a common refrain began to circulate, sotto voce: the government had promised we'd be safe. Red Star had sworn this trip was zero risk, the superscreens infallible. How had this been allowed to happen?

Each day, my body came back to me by increments. Dizziness still struck without warning, but worse was the fatigue – a bone-deep exhaustion, both mental and physical. As if I was operating on half the normal blood supply. As if a vampire had sucked the life out of me, guzzled my energy, sapped my spark. Drunk me dry.

Privacy was non-existent. We became familiar with each other's bowel movements and physical ailments, our dietary preferences and drug requests, the pleas for messages to be conveyed to worried loved ones.

To stave off cabin fever, I'd stretch my legs in the short passageway outside. Eight steps up, eight back, leaning into the walls for the big swells. I tried the door at the end: firmly locked.

Despite the grief and disbelief that permeated that cramped room, at times a strange elation would steal over me. A keen awareness that by some fluke – some accident of timing, blind luck or chemistry – I was not amongst the dead.

An announcement came: land was just over a week away.

Animated by this news, we sat up in our beds, a new brightness in our faces, talk flowing back and forth: speculation, expectations, hopes. We had no idea what lay in wait for us out there, but we'd be glad to see the back of this ship, return to an even keel. (Yes, the dreaded puns had returned: I was on the mend.)

8

CLEARY

Was he lost? The layout felt familiar, but he'd been fooled before. The lower decks were a tangle of identical passages that seemed to double back upon themselves, to crisscross in shifting configurations. The signs were confusing: figures, arrows and symbols, strange seafaring terms. *Orlop. Stowage. Chain Locker.*

Heading for the saloon, planning to kill some time on the gamescreens, he'd discovered a door wedged ajar, a set of steps leading below. *Crew Only*, said the sign.

His ma was down there somewhere. Without thinking he'd slipped through the door, but soon lost his bearings and wound up in this deserted section of the ship. Intersecting corridors doglegged off in unknown directions. Standing at this junction, he had an uneasy sense of having blundered into the crosshairs of a target: *X marks the spot.*

Stay calm, his ma always said. *Slow breaths.* They'd visited the Kildare Maze one winter, ended up wandering in futile circles, hemmed in by high green walls that hid whatever lay around the corner. Trudged those muddy paths for what seemed like hours before finally emerging into the open air. A lesson learnt: once your compass points were scrambled, keeping your cool was vital; panicking only made things worse.

Sweet for a split-second, these memories fast turned painful, like

116

a hand reaching into his chest and squeezing his heart, a grip so strong he could hardly breathe. They set off a longing with only one possible cure: being back in her arms.

One wish: to be with her. Cleary didn't care if he got sick, or died. He'd made every silent bargain he could think of: promised to give up birthdays, forgo Christmas; sworn to never taste another sweet, never open another gift or stay up past bedtime. He'd learn his times tables backwards, brush his teeth five times a day, fight monsters in dark cellars.

She was down here somewhere – but which direction? His carefully placed sticking plasters had been disappearing lately, peeled off the walls by some passer-by or cleaner, leaving a faint tacky residue.

Here the corridor walls were blank, nothing to navigate by.

A prickle at his neck; a sense that he was not alone. Cleary spun around: down the far end of the corridor stood a metal bucket, a mop handle swaying slightly with the pitch and roll of the ship. A minute ago, he'd swear, that passage had been empty. Who had put that bucket there?

Was someone spying on him?

A door flung open down the hallway. A bear-like figure lumbered into view, a misshapen thing without a head; a moment's horror before the apparition resolved itself into human form – a man walking in reverse, hunched with effort, lugging something heavy. Swaddled in white coveralls, a full-face respirator and gloves, he was carrying an object that resembled a black sleeping-bag. A second figure appeared, holding the other end of the bag.

Whatever was inside the bag looked large and heavy, the crewmen struggling under its weight. An unfamiliar bulk. Man-sized, surely.

As the men manoeuvred their load, a big swell hit the ship, tossing the world loose from its moorings. The bag and its contents hovered a moment at the apex, then crashed to the floor. Bending to retrieve it, the men spotted their observer.

Cleary froze. These crewmen could be anyone. Both tall and faceless, stooped beneath the weight of their load, the respirators lending them an alien appearance. One man was gesturing at him, as if shooing away a dog: ordering Cleary to retreat, get out of here.

Which direction? He chose a corridor at random and walked rapidly out of sight. After several blind turns it ended abruptly, a ladder set into the wall. He scrambled up into a small companionway. Through a salt-crusted porthole he saw passengers bundled against the cold, and beyond them that endless reach of blue. He shoved the door open.

With his back to the wall, his heart beating on staccato, he counted out slow breaths. It was nothing. He'd lost his way, that's all. His eyes lit on Declan, sitting on a bench, between his parents. His friend waggled his fingers in surreptitious greeting, then his attention flicked to Cleary's left.

A man appeared from the hatchway. No mistaking him: that rangy body, the stoop, that dark beard bristling from the white mask. Blackbeard leant against the wall beside him, hands in pockets, boots braced apart, like they were old friends surveying a shared territory. The man was so close Cleary could smell him – unwashed hair, dank sweat, a whiff of mechanical grease. His body odour earthy, almost zoological.

Without conscious effort, moving of their own accord, Cleary's legs propelled him across the deck. Sinking onto the bench near Declan and his parents, in plain sight of everyone, he lifted his binoculars and turned towards the sea.

~

Mealtimes were a welcome lull. The nurses formed a warm human barricade, a buffer against dark thoughts; a safe place to switch off, to drop the constant vigilance that left Cleary frazzled and wrung out. They ate together around the kitchenette table, masks off for the duration of the meal, knives and forks strictly allocated, a cup set above each individual plate at twelve o'clock so they wouldn't get mixed up. Meals arrived on a trolley, identical serves in covered trays, like in hospital. Dessert was jelly, custard, canned fruit, some mysterious sweet mush; Cleary often devoured a double serve, the women marvelling at how much a boy his size could put away.

Whenever someone spilt salt, Holly, the pretty blonde one, would flick a pinch over her shoulder for luck, and Cleary would send out a silent prayer: *Come back to me.*

After dinner the nurses sat and talked, drank tea, played chess or cards, the smokers taking turns off the tiny balcony while Holly worked through a dog-eared book of crossword puzzles. Cleary would sit and draw, lose himself in a world of colours and shapes, where bad dreams could be tamed and worries pinned to the page with careful strokes of ink: a skull and crossbones flapping in the wind, the pink tresses of a jellyfish, a gunmetal shark fin spiking a cobalt wave. The kitchenette walls were decorated with his best work.

A waft of smoke as Billie leant in close behind him. Cleary focused on the page, filling in the outlines with steady strokes: two masked figures trapped in a labyrinth, a black shape slung between them; a mop poking from a bucket, corridors branching off in all directions. Only one possible exit: a zigzag path winding through bird-filled trees, a wide green field, and the columns of a city sparkling in the distance. Along this path, free of the maze, a child and his mother walked hand in hand.

BILLIE

Summoned without warning to the captain's quarters, Billie was relieved to find Kellahan amongst the senior staff in attendance. She submitted to the san pump then squeezed onto a settee beside the head doctor. The crew remained stationed around the walls, as if standing to attention. Juliette gave her a faint nod.

Captain Lewis sat behind his desk, scrolling through a screen, a stack of fresh masks at his elbow. The frown he wore seemed to have become permanent.

'That's everyone, sir,' said Cutler, locking the door.

The captain turned to Billie. 'Ms Galloway, welcome. Doctor Kellahan is usually the designated medical presence at these meetings, but I've requested your attendance too. Given your role.' He cleared his throat. 'Your expertise.'

She'd been prodded awake by Holly, saying a crewman was waiting outside the door. She'd followed him reluctantly, her sleep-scrambled brain still trying to shake off an uneasy dream. Buckets full of bones and dirty hypodermics, a singing contest with a broken microphone.

Earlier that morning they'd lost another one: Prisha, a young woman from Hounslow. Time of death: 3.42. Long black hair matted with sweat, wide hazel eyes, chipped silver polish on her fingernails. Holding the sick woman's hand Billie had admired the colour aloud, hoping to stir a response, but she was too far gone. One of those reserved patients who buried pain deep inside themselves, faded away without a visible fight, unable or unwilling to vocalise what their bodies knew was happening. Prisha's sister, dosed up on Calmex, would now have been informed.

Number ten. A stab of guilt: Billie was relieved the girl had not died on her shift.

'I cannot allow any further loss of life,' said Captain Lewis now, fixing a stare on Billie, then the doctor. 'There must be no more deaths.' It had the weight of an order.

Kellahan removed his glasses. His eyes looked raw and sleepless. 'None of us wants to see more deaths,' he said. 'We're fighting this as best we can. But the ship was not equipped to deal with this. And we don't know exactly what we're up against.'

'What more can we do?' asked Captain Lewis. 'Why haven't we been able to contain this thing?' An edge to his voice she'd never heard before.

Billie spoke up. 'Our containment strategy is absolutely by the book. But in a setting like this – everyone squeezed in together, communal meals and bathrooms, the ventilation system—'

'What more can we do?' the captain broke in. 'What *else*?'

'We're doing everything we can,' said Kellahan, replacing his glasses. 'Your staff are scanning everyone twice daily. We're running surveillance, hygiene protocols, contact tracing, a buffer zone ...' He trailed off, and Billie took up the list.

'Perimeter controls, a strict donning and doffing regime,' she counted on her fingers. 'But in this setting, social distancing's near-impossible. We have to assume human-to-human transmission, but there may be other vectors too. And we don't know the incubation period. No lab analysis, no anti-virals.'

'Spare us the jargon,' spat Cutler. 'The captain's asking you a question: why is this thing still spreading?'

Kellahan bristled. 'Perhaps you should direct that question at your staff. They're responsible for hygiene compliance. For the scans, the decon regime, patient meals. Are *they* doing everything by the book?'

'Meals?' said Juliette sharply.

Cutler stepped forward, ready to arc up, but the captain planted his fist on the desk. 'No-one's laying blame here. Blame is not the issue. The issue is that people are dying on board my ship. We must prevent further fatalities. What more can we do?'

A hush fell as Captain Lewis surveyed the room. He'd always seemed to Billie like a man of no great conviction, slightly bloodless, not quite real. Dapper, with the kind of blandly handsome face you saw on ageing newsreaders or soap actors: pink skin, a thick head of silver hair, white teeth, a hint of jowls. But lately his presence had sharpened, taken on a more urgent cast.

'I've said this from the start,' said Kellahan into the hush. 'We need to break course and seek emergency assistance. Demand a medical evacuation.'

'No government will grant permission,' someone objected, and Billie realised it was the chief steward, Marshall. 'We've tried them all: Brazil, Argentina, South Africa. Even Madagascar. We're barred from docking. Nobody will take us.' Marshall eyed the doctor. 'You seen a map lately? You understand where we are, right?'

Kellahan ignored this. 'What about medevac?'

'We've been told that's not a viable option for a population this size,' said an officer. 'We got you the airdrop. That's the best we could do.'

'I've been instructed to continue to our destination,' said Captain Lewis. 'The Australian government has assured me they're fully equipped to deal with this. They're waiting for us.'

'We're a week from land,' said Cutler. 'We just have to make it through the next seven days. Keep as many alive as possible.'

Kellahan sat forward. 'Alright. I think we should increase the crew screens – up the scans on stewards, cleaners, kitchen staff. Anyone involved in food handling or waste disposal. Thrice daily, before meals.' The captain nodded, flicked some data into his screen.

Smart to offer options, give them concrete things to do. Spread responsibility. Billie took up the theme. 'Let's ramp up the hygiene comms too. Really press it home. Broadcast it every few hours – and keep changing the wording, so people don't tune out.'

'They're all terrified,' an officer put in quietly. 'I don't know what to tell them. All those kids ...' This was the man working with Owen on family liaison.

'How's the young girl?' asked the captain, and Billie saw it: he was frightened too.

'She's stabilised,' said Kellahan. 'We're hopeful she'll pull through.'

Marshall pointed at Billie. 'This one's got a little kid staying in her cabin,' he said, addressing the doctor. 'With all those *nurses*.' He spat the word. 'You call that safe?'

Beside her, Billie felt Kellahan tense up, but the captain spoke first.

'I've approved that arrangement,' he said firmly. 'Ms Galloway knows more about disease containment than anyone on this ship.'

There was a silence.

'What about the rumours?' asked the liaison man. 'What are we meant to do about them? It's rampant. All sorts of bad stuff flying around.'

'Fear does that,' said Kellahan, pointedly. 'And grief. People get angry, latch on to any explanation.'

'We all saw those protesters,' said Juliette. 'The day we left – the lunatics with the signs. Vigilante nutters. Wouldn't put it past them.'

Billie had seen the placards: *Ship rats! Deserters!*

'That lot are headcases,' agreed the officer. 'But murderers? That's never been proven.'

'Maybe they got it wrong,' said Marshall. 'Maybe it wasn't meant to be fatal.'

The captain fixed a warning eye on his chief steward. 'Crew are not to engage in rumour-mongering. Consider that an order. Speculation is unhelpful. Dangerous. Now,' he said, turning back to Billie and the doctor, 'how can we support your work? Tell us what you need.'

~

Before her shift she met Robbie on the foredeck. The wind was up, the sea a ruffled black expanse, clouds scudding across the star-speckled void above.

'Wasn't sure you'd be here,' said Billie, easing down next to him. 'It's late.'

'Can't sleep, hen,' he said. 'Those pills you gave me are mince.' He was bleary-eyed and smelt of booze. Bundled in thick layers of scarf, he seemed older, more fragile.

'Don't take double,' she warned. 'It's strong stuff. I told you not to drink on them, right?'

Robbie waved a hand. 'I won't drop dead from a wee drop of whiskey and a sleeper.'

She was too tired to nag a man this stubborn.

'It's pure shan having both pubs shut,' he said glumly. 'Especially now – medicinal purposes, stress relief etcetera. You'd think brass would see the logic.'

For a virus seeking a fresh host, a pub packed full of sloppy drunks was heaven. They'd discussed this: Robbie understood the facts, but Billie knew he missed the booze and camaraderie.

'How's Mona doing?' she asked. Terrified he would fall sick, Robbie's wife was triple-sanning his cutlery and slathering him in decon at every opportunity.

Robbie gestured at the sky, as if lamenting madness in a loved one. 'Mona's all worries. Made me chuck my baccy out the other day, saw me drop someone a pinch and got all paranoid.'

Her turn to speak, but Billie found her mouth empty. A stillness had taken hold, fatigue pressing down like gravity. Clouds churned overhead, grey scraps of vapour wiping out the stars.

He peered at her. 'You alright, hen?'

'I'm pooched,' she admitted. 'They keep switching our shifts around, my head's a muddle.' Nursing the sick and dying was gruelling stuff, no matter how strictly you cordoned off emotion. She'd forgotten how draining it was, how much it took from you.

He rummaged in his pocket, surfaced with a jar. 'Here,' he declared, triumphant. 'A healthy amount. Clean as a whistle, I sanned the fuck out of it.'

Amber liquid glowed beneath the deck lights, the jar almost full.

'Thanks, Robbie,' she said, sanning her hands. She held the container up to the light. Its weight was satisfying, no visible smudges on the glass. 'What do I owe you?'

'Don't be daft. You're keeping the lot of us alive.'

A poor choice of words, but she resisted the obvious rejoinder: *Not all of you.* Regarded the alcohol with a mix of ardour and mistrust. This was foolish – her, of all people, taking contraband under these circumstances; accepting a jar of grey booze whose provenance she couldn't track, no clue as to the hands it might have passed through, the mouths that may have taxed a sly swig in passing. People did all sorts of things when nobody was watching.

'Got it from Juliette,' he said. 'A peace offering. It's clean.'

'You saw this poured out with your own eyes?' she asked, weighing the liquid in her hand.

'Poured it myself from a fresh bottle,' said Robbie. He sounded miffed, as if she'd questioned his integrity. 'Wiped the whole thing down before I cracked the seal, new gloves and all. Jar fresh out of the bloody dishwasher too.'

Fire with fire, that was the way to handle Robbie. 'Don't blame me for being careful. If you'd seen half the things I see, you'd be double-checking too.'

'Alright, love,' he said, contrite. 'But you know I'd never risk it. Couldn't live with myself if you got sick.'

'Thanks,' she said, curbing an urge to pat his arm. 'You're a good egg, Robbie. Get some sleep. I'm off to stash this. Duty calls.'

TOM

When the next survivor was carried into recovery, I didn't recognise him at first. A pale skeletal presence, all ribs and eye sockets. My former Romeo.

Once the nurses had retreated, I levered myself out of bed and shuffled down the row to his bedside. He lay motionless on his back, staring at the ceiling.

'Hey,' I said softly. 'You made it.'

No response, but I sensed a shift, a tension in his body. He was listening.

'Not long now. A few more days and we'll all be off this thing.'

Still nothing. Feeling foolish, I spoke a little louder. 'That's right, don't talk, save your strength. Blink twice for yes.' A feeble joke.

His eyes remained wide open, fighting the urge to blink, and I felt ashamed: what was I doing? But a churlish part of me, some small hurt child, persisted. 'Hey,' I said, laying my hand on his leg. 'Remember me?'

'Back to bed,' said a stern voice. 'Let Stewart rest.' The head nurse, Billie.

I shuffled off, embarrassed, as if I'd been caught harassing a senior citizen for spare change.

Cooped up in that limbo-place, your mind went round in circles. Musing on Stewart's silence got me nowhere – was he in the closet? Regretting our encounters? Was he traumatised, or did he blame me for his ordeal, assume I had infected him, and not vice versa?

From then on, walking to the loo became a grand production:

I had to shuffle right past him, close enough to touch, while he stared off at nothing, avoiding my eye.

But the sight of him had sparked a memory. Before I'd escaped that terrible sick room, as the fog of my own illness began to lift and consciousness returned in snatches, I'd witnessed a distressing scene: my handsome sailor in the grips of fever, acting like a man possessed – rambling madly, fighting the nurses, screaming for a priest; hysterical and paranoid, yelling the place down, convinced he was not long for this world. Too weak to move, I was reduced to watching in horror.

He didn't get his priest. But some strange things passed his lips. *It wasn't me, I swear! Bastard took it. Poison money … Devil water …*

So unlike the cool, assured man who held me close in that dim-lit cupboard, kissed my throat as mops swayed and buckets clanked and oblivious boots tramped overhead.

Poison money. What feverish scenario had sunk its hooks into him? Asking him outright was clearly not an option. No hallucinatory bonding on the cards for us; my fascination with this beautiful Scotsman now a one-way street.

Pointless trying to untangle the fevered ramblings of a man I did not know: just an excuse to fixate on him, I scolded myself. No doubt I'd also blathered nonsense, in my own delirious haze. Agnostic or not, I too had fallen back on religion, my addled brain conjuring up that exercise in solemn optimism, sung in B-flat major: *Where is death's sting? Where, grave, thy victory?*

Where was it? Just on the other side of that door, my friends. Right next door.

~

Pacing the short passageway, wrestling with a bout of cabin fever, I was caught off guard when the door to the recovery ward flew open.

The Scots nurse: Billie.

'You okay out here?' she asked. 'What you doing?'

I jerked my head towards the clinic. 'Feeling cooped up. Just checking my legs still work.'

'Know what you mean. It's cramped alright.' She stepped into my small oblong of space, pulled the door shut behind her. 'Mind if I sit? Need a breather. I'm due to knock off but my doffer's gone AWOL.'

'Make yourself comfortable,' I said, gesturing at the floor, and we sat down opposite each other. Her suit crackled as she settled against the wall. 'Your doffer?' I asked, making conversation.

She waved a weary arm across her hazmat. 'Cleaning crew. They help us in decon, change our gear, make sure we don't spread infection.'

'Aha,' I said. Hadn't thought about the backstage stuff.

'I'd kill for a smoke.' Her sigh muffled by the ventilator. 'Not very medical of me, I know.'

'It must be exhausting. Wouldn't want to be in your shoes.'

She gave me a funny look. 'Likewise, Teach.'

I stared down at my bony knees, my emaciated legs. Recalled her voice urging me awake, her hands cupping my skull as my body lurched beneath me like a demon. Holding the bucket ready, soothing the retch. Expertly catching my stomach contents as they gushed from my throat, like it was no big deal.

'We owe our lives to you,' I declared, like some half-rate actor. 'To all the nurses, the doctors.' Billie made a dismissive gesture. 'You know it's true,' I insisted. 'There's no way to ever pay you back, but I want to thank you.'

She'd gone quiet now, staring at the floor, and I feared I had embarrassed her.

'You're a great nurse,' I ventured. 'I've seen you with Mia.'

'I'm not a real nurse.' A pause. 'And we haven't saved everyone.'

I let this sit awhile, then couldn't help asking: 'How many?'

'Dead?' She examined her gloved hands, adopted a cool tone. 'Too many.'

I took the hint. 'How are the kids? The deaf boy?'

She lit up at this. 'Cleary? Doing his best. Stoic little fella. I've promised him Cate's on the mend, but I'm not sure he believes me.'

'Would you say hello from me?' A shameless bid to remind her of my own connection to the kids, my personal stake in their wellbeing. 'Could you ask him … is he looking after my binoculars? He borrowed them just before everything went to hell.'

'He loves those binoculars.' An unexpected smile, a short laugh, a glimpse of crooked teeth. 'Wore them to bed once, got the cord all tangled up around his neck.' When I heard the warmth in her voice it dawned on me: someone was taking care of the kid.

'He watches the seabirds,' she said. 'Makes up names for them.'

She was more open than usual – fatigue, or just a rare moment of privacy. So I broached the subject that had been looping in my head, a rumour passed from bed to bed.

'The other doctor, the Welsh guy …'

'Owen,' she said, making no effort to hide her disdain.

'He reckons there's been talk. That this was some kind of terror attack. Biovigilantes, anti-migration gangs.'

A snort of irritation. 'Fucking bampot. He's paid to be a doctor, not a gossip.'

'*Potentially* a terror attack, he said. But how? And why?'

'You're asking the wrong person. Got my hands too full for rumours.'

I pressed on: 'But what do you think? Is it possible?'

She eyed me warily. 'Who knows what's possible these days?

The world's fucked up.' I didn't contradict her. 'Listen,' she went on, 'rumours can be poison. Why tie yourself in knots? You should be resting, recovering.'

'But …' I prompted.

'Yeah,' she conceded, 'I know. Something doesn't add up.'

'We all did the superscreen. It was guaranteed failsafe. I've got that in writing.'

'Sure,' she said. 'But remember the airports. Chimera 9 – they dropped that thing direct into the water supply.'

A bell chimed faintly in my head: *It wasn't me, I swear! Bastard took it. Poison money … Devil water …*

'Devil water,' I heard myself say.

'What?' Her voice sharp, suspicious.

'Stewart. When he was ranting and raving, wanting a priest. That's what he said: *There's something in the water.*'

Billie launched herself upright. 'It's cold out here,' she said. 'You should be back in bed.' Conversation over.

Struggling to rise I faltered, my muscles unresponsive. She took my arm in a practised grip, lifted me upright, held the door open.

I paused on the threshold. 'You'll say hello to Cleary for me? He's welcome to keep those binoculars, they're all his. Will you tell him that?'

'Course I will,' she said, then moved her head close. 'Watch what you say in there. Don't upset the other patients.'

~

Surfacing from a doze, I discovered we had company. At first I thought it was some foreign insect, an oversized bug hovering at the porthole. Then I recognised its shape; the way it floated and dipped with a mechanical intelligence, as if driven by a joystick. Mineral, not animal.

Finger raised, voice croaky from sleep, I announced our visitor: 'Drone!'

The guard swore, leapt up to slam the porthole shut and taped a towel over it, blocking the thing's view. Its survey of our wasted selves.

A piece of trivia sprang to mind: there are no insects at sea.

This horror was almost over. Drones are a sign you're nearing land.

THE
NIGHTINGALE

9

CLEARY

A low smudge on the horizon: Cleary's heart clenched in recognition. Everyone crowded onto the upper decks to watch that far-off line become a solid mass. Land at last. People were crying openly, men and women both. Billie put her arms around his chest and hugged him close.

With this new country in sight the ship felt more substantial, no longer dwarfed by the surrounding vastness of the sea. Help was close, if his ma could just hold on.

I'll see you soon, my darling: her last message. Six words penned in Billie's spiky hand. An ache in his chest, like a stone lodged there.

Please get better, he prayed. *Please be well again. Please come back to me.*

But the land stretched on and on, the ship giving no sign of stopping. For days they sailed along an empty coastline, skimming the belly of this new landmass, a low-slung presence over to portside. Not long now, Billie promised him. Doctors were waiting with new medicines, hot showers and clean sheets. His ma was going to be fine.

One evening, as dusk descended, they drew close enough to make out signs of life: a lighthouse perched on a cliff, homes scattered amongst trees, the twinkling progress of car headlights. New smells, the warm greens of plant life mingled with the ocean's mineral tang.

Just on dark the *Steadfast* dropped anchor outside a narrow harbour entrance, a stretch of water that boiled and bulged with hidden currents. Beyond the headlands, in the inner reaches of the bay, glittered the lights of a distant city. Then everyone was ordered below decks, the portholes covered up. The screens in the saloons went black.

~

The spacemen came that night. Woken by the cabin lights Cleary saw a man's face floating centimetres from his own, encased in a yellow helmet. As the man's lips moved behind his visor, Cleary caught the faint buzz of his voice, just audible, as if amplified.

Lumbering men in yellow spacesuits were ushering the nurses out of bed. Billie stood defiant, hands on hips, bare-legged in a t-shirt. Holly clutched her blankets to her chest, jabbing a finger at the door: 'Out! Get out!'

The intruders withdrew, leaving a single guard in the doorway, his broad back to the room as the women hurriedly dressed. Billie helped Cleary down from his bunk, and they set off through the maze of corridors, his shoelaces flapping. As she took his hand, he realised they'd left their masks behind.

Outside the air was warm, the deck awash with people. Searchlights swung pale arcs into the darkness. A buffeting wind, the air flickering overhead as a chopper dipped over the ship. Billie wound her shirt around his head like a turban, leaving a gap to see through. It smelt of disinfectant and her sweat.

Confusion, flashing lights, the crowd milling. Burly yellow spacemen herding people into lines, strangers in white hazmats waving blinking devices. Soldiers in gasmasks prowled the edges, rifles at the ready and batons thrusting from their belts.

He'd expected a city, but the air smelt of dry grass and trees.

Across the water floodlights revealed a small pier and a pale strip of beach. Boats zipped between ship and shore, the blackness beyond pinpricked with intermittent lights. He could just make out a hillside thick with trees, a low-hanging slice of moon.

The chemical stink of decon wafted from a strange machine. Manned by two yellow-clad astronauts, it sprouted a spaghetti-snarl of tubes culminating in an empty doorway. People filed towards it, adults and kids, passengers and crew, each person photographed in a pop of light then scanned with a twinkling device. Then one by one they raised their arms and stepped into the doorway that led nowhere. Pale jets of foam shot down from all directions, drenching pyjamas, soaking uniforms, plastering hair to skulls.

Billie raised her arms and moved forward into the machine. Reappearing soaked on the far side, she waved for Cleary to follow. Dazzled by the camera, he hung back, but hands pushed him forward; acrid white foam splattered across his face, blinding him, cutting off his air. Close to panic, he surfaced coughing and spluttering into Billie's waiting arms.

Hours passed, stillness falling across the crowded deck. Children slept in parents' laps, wet clothes drying in the warm night air. Ghostly figures trod between prone bodies, handing out fresh face masks and bottles of water, while down the far end an army of yellow men hoisted mattresses and pillows over the gunwale, out of sight.

Back in their cabin at last, Cleary realised what the yellow spacemen had been doing: their bedding was gone, their bunks stripped down to bare hard surfaces.

In the small hours of that morning, while they slept, the ship crept into the harbour.

~

Billie squeezed his foot to wake him. As they headed up to the top deck, the floor seemed to ripple beneath his feet. The ship was at anchor, the harbour flat, but his body still retained the surge of those great ocean swells.

Outside, a lazy sea flashed and glittered. Hazmatted officials swarmed the upper decks and soldiers scanned the sky, heads swivelling like robots. The air was thick with heat, the sky a vast blue dome, the light raw and unfiltered.

Cleary and Billie took turns peering through the binoculars, tracing the harbour's wide curve, the small settlement laid out beyond the pier. The place looked abandoned: old wooden buildings set on a sweeping lawn, a line of wonky gravestones, a tall brick chimney pointing at the sky. Seagulls perched atop a monument, opening and closing their beaks as if commentating. Armed soldiers paced the beach and burly men in yellow hazmats stacked boxes on the pier.

All that space: grass, sand, solid earth. An invitation to run freely, accelerate to his body's limits, charge around until he collapsed on the grass, spent and breathless, inhaling its green scent. The urge to run was like a kind of hunger.

Zooming in close, the image trembling, Cleary deciphered an ancient sign, its letters paled by time and coastal weather: *No person ordered into quarantine shall commit any breach of the regulations.* Along the coast lay a row of abandoned beachfront homes, their windows dark, their foundations half submerged in the sea. In the far distance a cluster of city towers poked through a brownish haze.

Strangers in white hazmat suits skimmed a fever scanner down the breakfast queue. The kitchen staff had been replaced by more hazmats, the usual stodge by fresh bread and fruit, huge vats of sausages and baked beans, a quivering mass of real scrambled eggs.

Unused to eating in the mess-room, the nurses formed a huddle.

Passengers and crew were all mixed in together, and the air carried a buzz of nervous energy. A dull-eyed officer forked eggs into his mouth, boxer shorts showing beneath his uniform jacket.

Cleary took great care to avoid the stare that lay in wait across the room; that dark blur of beard a warning beacon, a treacherous rock he must navigate around. He must perfect the trick: keep the man in sight, but don't look at him directly. And never turn your back on him.

He'd eaten half a watermelon when the white-suits came to take Billie away. She scribbled a promise: she'd bring news of his ma. *Meet me near the front mast after lunch.* She pinched his earlobe and was gone.

~

Lunchtime came and went, Billie nowhere to be seen. Seabirds flapped in the rigging, and Cleary watched a speckled juvenile jostle for a spot. Same size, same markings, same wonky leg: was this the bird he'd seen way out at sea? Could it have trailed the ship for such a distance?

He scanned the harbour, then trained his binoculars on the object now approaching from across the water. The new ship stopped a short distance away. Twice the size and bulk of the *Steadfast*, it dropped anchor with a whale-sized splash. The white hull marked with a red cross, a name spelt out in black letters across the bow: *Nightingale.*

BILLIE

Their new overseers swung into action with military zeal. Billie was marched onto a transfer boat where Kellahan and Owen waited. A soldier gunned the engine across the water to the hospital ship.

A floating cordon now encircled the *Steadfast*: yellow tape affixed to buoys, the words *Quarantine zone – do not cross* repeated in a loop. Soldiers hoisted the cordon aloft to let them through. A shadow skimmed the water, and Billie spotted a drone's black silhouette overhead.

The hospital ship was immaculate, all white paint and orderly signage: *Authorised Personnel Only. Sterile Zone. Infection Control Station. Outbound Waste.* Officials trussed up in full PPE escorted them to the local incident commander's office.

A no-nonsense man with minimal small-talk, the incident commander kept his audience standing and his summary short: the entire patient cohort had been transferred to this medical vessel. Several patients were still in serious condition, one deemed critical, but most had stabilised, and those in recovery appeared to be out of danger. There were grounds to hope the virus could be contained, any further deaths prevented.

'But we need to remain vigilant,' he warned. 'There's no guarantee this thing has run its course. That we won't see further cases.'

The entire incoming cohort, present company included, would be fitted with subdermal tracking devices as a precautionary measure. Regular fever scans should weed out any potential viral exposure, but their own responsibilities were not over yet.

'You've seen firsthand how this sickness manifests,' said the incident commander. 'We need you to actively monitor the population, be alert for any early signs. Keep your eyes and ears open.'

Owen tried to get a word in, some bluster about the limits of visual diagnosis, but the commander spoke over him. 'You can discuss the details with my medical staff,' he said, turning away. They were dismissed.

Two local medics in full protective gear led them to a state-of-the-art donning chamber. This was to be a 'briefing tour' of the onboard clinic – the briefing part, as it turned out, a largely one-way affair; the three of them were to provide verbal case notes to supplement the patchy written record. They were shadowed by silent lackeys in headcams, recording everything.

'You've done an incredible job,' said the female medic as they left the donning chamber, hazmatted to the gills. She'd introduced herself as Jane, but was badged as Doctor Hart. She paused before the door to the isolation ward.

'We helped with the evacuation,' said her colleague, Sullivan, who hadn't offered a first name. 'The conditions you were working under ...' He trailed off.

'And with untrained staff,' the woman added. 'I can't imagine how tough that must have been.' Sympathy in her voice, an invitation to elaborate.

Owen took the bait. 'No training for a scenario like that. You just do what you can.'

Billie rolled her eyes behind her visor, saw the female medic notice.

The door opened onto a long white room. The local medics encouraged them to do the rounds, stop at each bed, chat briefly with their former patients. This contact would help to 'personalise the transfer of care', as Hart put it.

The patients began to stir as they recognised their hazmatted visitors. Tom, the teacher, propped himself upright as Billie approached, gave a mock salute. 'Reporting for shore leave,' he said.

The *Nightingale*'s set-up was impressive: top-line gear, ample nursing staff, everyone decked out in proper PPE, a separate recovery ward for those deemed symptom-free. Nano-monitors ingested by each patient, data from their hand-scrawled charts already digitised to screens above each bed. Kellahan remarked wryly on how shipshape the place was – so clean and well appointed, the paint job clearly recent. Light poured in through translucent windows and the decon room had a sophisticated airlock. Textbook protes, Billie noted. They know what they're doing.

She'd assumed the patients would be rushed offsite, no chance to check on them or say goodbye. She was happy to see them, her survivors – a feeling tempered by relief that they were no longer her responsibility. Under scrutiny by the local medics and their mute spies she greeted each person, asked after them, passed on what limited news she could. They wanted to know how long they'd be kept here; when they could see their loved ones, contact home; what would happen next. All questions Billie wanted answers to herself. The local doctors deflected these queries, offering assurances that were scant on detail.

Cate slept beneath a white sheet, her body all slopes and ridges. Billie hovered, hoping she would wake, but her eyes remained closed, her breathing slow and regular. Her readout was good, but the IV was still in place. The Aberdeen crewman, Scoot, seemed to be feigning sleep, but his readout had steadied too.

Mia was sitting up in bed, bright-eyed, cheeks pink. Billie took the girl's small hand in her own gloved one. She spoke softly, her back to their observers. 'Your mum and dad are waiting for you.

You'll see them soon, I promise.' Met Mia's doubtful gaze, hoped there was some truth in this.

'When?' asked the girl. 'When can I see them?'

Sullivan tried to butt in but Billie held her ground, kept issuing calm reassurances until the child seemed to take them to heart.

Kellahan was peering around. 'Someone's missing.' There was a silence.

Hart pointed at the wall. 'There's one patient in critical. Not out of the woods yet.' A young man, the last person to fall sick. Outwardly strong, but his body had refused to rally. Had purged itself violently for three days, then fallen into an ominous stillness.

'How is he?' Billie asked.

'Critical,' Sullivan repeated. 'We'll let you know if anything changes.'

When the medics trooped them upstairs to see the onsite lab, the implications took a moment to compute. The facility was slick, clearly expensive. Through a plastic window they watched technicians label samples, squint into a high-tech microscope, scroll data up screens. Billie scanned the gear: at least a million pounds' worth, surely. She met Kellahan's eye, saw her surprise mirrored there.

'Why the onboard lab?' she asked, the answer already dawning. 'Aren't the patients being transferred to a proper hospital?'

'Nobody's going anywhere,' said Sullivan, then more gently: 'Not yet. And you'll all be required to make regular trips to the *Nightingale.*'

'Family liaison,' said Hart. 'The patients have been asking for you – their own doctors, their head nurse. Keeping that channel open will help foster community resilience.'

Billie untangled this jargon: so her services were still required.

Next up, three hours in a windowless room, verbally logging

patient case notes and timelines, Sullivan and Hart asking the questions. The discussion went beyond due care and viral analytics. Their observers had vanished, but Billie had no doubt the room was wired. *You do not have to say anything, but anything you do say …*

She had to hand it to Kellahan. The doctor's demeanour was courteous, collegial, disarming. Confiding details in a candid way, while hinting at the unreasonable pressure they'd been under, how under-equipped the ship had been, how they'd had to improvise to cope, to save as many lives as possible. No bad-mouthing of brass, just a gentle inkling that the guilt lay further up the food chain. A bid for absolution that covered their whole team of press-ganged nurses. A subtle refusal to take the blame for all the horror they'd endured. For those twelve lives erased.

Weeks ago now, Kellahan had warned them: once they reached dry land they must present a united front. Owen wasn't making that easy here, with his self-effacing hero act. The big balloon was acting breezy, tossing medical jargon around – *neurovirulence, mutation rates, gestation period* – while dropping mentions of the few work-arounds he'd devised, in truth a scant list against all the innovations Billie had dreamt up. She felt irritation rising: twelve people dead. Nobody was up for a medal here.

'This virus, its clinical manifestation: how does it compare to what you encountered back home?' Hart, directing this at Kellahan.

'I've worked outside the UK these past few years,' said the ship doctor. 'Missed the worst of the pandemic, left six months before it hit. Billie's the one who's been at the coalface.'

Doctor Hart glanced down at her device, flicked unseen docs across the screen; a subtle movement, one finger. She turned to Billie. 'You worked as a healthcare assistant back in Scotland? Forgive me, we use different designations here. Is that a nursing role?'

'An orderly, I think,' Owen broke in helpfully. 'Is that what you'd call it here?'

Billie glared at him, felt Kellahan watching her. 'A nurse's auxiliary,' she said. 'Patient monitoring and transfer, wash and dress, prep. PPE compliance, waste disposal protes. I worked the isolation wards at Glasgow South. Hands-on, worst cases.'

Kellahan spoke up. 'We were incredibly lucky to have Billie on our team. Without her experience, her training in ID containment, patient care ...' He trailed off.

Owen yawned and examined the ceiling, telegraphing disdain.

'What's your sense, Billie?' asked Sullivan. 'How does this thing compare with what you saw back home?'

'The ALT virus mutates so fast,' she hedged. 'The stats were never constant.'

'Just a general picture.'

She recalled the death wards: the sense of hopelessness, the reek of death and its entangled stinks, the chemical efforts to keep it at bay. Braced herself to muster up a neutral account.

'Mortality's slightly lower with this bug. We lost around fifty per cent of the sick ones, and that was under hugely sub-par conditions. With ALT, in a hospital setting, mortality was just over seventy. Although we had superbugs to deal with too, the AB-resistants – that ramped up the stats.'

The local medics waited, their full attention on Billie.

'ALT's airborne,' she went on. 'It's an enterovirus, so encephalitis was a major risk. This new thing ... the onset's quicker. More febrility – confusion, delirium, hallucinations. Getting the fever down was a real battle.' A wave of fatigue washed over her. She needed rest, food; to find the kid, lie on the deck and watch the clouds change shape.

Owen again: 'What's the nano-data showing?'

'We're running diagnostics,' said Sullivan, with a frown. 'But so far it doesn't match the profile of anything on record, ALT included.' He pawed at his neck, hunting an itch trapped beneath his suit. Despite the heat the locals were all fully kitted up, ventilators and the whole shebang. Billie's own team had been issued more minimal gear.

'Do we have any treatment options?' asked Kellahan.

'Nothing tailored,' said Sullivan. 'This bug looks novel.'

'We'll be trialling three,' said Hart. 'A nano-viricide, laser deactivation and a broad-spectrum anti-viral. We're optimistic, but it's too soon to tell.'

A sigh escaped Kellahan.

'Let's wind up,' said Hart. 'You must be exhausted. We don't want to overtax you.'

Bit late for that, thought Billie. 'What do we tell everyone? When can we go ashore?'

Hart performed a helpless shrug. 'I wish we knew. If it's any consolation, you're not alone.'

'None of us can leave,' said Sullivan. 'Not until we know exactly what we're dealing with.'

Viral profiling was just part of the mystery. The superscreen – that intense regime of pre-departure scans – had granted all on board a clean bill of health. They'd been at sea three weeks before the first symptoms appeared. Either this bug had lain latent all that time, somehow dodging the screening – or what? Kellahan had raised the issue of a stealth virus, or deliberate onboard contamination, but the locals had swiftly moved the conversation on.

'There'll be an investigation?' Owen asked as they stood to leave.

'Is,' corrected Sullivan as he swiped the door, releasing them. 'It's already underway.'

Outside the sky was wide and cloudless, the air tepid as they filed into the boat and returned to the *Steadfast* in the wordless company of soldiers.

Back on deck, in the shadow of the foremast, Kellahan removed his glasses and rubbed them on his shirt. Owen stood back, fists on hips, awkward now. Nearby a group of kids attempted cartwheels across the *Steadfast*'s deck, their laughter floating out across the water. Billie spotted Robbie by the wheelhouse, deep in conversation with a yellow-clad man, waving his arms, like the two of them were down the boozer together. She'd talk to him later, tell him Scoot had pulled through.

Boats milled around the ship like misdirected ducklings: a forensics team collecting evidence. A stink hung heavy in the air, and on the shore a yellow figure hosed down a smoking heap of mattresses. From what Billie could tell the yellow-clad men were assigned to do the grunt work; the white hazmats were the ones in charge.

'I'm off to find Captain Lewis,' said Kellahan. 'See what he knows.' He levelled a look at them both. 'We're a unit now. Heads will roll for this. Let's not make it easy for them.'

Billie found a private spot to roll a smoke. She'd kept up a professional front on the *Nightingale*. A sense of duty to her patients, plus a strong dash of self-protection, rather than any official capacity she might still hold. No doubt the nurses' wages had ceased, if they'd been paid at all. She tried to envisage the freedoms all those zeroes might offer, but couldn't fix on it.

Cut off: the feeling was palpable. During the journey she'd adjusted to going dry – unable to speak home, hear her parents' voices or see Jamie's toothy grin. The silence had been bearable for knowing it was finite. Now that there was no clear endpoint, no way to reassure her family, she felt the separation keenly – a tangle of pining, worry, guilt.

Her parents had never endorsed her decision to leave. But nor had they persuaded her to stay. Glasgow they mistrusted; the hospital more so, an unvoiced fear of her daily proximity to death. There'd been mention of alternatives – aged care, disability. Things that weren't contagious. Unable to secure another medical job, she'd presented this trip as a safer and more promising path.

'Will you get a boyfriend?' her brother had asked. 'A nice Australian man, with a hat?' She'd promised to call at Christmas and sing 'Auld Lang Syne' together. Jamie had a terrible ear, but sang with wild enthusiasm, striving to match his sister's range. Despite the racket, his efforts never failed to light her up. How would her parents explain her silence? Jamie was sensitive, stubborn. Wore his anguish close to the surface. What kind of distress were they enduring right now?

Enough. This would lead nowhere. She should go and check on the kid.

TOM

Our new ward was a vast improvement: a long narrow room suffused with milky light, that hospital hush. Clean sheets and nourishing meals, room to stretch our legs.

But no word on what would happen next. The portholes were screened and nobody could leave. A locked ward on a hospital ship ... best not to think of it as a prison, we agreed. White on white, all surfaces scrubbed clinically clean: white walls and floor, white equipment, white sheets and screens and furniture, the nurses' coveralls. Our new pyjamas the one exception, random splotches of colour in that ghostly room.

When our *Steadfast* medical team was first escorted in, it was clear that they were no longer in charge. There'd been a changing of the guard: now they were merely visitors.

Instead local nurses tended to us. A drawling accent, all flattened vowels and rising inflections. They were friendly, but hard to tell apart: white hazmats and respirators, red armbands marking them out as medical. The plump one, Ally, was my favourite. Asked me why such a posh-sounding guy was wearing these bog-standard pyjamas. Wasn't I a duke or something? Where were my velvet slippers, my silk dressing-gown?

Ally won me over, too, because she broke the rules, shared whispered snippets: we were anchored offshore from an old quarantine station, she told me, on a sleepy peninsula south of Melbourne. A heritage site, protected parklands, ocean research and ecotourism, not used for quarantine in half a century or more. A place where rich people holidayed and scuba-diving scientists measured crabs.

A few days in, a social-worker type showed up for a 'chat'. Nice enough, on the surface – blue armband, convoluted job title, the word 'support' in there somewhere – but what began with routine pleasantries soon strayed into outright quizzing. Did I have family back in England? Did I enjoy teaching? Didn't I find it stressful? Why had I applied to the BIM program? Her insincerity was grating, and my answers verged on flip.

'They promised us pina coladas,' I said. 'I'm thinking of suing.'

Her response: earnest nodding. She soon progressed down the row, plying my wardmates with the same routine.

Officially we were in Isolation, our lucky subgroup in Recovery. States of limbo, cut off from the world. But alive: that fact kept returning to me. Each time, without fail, it carried a sweet charge of exhilaration. A twinge almost sexual in its intensity.

They'd moved us off the *Steadfast* in the depths of night. Big hulking men in yellow suits, the muscle of the operation; white-clad medical staff standing back, courteous and efficient, as if the dirty work was not their business. Everyone in hazmats, like a disaster flick.

I'd protested, said my legs worked fine, but they'd insisted on lugging us here on stretchers – strapped flat on our backs, filing out into the night. Manhandled by torchlight into boats, then jostled onto this new vessel, through a complicated antechamber, and deposited in our beds. Smuggled aboard and stowed away, like human contraband. Contaminated cargo.

The nurses were generous with the meds. 'After what you've been through,' said Ally, waving a latex glove in gay abandon. 'Ask and you shall receive!'

But to my surprise, I didn't feel the need. Yes, I dabbled, softened the edges. But that old hunger, that urge for oblivion, had receded. I found myself lit by a strong desire to remain completely present.

The afterglow of having cheated death, perhaps.

Risky detox strategy, but surprisingly effective.

I hankered for something to read, something to watch besides my own internal data flickering up the wall, but strict rules governed what was permitted in and out.

Trauma: our official diagnosis, head-wise. On the physical front they were at a loss. Whatever struck us down remained unnamed.

The *Steadfast* medics made regular visits, bringing what news they could, but their stopovers were short, the info scant, the conversations monitored. I always asked Billie about the children. Most were doing well, she reported, but at least four had lost a parent. She couldn't provide surnames, so I couldn't connect all the faces.

'What happened to us out there?' I asked her once. A simple question, on the surface of it.

'They're saying—' she began.

Doctor Sullivan interrupted: 'Your wellbeing is our primary focus right now. How's the fatigue? Any more headaches?'

Isolation: an apt term. Mum, Dad, Rosa – there was still no word in either direction. Outbound comms remained banned, no inbounds being relayed. But our families had apparently been notified: now at least they knew we were alive.

In fact, Ally told me, the whole world knew: our names, and the names of the dead, had been released into the stream. The shitstorm had begun.

I yearned to call home. Had no idea how long they'd waited for news, fearing I was dead. Picturing them fretting, hoping I'd made it through … the thought of it broke my heart. Made me angry too, or would have done, if I'd had the energy to spare.

Little Mia was a trouper. Each day we chatted about her family and friends, made up stories about the world awaiting us outside – giant kangaroos, fruit trees thick with peaches, sun-tanned locals bearing get-well cards. She was restless, wanting her parents, worried about her little brother. Said he refused to sleep unless she'd given him his goodnight tickle. At times this had seemed like a chore to her, but now she'd tickle him forever if only she could.

Talking to Mia was no chore: she was a sweet kid. I'd have done it anyway, regardless. As for how she'd fallen sick ... Her sunhat, dropped on the deck; me bending to retrieve it, handing it back to her ... I tried not to dwell on that.

For the parents amongst us, this prolonged limbo was a source of great distress. Single mother to a vulnerable child, Cate took it particularly hard. Hungry for news of Cleary, angered by the bland doublespeak of our keepers, she got some of the local nurses offside. Bit back at their gentle admonishments to rest, their suggestions she might benefit from a sedative.

'I need to see my child,' she'd say. 'Is that so hard to understand? Are you robots?'

The desire for dry ground was palpable. On one visit Doctor Kellahan told me there was an inquiry underway, a mass inquest of sorts – to uncover how the outbreak had occurred, how it was handled. Adept at micromanaging our conversations, the local medics cut him off, said not to tire me out.

My strength slowly returned, that deadening fatigue receding. The nurses encouraged us to pace the length of the ward, move our limbs so they wouldn't atrophy. Without fail, each time Max and I shuffled past each other in our pyjamas, he delivered a cheery greeting: 'Lovely day for a walk!'

Max had no memory of when the fever hit. He knew he'd tried to throw himself overboard, but it wasn't something we discussed. Ditto the broomstick he'd brandished, the one I'd helpfully picked up and stashed away. What would be the point?

On the *Nightingale* we existed in a state of suspended animation, as if waiting for some unspecified announcement. We were like dazed survivors from a war zone: all the recent horrors, the sharp edges, were muffled by medication, or sheer gratitude at being alive.

One image from that time persisted: a figure slumped over at the far end of the ward. The man who'd lost his wife, face buried in his hands, a nurse rubbing his back as if comforting a child.

He was on the *Nightingale* too, of course: my holiday romance. Fool that I was, I hadn't quite given up hope, still imagined we might yet become comrades in arms.

One day, fortified by two coffees, I stopped by his bed, loitering with intent. He closed his eyes and lay there like a corpse.

'Hey,' I said softly. 'Stewart. You still alive in there?' No response, so I gave up and shuffled off.

I couldn't work it out: why pretend we're strangers? Did he blame me, assume I'd made him sick? Or was his coldness a silent plea, an appeal to keep our brief affair a secret? Was anyone still that repressed?

He shouldn't worry on that count, I thought with a trace of bitterness. *Privacy's a scarce enough commodity. I won't help drive it to extinction.*

10

CLEARY

The spooks came for him after lunch. That's what Declan called the strangers in white hazmats – *spooks*. The men in yellow hazmats were code-named bananas.

A female spook led Cleary to a room set up like a doctor's clinic: a low bed, a trolley with gauze and swabs, a tray of scary implements. A male spook held a scanner to his brow, and the woman tilted a talk-screen at him. As she spoke, her words popped up on the screen, spelt out in big letters.

Just a little injection, she said. *To keep you safe. Don't be scared. Everyone's getting one.*

She waggled a red lollipop wrapped in plastic. *For after. Just a tiny sting. I'll hold your hand, okay?*

A sharp white pain, then a burning feeling. She'd lied to him.

The woman patted his back and pressed the lollipop into his hand. *Well done*, she said into the talk-screen. *Brave boy.*

Tears prickling his eyes, he examined the place where the jab had gone in. Beneath the skin rose a small bump, as if a matchhead was stuck under there. He reached for it, but the male spook caught his wrist, then taped a wad of cotton to his arm.

Don't touch it, mate, the man said into the talk-screen. *And keep that dressing on till bedtime.*

Led to another room, Cleary found a matching pair of spooks

waiting. Splayed across the table were coloured pens and sheets of thick blank paper. They gestured at the empty chair between them, and warily he took a seat. Another talk-screen appeared. Cleary pulled out his notebook and flicked to a fresh page.

Hi Cleary. You like to draw, don't you?

Left alone with these treasures Cleary would have been content, but the spooks had other plans: they kept breaking his concentration, shoving the talk-screen under his nose, bombarding him with odd requests: draw this, draw that. He tried to be polite, and they gave him real orange juice, plus biscuits with icing in the middle, but some of their questions were so dense they left him at a loss.

Could he draw his family? Easy: he sketched his ma, himself, Granda, Gran and Uncle Liam, down the fish pond at Phoenix Park. Added a sun, flowers, and one of the park deer, antlers spread like wings above his head. The woman pointed to the deer: *Who's this?* she said into the talk-screen. *A deer*, he wrote, puzzled. Had she not seen a deer before? Her next question was no better: *That deer looks like it's got something on its mind. What do you think it might be?* How would he know what the animal was thinking? He wasn't a mind-reader. It was just standing around, doing deer stuff, but he knew that wasn't much of an answer. He racked his brains, then replied: *He wants one of Gran's Jaffa Cakes.*

Why does your mum look sad? the male spook asked.

His drawing showed the day of Granny's birthday, a Saturday afternoon, not long before they'd left Dublin. *She's not sad*, he wrote. *She's cheesed off cos she left Gran's present on the train.*

Winter had been coming, and his ma had bought Gran a soft green scarf to keep her cough away. When she'd realised the gift was lost, she dropped the bag of bread and clapped her hands over her eyes, a childlike gesture of despair. Gran had hugged her tight, patting her back as the ducks squabbled at their feet.

Cleary blinked, willed his tears into reverse. He would not cry in front of these spooks.

Asked to draw his da, he reproduced the only image he remembered. An old pic, shot from some distance away: a man dangling a fish from an invisible line, his features indistinct beneath the shadowed peak of a cap. Did his dad like fishing? Cleary had no idea. He couldn't remember his da. He put the drawing aside, asked for another biscuit.

Next question: could he draw his friends?

It would take ages to sketch his pals from back home – the gang from the Pearse Street flats, and his best mate, Ben, who'd moved up north last summer with his family, his ma a wreck from worry, afraid of losing another one to the bug. So he sketched Declan in a fighting stance, waving a sword, scowling ferociously. The pose came out a bit bow-legged, but his pal would be rapt with the biceps.

Then he drew Billie, a smoking fag tucked in her fist. Billie wasn't big on smiling, but the spooks wanted happy pictures, so he plastered a wide grin across her face.

The *Steadfast*, said the lady spook. Could he draw the ship, out at sea? The picture came out flat and lifeless, the vessel lost amongst blue waves, so he added a sea-serpent. The monster was pure class, all coiled muscle and bloodshot eyes. Below its jagged snarl the ship resembled a bath toy, a snack to be devoured in a single crunch. The sight of it gave him a chill.

Now the questions came thick and fast. What was the monster up to? Where had it come from? Why was it angry? There was too much to explain: the ocean's lukewarm dead zones, all the sea creatures sickened by chemical waste; diseased squid and poisoned sharks, jellyfish hordes sifting the desolate currents, acid-ravaged mutants roaming the sea floor. The way deep water sheltered fearful things. Even back home, you never knew what was down there: selkies and merrows up the coast, the serpent lurking in Lough Foyle. *Sea monsters are real,* he wrote. *Granda saw one once.*

The spooks turned aside, conferred. Then tilted the talk-screen at him: *Just one more picture, Cleary. Something you saw on the ship. The night you found that man, the one who got hurt. Could you draw that for us?*

He drew the bare facts, no more: the window framed by darkness, the shelves stacked with supplies, the dead man's legs, the blood on the floor. Then he pushed the drawing aside: *Can I go now please.*

~

Escaping the gloom for the bright sunlight of the upper deck, he saw a crowd gathered around a ladder propped against the kiosk wall. A line of soldiers was padding up the rungs.

On the kiosk roof a group of passengers huddled together, holding a white sheet. Against the sky, Cleary glimpsed smeared black letters: *HELP US!* High in the blue, he spotted a small aircraft, a rare sight. Someone rich, a prime minister or a millionaire, circling overhead, peering down at them.

The first soldier paused at the top of the ladder, his pals crammed in behind him, nose to bum. He spoke to the men on the rooftop, gesturing for them to come down, but although they seemed frightened they clearly did not plan to obey the order. Instead they edged further out of reach, moving in an awkward bunch, struggling to hold the sheet taut.

The crowd below was getting rowdy: a raised fist, a woman shouting through cupped hands. As the first soldier heaved himself up onto the roof, the crowd surged forward, and Cleary was jostled to the back.

He turned to see more soldiers lining the gunwale, their weapons aimed out to sea or overhead, tracking unseen prey. Out on the water, white flashes: boats speeding past.

Then he was hemmed in, the crowd in motion, a blind surge of bodies; a woman was dragged under, then hauled upright like a sack of spuds – a fistful of shirt, flesh, any handhold. Sweat and trampling feet, the smell of a panicked mob. Cleary was swept along in the crush, fighting to stay afloat, as the soldiers herded everyone below decks.

BILLIE

About to disembark from the *Nightingale,* Billie spotted chaos across the water: boats circling the *Steadfast,* the upper deck swarming with people. A crack of gunshot. Then she and the ship doctors were hustled back into the depths of the hospital ship.

The incident commander strode past, radio crackling, staff hurrying after him.

'Keep them out of sight,' he ordered. 'Media incident.'

Directed to a narrow bench in a windowless room, minders standing guard, they waited in silence. Owen stared at the floor, head in hands. With bad news to be broken, none of them were in a hurry to get back.

The first death at anchor: the man who'd looked so strong, but had succumbed so swiftly. The local medics clearly rattled, shaken to have lost a life, despite all their superior equipment. Their confidence taken down a notch.

These regular ward visits – brief trips to the hospital ship, conducted in the name of 'social continuity', as their overseers put it – were bringing unwelcome attention. Kellahan had voiced what Billie herself suspected: their role as go-betweens less a compassionate measure than a bid to quell disquiet, keep them implicated.

Ferried between the two vessels, Billie felt scrutiny from both sides. People approached her daily now, passengers and crew, even those who'd shunned her or been outright hostile during the trip. A few voiced gratitude or apologies; others left such things unsaid, but let their shame show through. Some acted as though they'd never spoken a bad word to her. She remembered every slight, but lacked the will to conjure it all back up. Fear cornered people, hit their panic buttons. You couldn't take it personally.

They sidled up to her in passageways, seeking inside knowledge she wasn't privy to: how long they'd all be kept here, when they'd be taken ashore, or sent home. *You tell me*, was the gist of her response. She was gentler with those seeking news of the patients. She'd tried to reassure Mia's parents – faced down the father's helpless anger, the mother's raw distress. So much for family liaison. Owen had well and truly dropped that ball, left her and Kellahan to field the questions: is my husband out of danger? How is my wife's mood? Can you pass my cousin a message?

And the bereaved: the spouses, siblings, children of those twelve dead. Families shattered, their loved ones rendered into the past tense. Broken by grief, many had retreated into private cabins deep below decks.

She didn't know them all by sight. There was no helpful map of all the faces on the ship, how one related to another. At night she lay awake, recalling the features of a person racked by pain and fever, the names they'd called out near the end, weighing them against a person she'd passed that morning in a passageway, their own expression distorted by grief and shock; scanning their face, appraising skin tones, trying to pick the family resemblance.

This latest death: another blow. Another hole left in the world. This ragged collection of souls again reduced by one. How much more could people bear?

She took the sleepers Kellahan prescribed, but not the Calmex: mistrusted its balmy numbness. Half the nurses were now dosed up on the stuff, haunted by images that neither sunlight nor safety could quash. But so far she'd resisted, knowing that any moment she could turn a corner and encounter one of the bereaved, that empty Calmex grin plastered across her face. A face that had no business smiling – not given what she'd seen, and what they'd lost.

Owen lifted his head from his hands. His eyes were bloodshot, his skin blotchy.

'I can't do it,' he said to Kellahan. 'You'll have to tell them.'

The doctor just nodded, his gaze fixed on the wall.

'I never signed up for this,' said Owen, defensive. 'I'm not a grief counsellor.'

Kellahan did not respond, and Billie held her tongue. No point stating the obvious.

An hour later they were released and ushered into the transfer boat. Climbing the gangway, Billie braced herself for questions. But soldiers aside, the deck of the *Steadfast* was empty.

She found Cleary in the fore saloon, playing cards with Holly. Billie wove through the crowd, avoiding the anxious looks that followed her. The kid was her first priority.

A wail rose, and she turned to see a young woman drop to the floor, Kellahan kneeling to comfort her. The dead man's girlfriend: felled by shock, her sobs now audible to everyone.

Head down, Billie made her way towards the boy.

'All okay?' she asked Holly.

'He's a card shark,' said the nurse, but Cleary's sights were set on Billie.

He snatched the note from her outstretched hand, bent over it as if trying to translate a foreign tongue. Scribbled in haste on the transfer boat, the message bore the lurch and wobble of the crossing: *How is my sweet boy? Behaving yourself? Be patient, darling. I'm getting stronger every day.*

'No problems today?' she asked Holly.

'All fine,' said the nurse. 'Poor mouse. He should be with his mum.'

Billie bit back her irritation. 'Nothing I can do about that. Thanks for watching him.'

Holly indicated the sobbing woman now being led from the room. 'Another one?'

A curt nod: no death talk in front of the kid. He picked up more than he let on.

'No word on ...' Holly trailed off, but it was clear what she meant.

'No. We're all in the dark.' Billie touched Cleary's shoulder, and he dragged his eyes from the note. *Come on*, she signed. *Let's go eat.*

In the stairwell a familiar figure blocked their path. Cutler, wearing civvies, an incongruous sight. Brass had ditched their uniforms after a quiet word from their new masters, a reminder that they were no longer in charge.

So far Billie had managed to avoid the man, bar one brief conversation: she'd asked him whether the nurses would still get their pay. Yes, he'd said – they'd signed a legal contract, fulfilled their side of the pact. No word on when, however.

'Galloway,' said Cutler now, dour as ever. Her surname less a mark of comradeship than a reminder of rank. Former rank, the way she saw it.

'Cutler,' she shot back, giving his shorts and t-shirt the once-over. No epaulettes now, but neat as a pin, as always. A small, mean-minded man who still carried himself as if he was in full regalia.

He stepped back to let a family troop past, waited until they were alone. 'Government's holding formal hearings next week. You'll be summoned for questioning.'

'Right,' she said, a tendril of unease stirring. She drew Cleary close. The boy did not look up at the officer.

'They're trying to spring it on us, minimise the chance for any arse-covering. *Collusion*.' Cutler snorted. 'Not that colluding would do us any good.'

Us? They'd worked together passably, when forced, but that was the sticking point: brass had made it clear she had no choice.

'The nurses too?' she asked. Those with families had returned to their dorms, but the single women were still bunked together, as were the single men. United by their shared ordeal, their refusal to bear blame, the nurses had closed ranks.

'Everyone,' said Cutler. 'Be prepared. Captain's called a meeting for tomorrow night, all crew, to discuss what we'll be up against. Let your lot know.'

'We're crew now?' she asked, unable to help herself. 'I thought us lot were scabs.'

He directed a baleful stare over his mask. 'I never saw it like that. You were hired to save lives – and that's what you did. My crew might not be geniuses, but they've grasped that much.'

Billie said nothing. Through the worst of the journey Cutler and his cronies had let the crew's animosity go unchecked.

'No-one's laying out the welcome mat for us here,' he warned. 'We need to get our story straight.'

Your story, she thought. *Ours is already straight: we did all we could.*

'Message received,' she said, taking the boy's hand, and together they set off for the dim confines of what now passed for home.

~

Lugging a box of supplies back to their cabin later that day, she saw Cleary and Declan in an alcove, talking to a figure in a white hazmat suit.

'What's going on?' she asked, facing down the official. Not much to distinguish them: this one had brown eyes set in a rectangle of dark skin, a strand of black hair trapped against the visor.

'Just having a chat,' said the man.

Billie caught a whiff of sugar, saw the boys chomping enthusiastically beneath their masks. 'What's that in your gobs?' she demanded.

A grinning Declan pulled his mask aside to display a wad of masticated brown goo. 'Caramels,' he said with relish. 'He's got 'em in his pocket.'

Billie pointed at Cleary. 'I'm this one's legal guardian,' she told the man. 'You want to talk to him, you go through me.' Not strictly true, but worth reinforcing. 'And you've got no right to give them sweets. You're breaking protocol.'

The official raised his hands. 'Just being friendly.'

Billie made to leave, but the man laid a hand on her arm: another breach. On reflex Billie jerked away.

'Wait,' he said. 'I need to scan you all.'

The boys chomped happily as they were scanned. Then the man turned to Billie, pointed the machine at her temple. 'Those protesters,' he said, all casual. 'The ones up on the roof. Are they alright?'

'You tell me. They're still locked up in the bloody sin bin.'

'Yes,' said the man. 'But wasn't one guy injured?'

An odd question. 'Ask him yourself. He's the one on crutches, thanks to your army thugs.' The protest had been broken up by over-zealous soldiers, one passenger slipping off the roof in the fracas, landing badly, a nasty sprain to his ankle.

The man lowered his voice. 'Not everyone's against you. You do have supporters here.'

A prickle of nerves. Against her?

The official hurried on: 'There's a bunch of activists and media camped outside the quarantine station. Most of them are on your side. They're not happy about how this is being handled, how you're being treated.'

'Okay,' said Billie slowly, buying time. Something was amiss here: a fever scan should not take this long.

Two yellowsuits strode past their alcove. The man dipped his head at them, waited until they were out of sight, then thrust some folded papers into her hand. 'Quick, take this,' he said. 'Written by a local journo. There are people on your side.'

Billie shoved the papers in amongst her supplies, out of sight.

'Chin up,' said the man, and was gone.

~

That night she left the boy asleep, in Holly's care. She needed some fresh air and solitude. To escape their cell, stretch her legs.

She lit a cigarette, pocketed her lighter and exhaled grey twirls into the darkness. Across the water a lighthouse blinked out its steady pulse. On the horizon glowed the city whose streets she'd walked so often in her head. Touted as a cultural centre, a humming grid of music and coffee, sports and commerce, art and opportunity – all the official markers of liveability. The vast sprawl of its suburbs gradually petering out into factories, industrial zones, vertical food farms.

She'd browsed the promo pics for hours: gated compounds, compact rows of tiny flats, hot running water, communal laundries and barbecue areas. The promise of disposable income, enough to send some money home – get her mum's teeth fixed, buy Jamie a new bike. Weekends off, new streets to roam, alleyway bars and music venues. A whole world of possibilities. Certain restrictions, sure: BIM workers were not citizens. But no curfews, no plague vans. No round-the-clock crematoriums belching ash into the saturated sky.

A white-clad figure slipped in beside her at the rail. Under the deck lights she could just make out his features: warm brown eyes, dark skin. The guy with the caramels.

'Hey,' he said. 'You're the singer.' Not a question.

Taken by surprise, Billie did not reply. How could he know that? She hadn't sung a note since they'd dropped anchor.

'Hold still a sec,' he said, raising a scanner to her brow. 'Sorry, must be annoying, all these scans. We haven't met properly – I'm Mitch.'

A first: a hazmat with a name. Billie continued staring ahead, let her smoke drift over his respirator as the scanner flickered.

'You read those articles?' he asked, voice low.

She nodded. They'd offered reassurance, of a sort: the journalist had slammed the zipped investigation, the government's refusal to comment; criticised the sub rosa terms of BIM contracts, the credentials of the companies engaged to ship cheap labour to this former colony. Raised questions about the killing of Davy Whelan. Even taken a shot at the 'hatemongers', the mob of howlers and public stirrers saying the passengers only got what they deserved: condemning them for signing up, for taking local jobs at lower pay.

'Why give them to me?' she asked. 'Aren't you taking a risk?'

'Nobody gave them to you,' Mitch said lightly. 'You just found them in amongst your shampoo and stuff. Right?'

Billie scrutinised him. What was he up to?

'I've been trying to extract some info from HQ,' he continued in a chatty tone, as if they were allies. 'Forward plans, when you'll be taken ashore, all that. Bastards are being tight-lipped.'

The scanner still hovering at her temple: clearly a charade.

'That thing broken?' she asked, blowing smoke in his face. Being plain rude now. 'I've not got all night to stand out here.'

'I dug out a few facts,' he went on, unfazed. 'For instance: Davy Whelan. Cause of death, *exsanguination*. Bleeding out, that means.'

'I know what it means,' she said, meeting him head-on now. His eyes were steady, no hint of a joke in them. 'What do you want?'

'I want to help,' said Mitch, his voice low. 'But I need information. Facts.' He made a show of checking the scanner, repositioning the device. Acknowledged a passing soldier. 'Davy Whelan's murder,' he said. 'I think it was connected to the outbreak.'

Billie's cigarette was out. She flicked the lighter, Davy's lighter. Answered despite herself. 'People are saying this ship is cursed.'

'It's a total shitstorm,' he said. 'The stream's full of howlers: hate talk, finger-pointing. Blame.'

'Blame?' The word made her uneasy. 'Blaming who?'

But the man did not elaborate. 'Government's nervous about you lot. They're in the middle of an election campaign. This mess has thrown a real spanner in the works.'

The scanner beeped and he checked the display, spoke out loud: 'All clear. Wristband, please.' Footsteps approached as he scanned her wrist.

'You done the upper decks?' asked a voice.

'Yup,' said her guy. 'Not many around.'

'Do the saloons next. Anyone you spot on the way. And get a move on, it's almost midnight.'

'Listen,' said Mitch as his superior walked off. 'You'll be called before the inquiry in a few days. I'll do what I can behind the scenes – advocate for the nurses, try to reframe the story. But I need info.'

So, a trade-off. He was fishing for a snitch.

'*You* need info?' She made an effort to control her voice. 'Look around you. Who's running this mess? You think I have any idea what the fuck is going on?'

'I get it,' he said. 'It's been badly mishandled. But I've seen the lab report: the virus doesn't match any known pathogen. Forensics think—' He broke off at the sound of approaching boots. 'Mitch, remember,' he said quietly. 'See you round, Billie.'

TOM

There was someone here to see me, Ally said. The ward felt claustrophobic, the idea of visitors welcome. Eager for distraction, I followed the nurse out the door.

'Bring us back some grapes,' Max called out as we left. 'No pips.'

Two goons in yellow hazmat suits escorted me down a series of passageways to a closet-sized room with a table set dead centre. Ally was unusually subdued, shooting me unreadable glances, but I was oblivious, happy to be out of that ward. She sat me down, offered a cup of tea, then withdrew. The goons stood right outside the door, their helmets visible through the glass partition.

The cup had hardly touched my lips when the door slid open. Two men in white hazmats, only their eyes visible: local accents, curt and autocratic. They set a device between us on the table.

And so it began. Two interminable hours, a steady barrage of questions, the tenor hovering somewhere between interview and interrogation.

'Thomas William Garnett, born 20 March 2034 – that's you?' No introduction from their side.

'That's me,' I agreed, trying to sound upbeat.

The younger guy made a point of telling me our interview was being recorded.

'No problem,' I said. 'But an interview about what?'

They ignored this, and all my subsequent questions. They did all the asking.

Personal history came first: where I grew up, schooling and further education, the family fortune and its abrupt decline, my own backslide into the borderlands of poverty. The patchy relief assignments and low-paid virtual work, the overdue bills, the struggle to stay out of debt. They knew all this, of course. It was just their opening sally, your standard transparency check.

But they soon changed tack.

'You applied for BIM eight months ago, correct?' This from the older copper – that's what they were, I'd realised: police.

'Yes,' I agreed. 'That sounds about right.'

'And in the intervening months, before you left England, were you approached by anyone about your participation in the BIM program?'

At first this stumped me. Approached? Then I remembered: that dubious-looking stringer who'd sidled up to me in a Newham pub, sniffing for info. Our names had all been leaked by then; I wasn't difficult to find.

'And what information did you share with this person?' The younger one, as if he was asking what I had for lunch.

'Nothing,' I said. 'I refused to speak to him. When you apply for BIM they make you sign a non-disclose. The wording's pretty strict.'

They harangued me for a bit longer, demanded dates and details. Who had I discussed the program with: friends, family, colleagues, acquaintances, strangers?

It wasn't something you bragged about, I told them. BIM had its detractors. We were often branded as deserters – sometimes by people who'd failed to make the cut themselves, been rejected in the screening process.

This pricked their interest. Had I applied for BIM through any other companies? No, I said, just Red Star. What made me choose them? I told the truth: they had the best ads, the least intrusive background checks, and headquarters in London's outer east, less than ten kilometres from my front door. Not satisfied, they pressed the point. Had I ever had contact with any rival BIM contractors? Suppliers, crew or officers who'd worked for other shippers, past or present? They named two other companies who ran labour to Australia. The names were familiar – I'd seen their ads, skimmed their info, but never made contact.

Next up came meds and heads: past illnesses, telomere scores, diagnoses, that period of stress leave. Psychopharms: they made me confirm brand names and dosages, availability and cost. They fished for other drug use too, fly stuff, greymarket. The sanctioned meds worked for me, I said. They were economical and effective – and, in my case, bio-tailored and prescribed. Not random or recreational.

'All this is in my file,' I pointed out, trying not to sound defensive. 'I'm not telling you anything new.' Wished I'd resisted the sick-room habit, gotten properly dressed. Hard to maintain your dignity in borrowed pyjamas.

They did answer one of my questions: why was I being singled out? 'You're not a special case,' they said. 'We're interviewing everyone.'

And on it went. Could I describe my relationship with the ship's officers: any friendships, any frictions? Captain Lewis: had I spent much time with him? And the crew: did I befriend anyone during the journey? No, I answered: we didn't really mingle. They saw me as a passenger, not one of them.

I held my gaze steady, my voice neutral. How could our brief liaison be relevant? It was nobody's business.

'That dead body you saw,' said the older cop. 'Tell us about that.'

Fuel for bad dreams, that sight: I described the rotting flesh and empty eye sockets, the body's proximity to the hull, the crew's response. Not a blink, the cops relishing their hard-man act.

They saved the murder for last.

'September fourth. That date mean anything to you?'

Not at first, it didn't.

It was a Wednesday, they prompted. Presumably I'd have been teaching? Yes, I said. But that date rang no particular bells.

'A man was killed in the small hours of that morning,' said the older cop. 'What can you tell us about that?' Phrased as if I had some inside knowledge. I told them what I knew: about the young boy, my student, who found the body. Management's request that I spread the official word, frame it as an accident.

No, I hadn't known the dead man. I'd since seen pics, of course, and his face did seem familiar – perhaps he'd served me at the kiosk, or passed me on the stairs – but to my knowledge we had never met.

Where did I sleep the night Davy Whelan died? I repeated what I'd told Cutler: in the schoolroom, on the sofa. Didn't budge until early morning, when I went back to my dorm to get ready for the day's lesson.

They took notes, fired out a few more questions. Then, at last, to my relief, they let me go.

Catching my breath back in the ward, I was struck by the way that first death, the sly violence of it, had been so quickly eclipsed by a more palpable threat. How the killing of Davy Whelan was all but forgotten in what followed. Now I wondered: were the two connected?

11

CLEARY

The blimp hung in the sky like a fat torpedo, its message stamped in tall black letters: *Keep Australia Clean!* This command was a puzzle to him: the *Steadfast* was free of litter, bins emptied swiftly, the cabins and hallways swabbed daily. No junk floated in the water, and even the beach was clear of rubbish. The air itself here seemed to sparkle.

The deck was a sea of upturned faces, soldiers' rifles trained on the apparition overhead. Cleary had never flown, except in dreams. How would it feel to float like that, so high and weightless, nothing but birds and clouds for company? He relinquished the binoculars, let Declan scan the airship, mouthing the man-sized words: *Keep Australia Clean!*

Patrol boats zoomed in anxious circles as bananas shouted through loudhailers. Cleary did his best to avoid them, spooks and bananas both. Each morning they made the kids line up to be scanned and sanned, then sprayed them with sunscreen that smelt like Club Rock Shandy.

Yesterday a spook had crouched beside him in the queue, given a playful wave, like he was a baby, and shoved a screen under his nose: *Come chat with me for a bit? Cook's made cake.*

Billie had cut in on the woman, made Cleary go through their act, signing back and forth, just like she'd shown him. As if

173

he understood the shapes Billie made, when most of them were nonsense.

He doesn't want to come with you, she'd told the spook. *He's with me.* Then she'd put her arm around his shoulders and turned her back on the official.

Every other day, Billie went over to the hospital ship. Without fail, she brought back a new message, penned in her own jagged handwriting: *I'm getting better all the time. Not long now, darling. I love you to the moon and back.* Their old bedtime routine, from when he was little. When Cleary's world had abruptly fallen silent, his ma had begun signing that phrase with her hands – one held aloft to form an 'O', the other rising from her heart, circling the moon, then down to his pyjama-clad chest. *To the moon and back, my darling.*

Those notes. Surely Billie wouldn't make them up? Not *to the moon and back.* There was no way she could know about that.

The fear never left him, a dark hum beneath the surface of his days: the unvoiced terror that his mother might never recover; that the person at the centre of his world would be lost to him forever. That Blackbeard might hurt her, though Cleary hadn't told a soul about what he'd seen. He tried to push the darkness down, watch for good omens. Yesterday: a splatter of white goo hitting his shoulder. A second's confusion, then Declan cracking up: *Shite! Bird shite!*

That was good luck, his gran had always said. Would it be cheating to help your luck along, stand underneath a bird or two?

He knew where Blackbeard slept. Knew the table he ate at, the people he sat with, the routes he used to move around the ship. Cleary tried to stay out of the man's orbit: avoided enclosed spaces, made note of the exits, and when alone gravitated towards the open space of the upper decks. Primed for avoidance or flight, ever alert to threats approaching from behind, he kept his back to walls and checked over his shoulder constantly.

At the rail beside him, Declan handed the binoculars back. Cleary was grateful to find his friend unchanged, no fallout from their separation during the journey. The boy's parents had even softened towards Cleary, making an effort to include him. This new attitude was evident in other adults too: wary looks replaced by invitations to join a family for dinner. He mixed with the kids, but steered clear of the parents. Who knew what they might do next.

Declan had made him a promise: one night he'd knock a guard out cold, steal a boat and drive Cleary across to the *Nightingale*. He'd sketched out the whole mission – the pilfered spanner clanging off the guard's skull, the knots he'd use to immobilise the man while they sped off in the boat. No word on where they'd get the ninja outfits, but that was a minor detail.

But Cleary knew better. Despite Declan's bravado, the plan would never work.

He felt a gentle weight on his shoulders: Billie, turning him towards her, beckoning now, urgent. *Quick – come with me!*

Swept along by a mix of hope and fear, Cleary followed. She led him through the ship's innards to a door guarded by two soldiers. It opened onto a musty room full of spooks working at desks. They were shown to a corner.

Billie scribbled, spun the pad so he could read it: *Surprise for you!*

A spook raised her arm, and a screen flickered to life on the wall. And there, sitting in a chair, looking straight at him, was his ma.

She wore a white smock but no mask. Her face had changed: her cheeks hollow, her bones sharper, skin pale as skimmed milk. The chair dwarfed her body. Her collarbones had surfaced, and her arms were thin as sticks.

She smiled, and his heart gave a kick: the screen was live, she could see him too. *My darling*, she mouthed, reaching out as if to cup his cheeks in her hands. As she spoke, her words popped up on the screen like bubbles. *Hello, my angel. Look at you.* She was trying not to cry, or laugh, or both.

Proof at last: his mother was alive. He'd buried it deep, the fear that Billie could be lying; that in truth his ma was gone forever. Now here she was, so close, but still out of reach. She looked so weak, and all at once he'd had enough of being brave. He wanted to bury his face in her neck, sniff her hair, take shelter in her arms.

Don't cry, darling, she said. *Look at you! Someone needs a haircut.* She snipped two fingers.

Cleary wiped his cheeks, signed back: *Are you okay?*

His ma nodded. *I'm good.* She tapped her chest. *How are you?* Her palms up, a juggling motion, finger pointing. The few formal phrases they'd learnt together, a hybrid vocab, mingled with their own invented or borrowed gestures.

He wiggled his loose tooth, made the sign for money. His ma laughed. *You're too old for the tooth fairy, you chancer.*

He was conscious of spooks hovering nearby, watching. Billie too.

His ma leant forward, her collarbones standing out like cords. *I'm feeling much better. They say I'll be allowed to be with you soon.*

When, when?

A headless torso dressed in white moved into shot. His ma waved the person away.

Not sure, she said, *but soon, my love. Billie will find out for us. You be good now.*

A flutter in his chest. She was signing off.

I have to go now, darling. I love you so much, my brave boy. She blew a kiss. Wrist-bones visible beneath the skin.

When are you coming back? But the screen had vanished.

Facing the blank wall he held one hand aloft, the thumb and fingers forming an 'O'; the other hand a rocket shooting up from his heart, tracing a loop, and home again. *To the moon and back.*

~

Sleep eluded him that night. Careful to avoid detection, Cleary slipped from the nurses' cabin and made his way to the upper decks. When the circling guards were out of view he climbed into the rigging and perched there like a bird, bare feet dangling above the yard. He'd be safe up here, out of sight.

Overhead the mast plunged up into a void prickled with stars. The bay was an arc of lights, a speckled horseshoe ending in the black mouth of the harbour. At regular intervals, like a slow heartbeat, the sweeping beam of the lighthouse winked out over the bay.

Just across the water lay the ghostly bulk of the hospital ship, his ma somewhere aboard. Seeing her alive, speaking to her, had changed everything. The *Steadfast* now seemed drowsy and remote, its inhabitants drugged or hypnotised, while Cleary felt alert, sharp, urgent. Abuzz with hope and impatience.

If anything the pain of separation had grown worse, his yearning now a physical pull, a magnet dragging his heart into crazy shapes. He must try to be patient: she was on the mend, out of harm's way, safe on the *Nightingale*. He would never speak a word of what he knew. He'd soon have her back, and one day they'd be free of this unlucky ship, would step ashore together. Leave the danger far behind.

Lost in these thoughts, he didn't spot the man's approach until it was too late.

Blackbeard came to a halt directly beneath him. Cleary froze as the deck lights revealed the top of the man's head, a whorl of thinning hair, a gleam of pale scalp. The man stood at the foot of the foremast, surveying the dark shoreline, fists on hips. Something fake or theatrical in his stance, like an adult playing at hide-and-seek, feigning ignorance of the child plainly visible nearby. His presence here no accident.

Alone with his enemy, the guards nowhere in sight, Cleary resorted to prayer: if he stayed completely still, melted into the mast, the man would not see him. His heart turned over in his chest, a heavy liquid roll.

Blackbeard patted his pockets, pulled his mask aside and lit a cigarette. The smoke snaked up through the rigging as if seeking Cleary out. He breathed in shallow sips.

Night offered no protection. The man was strong and could no doubt climb. Would anyone hear him scream? Could he edge along the yardarm, out of reach? Head up into the furthest reaches of the rigging, seek a line too delicate to bear the man's full weight? Or shimmy to the very top of the mast – but then what?

All at once Blackbeard was in motion, climbing swiftly up the ratbars, face upturned, a hunter seeking out his quarry. Coming for him. Before he could think, Cleary was scrambling up the rigging, away from his pursuer. Hand over foot, instinct in motion.

Above him the next platform stuck out at a daunting angle, the ratlines slanting backwards, a hurdle that would slow him, test his strength. He could sense the man gaining on him.

Up – or sideways?

No time to risk the obstacle: out along the yardarm his only option. He squeezed through a thicket of cables, stepped onto a foot rope slung beneath the yard, and began sidling away from the mast. His fingers scrabbled for purchase, latched on to a wire overhead. Bare toes gripping the foot rope, Cleary made his way out into the darkness. Far below glinted the hard surface of the deck.

A violent lurch, the rope bucking and wobbling beneath him.

Fighting to keep his balance, the wire digging into his fingers, he glanced back to see the man bent double against the mast, preparing to give the rope another heave.

This time Cleary braced himself, rode the wild oscillations; clung to the wire above, sought the rope below. Regained his footing and kept moving, taking neat tightrope steps, edging further out of reach, beyond the outline of the deck. Black water glittered far below.

Now the rigging trembled under a new weight: Blackbeard was coming after him, stepping quick and sure along the foot rope, nimble as a spider. Cleary sped up, but the man was gaining on him, the smell of stale sweat carried on the wind.

The next jolt tore the foot rope out from under him, left him dangling by his fingers, legs pedalling thin air. He swung over the void, feet seeking purchase, finding nothing.

The man was almost on him when Cleary shut his eyes and let go. A sickening drop, a blow to his knee, a sharp bolt of pain as he struck the rail – bone glancing off metal – then the full shock of impact, a blow punching all the air from his body.

An orb of light above him shimmered, shrank, blinked out. Then icy blackness closed over his head.

BILLIE

The paperwork was a mess – figures scrubbed out, entries missing, dosages indecipherable. The impression it gave was sloppy at best, verging on negligent to a less charitable eye. Instructed to fill in what blanks she could from memory, Billie had been given a less-than-subtle warning: resist the urge to fudge anything, to cover up mistakes or falsify the record. She pushed the files back into the folder. She'd deal with it tomorrow.

Alone beneath the kitchenette's weak light, she pulled out the other pages: eight neatly folded sheets, secured with an old-fashioned staple. She knew the words almost by heart. The comments too: they burnt with a rancour not easily forgotten.

Gov Must Right Wrongs to Migrant Workers. The first article had a zealous tone and ended with a teaser: *The blame for this disaster lies not with the traumatised victims. The blame lies with those who let this deadly sickness loose in what was effectively a floating prison. The burning question: was this negligence or malice? Updates to come.*

Backflow on the piece was split: roughly one-quarter agreed with the journo, another quarter were fence-sitters, and the remaining half voiced angry disagreement or outright venom. All those howlers, flooding the stream with hatred: *foreign filth, dirty scabs, ship rats, fuck off we're full.* Even the more measured responses carried a note of hostility: *These people are a biohazard. They must be sent back where they came from.* The public up in arms, outraged that a deadly illness might be allowed to breach their borders, terrified these new arrivals could spell the death of them.

What had that strange official told her? *You do have supporters here.*

But if there was indeed a cheer squad, they were clearly a minority.

The second article focused on Davy Whelan, the slain crewman, asked why the killing seemed to have sunk from sight. Given that the virus struck mere days after that violent death, were police investigating a possible link between the two?

Cause of death: exsanguination. Bleeding out. Poor Cleary, witnessing the aftermath.

She checked her watch: almost midnight. Time to turn in, check on the boy.

Her hands met with a tangle of blankets: his bunk empty. Billie swore aloud. When she'd last checked he'd still been awake, eyes wide in the dim cabin. She'd kissed his forehead, stroked his eyes shut. Then returned to her paperwork.

Why hadn't she made him a mug of hot milk, sat with him until he fell asleep? Some surrogate she was. How long had he been gone?

No sign of him on the top deck, but a huddle of officials and crew turned at her approach. Bad news plain on their faces.

'Where were you?' demanded a sailor. Len, the superstitious guy.

'There's been an accident,' said a hazmatted official. 'The boy.'

'Where is he?' A stab of fear and guilt. 'What happened?'

The sailor pointed. 'With the doc, down in the captain's cabin. Jumped in the fucking water, half drowned himself.'

She ran, pushed past the crewman guarding the door, barged into the captain's rooms.

Kellahan was bent over the boy, checking his pulse. He turned as Billie entered. 'He'll be okay,' he said, moving aside for her. 'Someone heard the splash and pulled him out.'

Cleary's gaze was unfocused, strangely blank. He gave a weak smile as she squeezed his hand, touched his cold cheek. His body so small in the big bed. Heatpacks tucked around him, the bedclothes tented halfway down. An officer stood against the wall, radiating disapproval.

'I've given him a shot of pseudopiate,' Kellahan was saying. 'His knee's blown up like a balloon, nasty bruise on the patella. We'll need to get that x-rayed.'

'I'm so sorry,' she whispered. 'Little fella, I'm so sorry. I'm here now.' She raised her mask and kissed his damp forehead, tried to keep the worry from her face. His lips made a smacking sound. The kid was jellied.

'Looks like he tried to swim across to the *Nightingale*,' said the officer. 'A media boat picked him up.' Displeasure plain in his voice. 'Captain Lewis is next door, getting quizzed by local military. He's not happy.'

'Captain said you can sleep in here tonight,' Kellahan said to Billie, ignoring the officer. 'Watch the boy. He'll need that ice pack changed and more pain relief in a few hours.' She felt the doctor's hand on her back, a light pressure. 'He'll be fine,' he said. 'Don't worry. Nobody's to blame.'

~

The judge's hologram shimmered on the wall, then settled into solid form. Below the woman's disembodied torso ran Billie's name, the date and the words *Maritime Incident R52*.

'Please remove your mask and state your full name,' said the judge, turning her attention onto Billie. The woman's eye contact was slightly off – just a minor miscue in the program, but the effect was disconcerting. Billie felt both exposed and oddly invisible.

'Billie Grace Galloway,' she said, trying to meet the judge's eye. Was the effect the same at the far end? She didn't need some tech glitch making her seem shifty. Breathe, she told herself.

'Ms Galloway, I'm going to ask you a series of questions,' said the hologram judge. 'Please answer to the best of your ability. This interview is being recorded.'

Billie inclined her head, not sure if she was meant to speak.

The judge indicated the glimmering presence beside her. 'My colleague, Mr Harper, will ask for clarification at times. Do you understand your obligations?'

Billie cleared her throat. 'Yes, your honour.'

'No need for formalities,' said the judge. 'This is a government inquiry, not a court of law. Yes or no will do just fine.'

They began gently, confirming dates and facts. Billie glanced around the room: these two holograms and a dozen ghostly strangers in white hazmats. At her elbow sat a 'personal liaison officer', a young woman apparently tasked with 'safeguarding' her 'emotional and physical wellbeing'. No passengers or crew, no brass in here. Just Billie, alone with all these apparitions, deep in the bowels of the hospital ship.

'Ms Galloway?' said the judge. 'Would you like Mr Harper to repeat the question?'

'Please,' she said. *Snap out of it. They've barely started.*

'How long did you work at Glasgow South Hospital?' He had a pudgy, patient face and a thatch of black hair that looked dyed, although that might be the optics.

'Almost four years.' She resisted the urge to add: *It's all in my file.* No doubt they were familiar with its contents.

'Why did you leave that position?'

'I was laid off.' She'd been good at her job. There was no red flag on her profile, just a suspicious gap: an empty space hinting at omission, erasure, obfuscation. One solitary lay-off, at a time when every pair of hands was needed.

Harper's expression remained benign. 'So, superfluity. No other reason? No other contributing factors?'

Here it was. This would become part of the official record. She could not risk a lie.

'I got ... involved with someone. A supervisor.' The holos waited. The room was still.

'Please go on, Ms Galloway,' prompted the man.

'He was a senior staff member, an ID specialist – Infectious Diseases. Married. It lasted maybe three months. I called it off.' How deep would they dig? The one work friend she'd confided in had disapproved, broken the confidence. No sympathy there when Billie had ended it.

'And your relationship with this man – how does that relate to your departure from the hospital?'

She sensed the hazmats stirring, their attention sharpening.

'He was using pseudopiates. I didn't realise, not at first.' No-one prompting her now. Just letting her stumble forward into the silence. 'The stock was closely monitored. So he asked me to ... obtain some for him.'

The judge remained impassive. 'And you agreed?'

'Just three times. Then I said no more – never again. And I broke it off with him.' Not until her affair with Luke was over did she realise how isolating it had been, how much time and energy it consumed – the waiting, the cautious frustration, the snatches of stolen time.

'Did hospital management discover you'd accessed these drugs without authorisation?'

'Yes,' she said. 'I was brought before a disciplinary panel.'

There was no avoiding Luke at work, but she'd been doing well – until the shock of being hauled before that grim-faced row of higher-ups.

'And what about this man, your supervisor?' The judge's image splintered, then drew in sharp again.

Billie tried to meet the woman's eye. 'He was there. On the panel. They had no idea. Nobody knew the stuff was for him.' Luke had kept his head down as she sat before them, telling the lies that saved his arse.

The judge frowned. 'You protected this man? Why?'

'He promised to advocate for me, make sure I wasn't blackmarked. I was going to lose my job anyway. No sense in us both going down.' How foolish it sounded now. How slow she'd been to admit it to herself: that Luke's appetite for chemicals far outweighed his affection for her. That his skewed desire had cost Billie her job.

'Did he offer you any incentive?' asked Harper. 'Any inducement to accept the blame?'

Billie hesitated. 'He made sure I was recorded as a lay-off. Agreed to be my vocational referee.' What kind of fool would fold without compensation? They'd have access to her bank records anyway. 'And he paid my rent for three months. That was the deal.'

It was a shock when Harper named the exact sum. Was that the payment she was referring to? It sounded like a lot, but without a job it hadn't lasted long. Not until actual hunger struck did she wish she'd set her price a little higher.

That mess she'd left behind: it was irrelevant. They were just muckraking, seeking dirt. But why?

Next topic, naturally, was drug use – prior, current, alleged. Nicotine and alcohol, she answered, the odd sleeper, all in moderation. The drugs she'd lifted had not been for her. She'd never failed a workplace drug test.

Had she been unwell during the past five years – any undisclosed physical or emotional issues? No, nothing; to disclose vocational trauma was to risk losing your job.

Then an odd string of questions: had she applied for BIM intake with any rival shipping companies? Known anyone who worked for other shippers? No and no. Billie snuck a glance at the official beside her: zero eye contact.

At last, the guts of it: describe your professional qualifications and experience. How you were recruited to care for patients on the ship. Your understanding of the agreed reimbursement and conditions. The virus' clinical manifestation, the care regime and medications used, how responsibility was delegated. The containment and waste-disposal protocols you put in place. Available equipment, workarounds devised, reasoning behind said workarounds. How your fellow recruits coped with the conditions, the mental strain. How you stored the bodies.

All this required careful answers, but it was firmer territory. And the recent bad news had put things on a more equal footing: *You lost one too. Someone died on your watch.*

It was a relief when they dropped the medical stuff and brought up Cleary's name.

'I understand you've been granted interim custody of the boy?' asked the judge.

'I requested it. He's a good kid. I nursed his mother. He's been alone since she got sick.'

The judge shot her a quick smile, a switch flicked on and off. 'And it seems you've taken good care of him. The wellbeing team commends your efforts.'

Harper spoke up. 'Although we are aware of a recent incident where the boy engaged in some risky behaviour. Sustained injuries. Almost drowned, in fact. You were sleeping at the time, is that correct?'

Billie swallowed a surge of guilt. 'No. Your people had me working, checking over the medical records. Cleary snuck out. He's desperate to see his ma.' No bones broken, but the bruise went deep. His limp a constant reminder of her negligence. He refused to discuss the incident, said he couldn't recall how or why he'd ended up in the water.

That's when they sprang the clip on her. A screen lit up: they had obtained some footage, which they'd like to share with her. An overcast sky, a glimpse of mast. People scattered across the deck.

Zooming in: two figures sitting cross-legged, in plain view. Billie stage right, Cleary facing her, their hands in motion, cutting shapes and scooting through the air. Signing to each other, taking turns. Saying nothing. A charade for all to see.

'You speak sign language?' asked Harper.

Her voice was small in the stillness of the room. 'A little. I'm not fluent.'

'And this footage: is this Irish Sign Language the two of you are speaking here?'

She could have said no, claimed this mime show as their own private language, home signs they had invented, gestures Cleary had taught her. But that would contradict what she'd told other officials: that she and the child shared a formal vocabulary, a fluency that bound them as a unit. A harmless lie, a bid to place herself between them and the boy, protect him.

Blindsided again, she stuck with the falsehood: yes, it was Irish Sign Language. At once the vidscreen went black.

The judge looked past Billie, beckoned to someone. In the doorway stood Cleary, an official at his side. The boy's eyes darted around the room, returning to Billie after each pass, his one familiar reference point. She attempted a jolly wave, but it didn't feel convincing.

She'd known Cleary would be questioned; been told that as his interim guardian, she'd be present to provide 'assistance and support', whatever that meant. But now his keeper was steering him to a separate table, away from Billie. As the boy lurched towards his seat, clumsy on his crutches, she fought the urge to rush over and reclaim him.

'Ms Galloway?' Harper now. 'We've located a fluent ISL speaker. She's reviewed this footage, and raised doubts about your claims to signing expertise. She will act as Cleary's interpreter at this hearing.'

Harper and the judge turned to Cleary, their expressions suffused with a new warmth.

Now the judge spoke with expert kindness. 'Hello, Cleary. I'm Caroline, and this is Mike. You can take your mask off. We'd like to ask you some questions about what happened on the ship. Would that be okay?'

The official beside Cleary touched his shoulder, turned him towards her and began to sign, her gloved hands cutting the air quick and sure, deft as birds. The boy frowned.

Cleary looked Billie's way. She gave the smallest nod, enough to reassure him. To make it seem that they remained a team; that they had any choice in all of this.

TOM

It began as a joke, my prison-style countdown, the struck-out days in blocks of five taped to the wall. But three weeks in, the joke had soured. Boredom buzzed, aimless as a blowfly.

We now had a lounge area: wipe-down sofas (white, of course), exercise machines, a vidstream full of flicks. No news channels, no outside contact. But it beat staring at the walls.

An exercise physiologist had been assigned to us, an earnest young woman who specialised in post-viral rehabilitation and bright lycra. Her presence a bid to reverse the damage done by forced idleness, to recondition our wasted bodies.

'What are we getting fit for?' I asked, gyrating like a breathless hamster in the grips of the machine. 'A Houdini job? A mass escape?' Fishing for information, but she wouldn't take the bait.

'Just life,' she answered sweetly. 'Let's get your heart rate up a bit.'

'They're bulking us up,' called Max from the sofa. 'They're gonna eat us!'

Mia, watching pop clips, looked up alarmed.

'I'm joking, pet,' Max reassured her. 'We're safe in here, nobody's going to hurt us.'

The image was hard to shake: animals on a treadmill, livestock being put through its paces. But my body no longer felt like a casualty of war. And I'd noticed a curious side-effect. Something was missing: that constant hum of worry, the grey dog that had shadowed me so long.

In its place was a steady, galvanising anger. Against those

who'd cut us off from our families, kept us in the dark, deprived of information. Those power-tripping cops, playing head-games. Anger at whoever let this happen – promised us zero risk, a clean journey; then let people die, left children bereaved. Treated us like units of exchange, damaged goods. Anger, too, at all the unknowns we still faced: the buried information, the rumours.

Anger is a dangerous emotion, so the experts say: too often misdirected, too easily turned inward. But surely there are times when it's the only just and right response.

Cate kept demanding to see her son, alternately haranguing and pleading with the doctors, not taking no for an answer. But that's the only answer they would give her.

Not everyone was coping with confinement. One man let loose at the nurses: *It's like a fooking morgue in here! Take those screens down for godsake, open a window. I can't breathe!* I heard the sounds of a brief scuffle, the pop and splash of breaking glass, then silence: a quick chemical cosh administered, no doubt.

The nosy official came back. She made no secret of digging for info this time, but still branded it as a 'chat'. A chat, she breezily noted, that would inform the official inquiry into 'the incident'. A woefully tame euphemism for all that death and suffering.

Her questions took a peculiar slant. She asked about odd moments from the journey, things I might have witnessed: a crate transferred mid-ocean from a passing ship. That decomposed body again – the nightmare thing we saw floating in a rubbish island near the equator. This time I was polite and helpful. Anything to keep those grim coppers at bay.

At last a 'personal' message was sent to my family back home, a three-minute vid. *Hi Mum, hi Dad, hi Rosa! Please don't worry: see, I'm almost upright!* Propped up in bed, hair combed for the camera, I did my best to assure them I was okay: *I'm still alive,*

I said, *unless the boredom kills me*. That crack got cut: content was heavily vetted. Five takes before we had a clip the gov-reps deemed acceptable, by which stage I was racking my brains for variations on bland platitudes: *The nurses are great. We're being looked after very well. I love you all very much.* Hostage-speak.

Info lockdown was still in force, but talk was impossible to quarantine. Ally said we'd sparked a full-blown panic in our host country, brought the Fear across the seas with us. The population was up in arms. There'd be no hiding now, no chance to fly beneath the radar, keep the BIM program low-profile. The cover had blown off; the story was streaming wild.

We were a threat, the enemy. They wanted to send us home.

~

This afternoon, lost in thought, I opened the bathroom door – and, bang, there he was.

My handsome Scotsman, washing his hands in the sink.

So close to my old flame, I couldn't keep pretending. 'Stewart,' I said, closing the door behind me. 'How are you?'

He froze, then went back to washing his hands. Rubbing his palms together like an OCD case, water hissing in the sink.

The words spilt out before my brain, or pride, could intervene. 'Please, look at me.'

I took a step forward. The room was narrow, no space to manoeuvre.

He shut off the tap and stood there, wet hands clenched at his sides. We were so close I could hear him breathing. The ceiling light fizzed and flickered.

'How are you?' I asked again. It came out slightly aggressive, not what I'd intended.

His pupils were huge, black and empty. An unnerving sight,

like staring into a well. *Get me a priest!* Up close, alone with him at last, it struck me: he was afraid.

'What do you want?' he asked.

'You've been ignoring me.' I heard the whine in my voice, that jilted intonation, like a sulky teenager. Was unable to check it. 'All this time, not a single word. Why?'

He stared at my hand, which I now realised was splayed flat against the opposite wall, my arm blocking his exit. 'Get out of my way,' he said quietly. 'I can't speak to you.' Fists clenched, ready for trouble.

'I just want to know if you're alright,' I said, dropping my arm, all trace of bravado gone. He brushed past and left me standing there, the taste of shame in my mouth.

~

At last some possible bright news arrived: a hint we might soon be declared fit for release. Ally promised nothing specific – she'd warned me our conversations might be monitored.

'You'll want to get out of those baggy-arsed pyjamas soon,' she said, with a meaningful look.

'Why? You find them too alluring?' One of our running jokes: she knew which team I batted for.

'You'll give the public a heart attack walking around like that,' she said, waggling her eyebrows, a pantomime conspirator. Hardly subtle, but I was slow to catch on.

'The public's safe from the sight of my baggy arse. Nobody's mentioned a release date.'

'Well, I'm guessing your baggy arse is about due for some fresh air.' She gave a smirk, a wink.

Now I'd caught her drift, and played along. 'But I'm contaminated. Riddled with bugs, a walking epidemic.'

'You seem fine to me,' she said. 'Same for this whole ward, bunch of bloody malingerers. You're all the picture of health. Be glad to see the back of you.'

I hoped she was right. If I didn't see the sky soon, I feared I might implode.

12

CLEARY

He was in the kitchenette, inching the peel off an orange in one long unbroken spiral, when Billie appeared in the doorway. It struck him at once: her face was bare, her mask gone. She knelt before him, holding up a piece of paper: the words he had been waiting for.

Your ma. She's back. Quarantine's over – the patients are out.

Cleary rose too fast, pain shooting through his knee, let Billie half carry him into the bunk room where he fumbled with his laces – *Hurry! Hurry!* – as she tied his other shoe. She shouldered his bag, hauled him to his feet and led him out into the sunlight. Lurching along behind her – too slow, his crutches not cooperating – he saw more bare faces: the spooks and bananas were gone, replaced by strangers in tidy grey uniforms. Passengers and crew had also re-appeared, their mouths now visible again.

He followed Billie around corners, down a tricky set of stairs. Past a red sticking plaster dangling from a wall, a sign they were nearing a crew-only area; sick with expectation, he gave it no more than a glance. Along an unfamiliar passageway, past a sign: *Officers' Quarters*.

At last they stopped at a pale blue door, half ajar, marked with the number eight. Sunlight was visible in the room beyond, and an familiar pair of shoes lay discarded on the floor. Billie knocked then swung the door wide.

His mother lay beneath an open porthole, illuminated like a person in a painting. Cleary flung himself upon her, their faces meeting in a bright band of sunlight; he burrowed into her, inhaling her scent. The smell of safety, of home, faint but still discernible beneath the hospital vapours. Through her nightdress he could feel the hard outlines of her ribs, like the frets of a kitchen chair. But her grip was strong, the hug tight.

You smell like oranges, she signed, grinning down at him. *I might just eat you up.*

He lay in her lap, gazing up at her. Flooded with light her skin was almost transparent, her features sharper, the shape of her skull now visible. Her hair had been chopped short, giving her head a girlish cast, but there were new lines around her eyes, purple smudges below the sockets. She bent to kiss his face, and Cleary let his head rest in her arms, cradled like some precious object; content to stay like this forever, to never leave this sunlit room.

After a while he felt her exploring the tiny bump on his upper arm, the spot where the needle had gone in. Cleary mimed an injection, wincing. His ma nodded. She reached for his hand, ran his fingertips over her own arm: a matching bump.

Then, with great care, she unrolled the bandage to expose his injured knee, laid her cool hand on the damage: the joint still puffy, the bruise a vivid mauve stain.

What happened?

Cleary mimed a clumsy stick-man tripping over nothing, colliding with the ship's rail, tumbling overboard; a puppet-show she made him repeat several times, watching him steadily, before finally bandaging the knee back up.

It hurts?

A bit, he admitted. His crutches lay forgotten on the floor. Without them he was reduced to a kind of artless hop-and-stagger, a gait both inefficient and painful. The kind of thing a predator could spot a mile off.

He clasped her wrist, his thumb and forefinger almost meeting around the bone: *Skinny Minnie.* A joke to cover his shock at the damage, how cruelly the bug had reduced her: all bones now, the padding gone. The gauntness did not suit her, made her look like someone else.

His mother pulled free of his grasp and tickled him, the laughter spilling out of him unbidden. Not caring, this time, who might overhear these strange noises he was making.

They lay together until darkness fell. The room had two narrow beds, and a faintly male smell: aftershave, sweat, musty socks. When the deck lights flickered on outside they knelt at the porthole and took turns with Cleary's binoculars, scanning the shoreline, pointing out dim landmarks and lighted windows, trying to fix the moon in their sights. Imagining the day they'd finally step ashore, wriggle their toes in the sand, wander that green expanse.

Dinner came on a trolley, and they ate in bed. Then they locked the door, nestled close and drifted off together into sleep.

~

They found the bird the next day, nailed to their cabin door. Its fragile body impaled on a long silver spike, dark feathers splayed in a parody of flight, a line of blood trailing towards the floor. His ma drew back, tried to block Cleary's view, as if the thing was dangerous. But it was too late.

Taking in those crumpled wings, that tiny body stilled forever, he read the threat for what it was. Registered his own response, as if from far away – terror, pity and disgust, all churned up together. He had no doubt who'd done this.

An officer was notified, a sailor dispatched. The man pried

the corpse off the nail and disposed of it, without ceremony or comment, as if this was an everyday event. The nail remained; so did the blood, still wet but thickening. Cleary scrubbed at it with a wad of tissue but the shadow of the stain persisted. He washed his hands then held them to his nose, sniffed: that faint scent, sweetly metallic.

His ma was plainly troubled, but had no inkling of the danger they were in. He must not leave her alone. Must make sure the cabin door was locked securely from the inside. Stay vigilant, alert for the worst. And now there was no question: he needed a weapon, a sharp knife or a hammer, something easy to conceal.

It was a land bird – the kind of dark-feathered creature that nested in treetops, not rocky cliffs or sand dunes. A bird that had no business being on a ship. Where had it come from? How had its life ended? Not with a nail through the heart, surely. An accident, perhaps – a burst of flight, a closed porthole, a broken neck. Something quick and final. The body a chance discovery, put to sinister use.

Extracting a promise that his ma would not leave him alone in the women's bathroom, not for a moment, he locked himself in a wash cube, cranked the water up so hot his chest and shoulders flushed crimson, and lathered himself from head to foot, trying to scrub away the fearful stink of death.

BILLIE

Without the respirator Doctor Hart was younger than she'd sounded, while Sullivan was grizzled, worn around the edges. Anonymous officials on both ships had been replaced by individual people in neat grey uniforms, their features exposed and strangely vulnerable. Sullivan was gruff as ever but minus the hazmat Billie thought she detected a sheepish note. He'd offered them coffee and dialled down the officious tone. *You lost one too,* she thought. *Not so easy, was it?*

'A huge relief,' he was saying. 'We weren't sure we'd be able to contain it, let alone deactivate the thing.'

'We want to thank you all for the way you've handled this whole situation,' said Hart.

Billie gave her a puzzled look. 'Handled …?' Realised this was code for being cooperative.

Kellahan stepped in. 'It's been a pleasure working with you. It's an impressive operation you've run here. And no-one's more relieved than us.' Ever the diplomat. Smart guy.

Owen was on about the nano-data again – how were the antibody profiles playing out? – but the locals didn't bite. They stayed on message: a combination of laser deactivation and nano-viricides had proven effective, the bug shut down, disarmed and discharged. There were no active cases, and viral latency did not appear to be an issue.

Still, Billie couldn't help asking. 'Any clue on where this came from? How it got on board in the first place?' She addressed Hart, always the warmer of the two.

Hart glanced at her colleague. 'No. But that remains a concern.'

'As they say, the investigation is ongoing,' said Sullivan. His tone verged on breezy, and Billie tried to keep the irritation from her voice.

'Surely this bug would've been picked up in the initial screenings? They scanned us daily, right up to departure. How could it lie dormant for three weeks?'

Hart spoke cautiously: 'We don't have any solid answers yet. I'm sorry.'

It was Kellahan who voiced it: 'I just can't fathom it, that this could be deliberate. Who'd do that? And why?'

'Those anti-migration nutters?' Owen suggested. 'StayPut and that lot – they've made threats before. Back when Heathrow was still running regular flights.'

Kellahan made a dismissive gesture. 'Just some fringe group, wouldn't have the resources. Makes no sense.'

'Did they test the drinking water?' asked Billie.

'We don't have oversight of forensics,' said Hart. 'We can't tell you anything. I'm sorry.'

'That crew member who was killed,' said Sullivan in the ensuing lull. 'Heard any word on that?' As if asking out of curiosity, making small-talk.

'There's been every rumour imaginable,' said Kellahan. 'Wild guesses galore. Standard behaviour when people are traumatised and grieving.' Unusually curt, for him. He drained his coffee, placed his palms flat on the table. 'Forgive me, I should get back. Another meeting with worried parents. More night terrors.'

Hart and Sullivan offered their first handshakes, bare palms extended: a rueful acknowledgement this was all over, at least for them. To Billie the cheer felt forced, somehow improper. As if all that suffering had never happened. As if the rest of them weren't still stuck here.

~

Robbie found her in a quiet corner of the deck, staring landward, imagining grass underfoot. 'Alright, hen?' he asked. 'Got my fiddle back. You in the mood for a singalong?'

'Not really.' A daunting prospect now, performing for a crowd. Her face too familiar for all the wrong reasons.

'Take your mind off things.' He waved a vague arm. 'Not to mention this lot. They could use some distraction.'

'I've done my share for this lot.' It sounded petty, she knew: some lingering resentment there, despite her efforts to dispel it.

Robbie nodded. 'Right you are, Songbird.' He offered his tobacco pouch, but she hesitated. 'Aren't we safe now?' he asked.

Billie sanned her hands, took pouch and papers, rolled a smoke, re-sanned and passed it all back. Held her lighter steady as Robbie cupped the flame, both careful not to touch each other. The old rituals now reinforced tenfold.

They watched a gang of kids play tag around the mast.

'How's the wee lad?' Robbie asked.

'Over the moon to have his ma back.'

'You've done a brilliant job looking out for him.'

'Thank god that's over. I was well out of my depth.'

Since she'd relinquished the boy, the walking habit had reclaimed her: tracing her old circuits of the ship, that mindless two-part rhythm, a bid to crowd out loss. It had taken her unawares, how much she missed the kid's presence – their daily routines and visual jokes, their private language of gestures, his small form sleeping in the bed above. The creaturely scent of his hair; the way his head fit into the crook of her neck, neat as an egg in an eggcup. Since his mother's return, the relief she'd expected to feel had not appeared. Instead there was an absence, a Cleary-shaped hole in the world, and a lot of free time.

Now Robbie interrupted her thoughts. 'I was speaking to

Juliette. She's come by some whiskey. A freebie, if you're keen.' Robbie had been attempting a reconciliation of sorts with what remained of the galley crew. They'd been grateful for her updates on Scoot's progress, he said.

'They didn't mean to desert you. Everyone was badly spooked.' She expelled a huff of smoke. No sense wasting words on this.

Robbie was right: diversion would be welcome. Relief had given way to frustration, then flashes of anger, spot fires hinting at a looming conflagration. Talk of hunger strikes, mass protests, sabotage. Starved of information, guarded by armed men, they all felt the pressure building. If anyone tried to escape, to brave the swim and strike out for land, rumour said the soldiers had orders to shoot on sight. No wonder anger was brewing. Billie felt its edge herself.

'Up on the sundeck, after lunch,' said Robbie. 'You can join in, or just listen.'

She knew she'd go – if not to sing, just to fill her head with music. Blot out the other stuff.

Robbie pointed. 'Here's your mate.'

That dear, dark head: Cleary wobbling towards her on his crutches, gawky as a foal, his mother close behind. The boy's smile almost shy; something different about him.

Billie pulled him into a hug while Cate stood back.

The boy broke free of the embrace, grabbed Billie's hand. An object dropped into her palm. She opened her hand, grimaced in mock disgust, and Cleary grinned, revealing a missing canine. In her hand lay a tooth, a rime of blood still clinging to the root.

~

Music drifted through the rigging as Billie piggybacked the boy across the deck: a fiddle's loop and whirl, the drone of an accordion. Resting in the saloon with a group of other parents, Cate had entrusted Cleary to her care. He still hadn't mastered the crutches; Billie had made a show of griping, said she wasn't a packhorse, but in truth the weight of him was welcome.

As they approached the sundeck, someone stepped from the crowd to block their way.

'Where you taking that kid?' demanded Marshall.

'Move,' said Billie. 'I don't answer to you.' They glared at each other. The boy's grip tightened around her neck, restricting her air; irritated, she tugged at his arms. 'Get to fuck, Marshall,' she snapped.

People were watching now, the chief steward clocking the scrutiny. He edged aside and Billie pushed past.

'That kid's not right in the head,' Marshall yelled after her.

Fucking walloper. The kid had more brains than all of them put together. Still, Cleary struck her as tense, subdued. Worried about his ma, no doubt: still weak and ghostly thin, her spark nowhere in evidence.

Robbie's wife, Mona, made room for them as he led the musicians in a reel: a kitchenhand wielding the accordion; a dad drumming on a bucket, his kids at his feet. A sulky-faced teen giving the odd honk on a moothie, in tune but never quite in time.

When the band broke off someone hollered out a request for 'Caledonia', and Robbie turned to Billie. He'd promised not to put her on the spot, but of course the man was full of it.

'Songbird?' he called, flourishing his bow. 'Will you lend us that magical voice?'

Applause, hoots and whistles. Juliette met her eye, offered a tentative smile. As Billie rose to join the band she squeezed the kid's hand, wondered who the reassurance was meant for.

Silence fell as she stood before them: no soldiers in sight, no grey-clad officials; a strategic withdrawal perhaps, a peace offering of sorts.

One deep lungful, and there it was: her voice still strong and ready, the melody bound up in muscle memory. The swell of music drowning out the recent past. As people stood to dance, to sing along or let out mindless whoops, Billie felt the world's sharp corners blur. She was inside the music, the song inside her body, sound pulsing through the drowsy air, coursing through them all. People singing along, clapping out the rhythm. Eyes closed, bodies swaying, brought together by pure sound.

The first bomb hit the children in the front row: violent red splatters, the kids' faces and clothes streaked scarlet. A moment's lull before the screaming.

Red gushes, bloody fountains; the deck a war zone, parents shielding children. A balloon burst against the gunwale, a glut of red liquid spraying into Billie's face. Cleary's mouth was open in a panicked wail, his cheeks streaked red. She dived for him, lost her footing on the slippery deck, fell heavily.

A sour taste in her mouth, a chemical tang: not blood.

She grabbed for the child, wrapped his screaming head in her arms.

Chaos as the crowd scrambled to escape the onslaught, bodies crashing to the deck, children shrieking. A red storm raining down, people cowering and slipping, blinded. The crack of gunshots, soldiers firing overhead.

Billie lifted the boy and staggered away from the carnage.

'It's paint!' someone was shouting. 'It's just paint!'

Then the drones were gone, the sky empty. Red-spattered officials helped the fallen to their feet as women consoled sobbing children. Cleaners appeared with mops and buckets. Cleary buried his head in Billie's shirt, a light tremble emanating from somewhere deep inside him.

~

A familiar room: the scene of her recruitment. The same line-up of senior crew and heavies, the ship doctors and nurses too, but the crew's uniforms now piecemeal or gone, the old hierarchies levelled.

Only Captain Lewis had retained his full regalia: seated behind a table draped with a Union Jack, all present and correct despite the heat, the dark smudges beneath his eyes. He gave a signal and one of his men locked the door.

Cutler, the first mate, called for quiet. 'We don't have long. They'll soon realise we're missing.' Still taking up maximum space, nothing in his stance suggesting a demotion. But geotagged no doubt, just like the rest of them.

'Before I hand over to Captain Lewis, a few points. Foreign Affairs back home is advocating for us, but they have no jurisdiction over this vessel.'

'So who's in charge?' someone called out. The atmosphere prickly.

'Authority rests with the local incident commander. The captain—' Cutler broke off, glanced at his superior. 'For our purposes, Captain Lewis is effectively next in command.'

'When do we get off this ship?' Ruben's voice, no hint of deference in it.

The captain took the floor. 'I ask that question daily. But our hosts are not being particularly forthcoming.'

'We're in swimming distance of a quarantine station,' said another nurse. 'Can't they take us ashore?'

'I'm pushing for that,' said Captain Lewis. 'But the situation is politically sensitive. The government's just weeks from an election, and public sentiment's not on our side.' A shimmer of sweat on his upper lip.

'We've got three passengers on hunger strike,' said Ruben.

'I've told them it's useless, there's no media presence. But they want off this ship.'

'It's the uncertainty,' said Holly. 'People need answers.'

Kellahan spoke up: 'The bereaved should not be kept here. Bad memories at every turn.' Faces too, thought Billie: no space to escape the grief of others.

'Can't they transfer us to the *Nightingale?*' asked Holly. 'She's twice the size.'

'The incident commander's vetoed that,' said Captain Lewis. 'He wants to keep their lab isolated.'

'But everyone's been cleared,' Billie objected. 'No active cases. Are we still in quarantine, or what?'

The captain blew a frustrated breath. 'The threat level's been downgraded, but—'

Ruben cut in. 'Are we still at risk, or not?'

'We're guinea pigs,' muttered a crewman, one of several still wearing his mask. 'It's a test, to see if anyone else gets sick. I'm keeping this thing on until those bastards take us ashore.'

'Let's not start with the conspiracy theories,' warned Cutler.

Billie met the captain's eye. 'Do you have stream access? You've seen what's being said?' Careful to phrase it as a question, not admit to prior knowledge.

He frowned. 'Some of it. We all know what happened yesterday.'

The drone attack: people seemed reluctant to refer to it by name.

'I meant the virus,' Billie countered. 'Theories on where it came from.' Recalled that smuggled article: *Was this negligence or malice?*

Cutler was quick to reply: 'That's for the investigators to determine. There's no point—'

'They're saying it was a terrorist attack,' said Owen. 'Some extremist cult, trying to shut down migrant labour.'

'I'd put money on it,' someone agreed. 'It was fucking StayPut hacked the ministry, leaked the passenger lists.'

'That was never proven,' an officer objected. 'No-one claimed responsibility.'

Cutler raised his hand for silence, but a sailor broke in: 'My bet is that Spanish ship. Cops harangued us for hours about that new bilge pump, the crate they winched across – who touched what, who pissed where.'

'That's one theory,' Captain Lewis conceded. 'But apparently there's been no outbreak in Spain. No mysterious deaths on Spanish vessels. They've been militant on border control. Aside from a few flu outbreaks, they're clean.'

'Was me and Jimmy unpacked that crate and fixed the pump,' said a crewman. 'We're still standing.'

'Only two crew fell sick,' said his mate. 'Neither one went near that crate.'

'That dead body in the water,' put in Juliette. 'Up near the equator. A bug could have got in through the seawater intake. Turn on the showers and bang, you're done for.'

'Impossible,' said an officer. 'That system's state of the art, the intake's fully purified.'

'You can't catch a virus from a corpse,' said someone. 'Can you?'

'Damn right you can. Look at the Arctic, all those germs leaking out when the ice melted.'

'Anthrax!' A loud interjection from up the back: Marshall. 'Dead reindeer. The bug came back to life when the carcasses defrosted.'

'We're talking about the equator,' someone objected, 'not the Arctic.'

'Alright.' Cutler, trying to restore order. 'We're wasting time here.'

'The kids,' said Doctor Kellahan. 'This is a terrible environment for them. Distressed adults acting out, that incident yesterday. The children should not be on this ship.'

The captain looked exhausted. 'I'm with you there. But the commander's position is that they've made services available. The counsellors ...' He trailed off.

Kellahan persisted. 'This is no place for children. How can this be legal?'

'When will they lift the comms ban?' This from Lauren, the flaky nurse. 'I need to call home.'

A pang: Billie saw her parents' worried faces, her brother's goofy grin.

'What do we tell the bereaved families?' Owen's voice. 'They're asking about funerals.'

Pounding, a heavy fist against the door. The room fell quiet.

'Open up!' A man's raised voice, that flat nasal accent. 'Unlock this door right now.'

'Let them in,' said the captain. He threw down his cap and sank into his chair, the gesture of a man defeated.

~

The official materialised at her side as she left the laundry room. Clad in the grey uniform of their overseers, dark and clean-shaven, close to her own age. *Mitch*. Not bad-looking, Billie had to admit. He flashed white teeth, a grin so guileless she almost returned it, just caught herself in time.

'Got a minute?'

She hung back. No reason to trust any of these people.

'Official business,' he said breezily, holding up a device. 'I'm doing some fact-checking for forensics. Zoning parameters, quarantine stuff. Won't take long.' He jerked his head: *this way*.

Another man expecting her to jump at his command. But

something off about this one: his manner too familiar, his loyalties unclear. She wavered, but curiosity won out.

He led her to a booth in a corner of the aft saloon. The room was near-empty, just a couple bickering in the corner and some kids immersed in a motion game. Screened by a vending machine, no cameras in sight, the spot offered a rare semblance of privacy.

'You know those articles?' Mitch asked as Billie slid into her seat. She did, almost word for word.

'You remember the journalist's name?'

No: the name hadn't mattered. The articles now committed to memory, interred at the bottom of her suitcase. Contraband documents in antique form, lone missives from the outside world.

'He's a contact of mine,' said Mitch. 'Specialises in advocacy, human rights stuff.'

'I don't follow.' Not content to let him parcel out scant clues and innuendo. This man had made vague promises last time, before the hearing; said he'd put in a good word. Look how that had ended: she'd been blindsided, her character called into question.

He showed his palms: *no weapons, nothing to hide.* Good looks aside, he had one of those trustworthy faces. 'We can help each other. I need info.'

Billie pressed her lips shut.

'I know,' said Mitch. 'You all signed a non-disclose. But I'll protect your identity. You have my word on that.'

'You'd trust some random stranger in uniform?'

'I'm taking a huge risk here,' he said, blinking. 'It goes both ways. You could get me fired, or worse.'

'Fired for what? Acting mysterious?'

'You think I'm government,' he said. 'I'm not. Emergency management's outsourced – we're mostly contractors.'

'Contractors for who?'

He pointed to the logo on his grey shirt: a parachute descending into a cupped hand. 'Pro-Tech. A national outfit. Natural disasters, industrial accidents, terrorism. As for my being here … well, let's just say it's not exactly legal.' A hint of self-importance, like he wanted to impress her.

'Aye, right,' she scoffed. 'So you're some kind of secret agent.'

Mitch didn't take the bait. 'Listen. I have a source in forensics. They suspect the virus was deliberately released. She reckons there's no way it could slip past the bioscreens.'

Billie dropped the flip tone. 'That theory's been doing the rounds since day one – border vigilantes.'

He shook his head. 'Forget all that. It's a blind alley, a distraction. I've done some digging. The facts point to commercial sabotage.'

He laid out his alternate theory in short, sharp bursts: three rival shipping companies were competing for BIM contracts worth many millions. There was a history of bad blood between them – dodgy deals, undercutting, claims of poached suppliers and corporate spying. If Red Star could be knocked out of the race, it would leave a lucrative gap for the other two to fill.

'These labour routes are worth big money,' insisted Mitch. 'Land a BIM contract and you stand to make a killing.'

A prickling unease, her head whirling. 'But all those deaths,' she countered. 'Nobody will sign up for BIM now, surely. Not after what's happened.'

'There's been a dip in applications, but people are still signing up,' he said. 'Just not to Red Star's intake. This will ruin the company.' Red Star's line had been shut down, but the rival shippers were still operating, with enhanced protocols at both ends; the workers screened to within an inch of their lives, then hustled off to remote inland food farms, out of the public eye. Back home the shippers had ramped up their recruitment efforts, he told her, launched aggressive new ad campaigns, were loudly trumpeting their credentials – foolproof ultrascreens, superior vetting, zero risk. Million-dollar guarantees. No chance this could ever happen on one of their vessels.

'But those deaths,' she said again. 'If this was deliberate, done to damage the company, surely whoever did it risked getting the whole program shut down?'

'Maybe. But the bug looks engineered. Perhaps it wasn't meant to be fatal? It's not a precise science, bioterrorism.'

All those warm bodies crammed in close together, breathing the same air; that claustrophobic horror, the sense of being trapped at the mercy of an invisible executioner.

'I can't believe people would risk it. Get on another ship.'

'The polls say otherwise. Look at all the push factors. No offence, but your homeland's a basket case. Why did you leave, Billie?' Using her name like they were friends.

She turned away. 'That's none of your business.'

He made an apologetic gesture. 'You're right. But the govs won't ditch BIM without a fight. High political stakes, too much money tied up in the program. And if this whole mess can be explained away, painted as an aberration – blamed on some floating corpse, or a mid-sea transfer ...' Mitch watched her process this. 'So you've heard those theories too. Far-fetched, but convenient. And they're gaining traction.'

Too much to take in here; a suspicion she was being manipulated. Who was this guy?

'The govs can keep BIM running if they can argue this was a one-off, a freak event,' he went on quickly. 'Say nothing malicious went down, nothing got through the bioscreens. We redesign the intake filters. Ban cargo transfers between ships. Bingo – problem solved.' He had this speech planned out.

'You want something from me.'

'I need your help. I'm leaving you a device.' Rummaging beneath the table, a subtle motion. 'It's fully streamed. And you can message me, there's a secure link. But don't get caught with it. And don't check your personal accounts – they'll be monitoring them.'

She held up her hands. 'No, I don't want it. This has nothing to do with me.'

'Billie,' he said, urgency in his voice now. 'It has everything to do with you. The howlers are out in force. You know who's being blamed for all those deaths? The quote, *incompetent ship medics*, unquote. The *so-called nurses*. They're blaming you.'

'But we *saved* lives.'

'Breach of duty, they're calling it. Medical negligence. People do time for that.'

'But the last one died right here—'

'They're out for blood,' he interrupted. 'I can help turn that around. Take the heat off you, shift the narrative. Work out what really happened. But I need your help. We need to find out who did this.'

She felt it in her guts, a cold trickle of dread. What was being said about her? Who was trawling her life, hunting for dirt? Her parents: she felt sick to think of them being harassed by journalists, seeing her mug plastered across the news, copping sidelong looks from the neighbours. Saw her dad shaking his head. *It's a big stooshie,* he'd say. *A terrible mess. We just want her safely home.* Absent-mindedly she rubbed her arm, felt the blip of the geotracker lodged beneath the skin.

'It's a bloodsport, all that public venting,' said Mitch. Was that concern in his eyes, or something more calculating? 'It's ugly, but it's not personal. The mob just wants a scapegoat. Don't take it to heart.'

'I went to that hearing,' she said. 'I didn't notice anyone taking my side.' He regarded her blankly.

'You said you'd help,' she reminded him. 'I guess you didn't have much sway over that judge.'

'I'm sorry it was rough. But there are people fighting for you out there. Me included. I'm doing my best.'

'You say you're not government. So who are you?' A short silence. She watched him weigh it, calculate the risk.

'My job is to uncover facts.' Then, more urgently: 'But, please, this conversation – I'm just some nameless Pro-Tech contractor. You walked me through your quarantine protocols. Donning and doffing, contact tracing, buffer zone, all that stuff. That's it. Nothing else.'

She found herself nodding.

'And if anyone asks, you don't know my name,' he said. 'I can't help you if I end up in prison.'

'Prison?' she echoed. 'They threatened us with prison. If we didn't cooperate – the nurses. We had no choice.'

Now he was all business. 'I'll make sure that message gets amplified. But we need to track the source of the contamination. Work out who brought this bug aboard, and how.'

She felt dazed, remote. A thought swam to the surface: 'Did they check the water?'

A quizzical look.

'The drinking water. Have forensics tested it?'

'Pretty sure they tested everything. Kitchen, mess, wash areas. Sleeping quarters, supplies.'

'What about the kiosk? They had water tanks in there. Did they test the tanks?'

'I'll check. You think—'

They both jumped as an alarm blared out. *Security personnel to bridge*, rasped a voice over insistent bleeps: *Incident alert, security personnel to bridge.*

'I'm investigating several crew members,' he said. 'People who've previously worked for a rival shipper, an outfit called Orion. Digging into their backgrounds, finances. I've narrowed it down to four names, but it's slow going.'

'Four names?'

Now Mitch was looking over Billie's shoulder. He gave a dazzling smile.

'You deaf, mate?' said a voice.

Billie turned to see an official standing behind her. She hadn't heard the man's approach.

Mitch waved his device. 'Just checking some details. Orders from above.'

'Get upstairs,' said the man. 'There's a code blue. Move it.'

Mitch eased out of the booth with a quiet warning: 'Best if we're not seen together. Don't get busted with that, and don't access your accounts. Your middle name – that's the password.'

Left alone, Billie sat motionless, trying to process what she'd heard, to weigh it against what she knew, sensed or half suspected. She felt numb, immobilised, and it was some time before her breathing returned to its usual soft loop.

Mitch: she'd placed it now, seen the word spelt out in print. On paper: the bylines on those articles he'd given her.

A noisy group had invaded the saloon, the adults debating some point, kids pestering on the sidelines. Billie switched seats, dug between cushions, found the contraband device. Tucked it into the waistband of her shorts, praying it wouldn't fall out and clatter to the floor.

Then she locked herself in a wash cube and keyed in a single word: *Grace*.

TOM

Soon after we rejoined the *Steadfast*, they summoned us into the sick room one by one. God knows what possessed them to choose that particular venue. The smell of the place alone set me reeling: dizzy, breathless, chest tight, my heart hammering out distress signals.

It was over in seconds, but more painful than your average jab. Like everyone else on the ship we were now geotagged, a tiny tracker embedded in the upper arm; you could feel the bump, like a grain of rice lodged beneath the skin.

Cutler stood observing as the local medics did their work. He was his usual self, officious as ever, as if he hadn't noticed his demotion. Unpleasant man, but not the tyrant he'd once seemed; his bully licence now revoked, his power dissipated.

Shutting the door on that acrid room, I joined a group of convalescents gathered along the ship's rail. A ragged crew, we were easy to pick out from the crowd: big heads on thin bodies, taking hesitant steps, faces tilted to the sun like flowers. Freshly released, we gravitated to the top deck, inhaling the air and view.

After that white ward, I couldn't get over the colours: hillsides jammed with foliage, a glimpse of jewel-toned vehicles on a distant road. A sky so huge and blue I tried to fill my lungs with it. The air thick with heat, the light so different from back home: high and stark and clear, the lens wiped clean.

'That place looks like a holiday camp,' said Max, pointing at the buildings beyond the beach. 'When do we go ashore?'

Drinking in the view, we heard a chorus of high voices.

'Teach! Teach!' A gaggle of red sunhats: the children, making a beeline for us.

'Hey, Pied Piper,' joked Max, 'it's your disciples.' Not the best analogy to level at a male teacher.

It lit me up, the sight of them, all wide eyes and scuffed knees. They crowded around, chattering: did I know there were war drones dropping paint bombs from the sky, and actual real dolphins swimming in the bay? I asked Emily if she'd written any new poems, let Troy marvel at my puny wrists. Avoided asking after their families. I'd requested a full list of the dead so I could start piecing it all together; match up surnames, offer solace where I could.

'When do we go back to school?' asked Tamila, squinting up at me earnestly.

'Once I get a bit fatter,' I hedged. 'Look! Over there, on the hill – is that a kangaroo?'

~

We'd been welcomed warmly back into the fold. The day the transfer boat ferried us once more to the *Steadfast*, people had been lined up along the rail, waving as we approached. I'd watched as Mia was reclaimed by her parents and brother, the raw relief as they clutched each other close, a circle of four; I saw families reunited, lovers back in each other's arms. All past quibbles, all doubts forgotten.

Back from the dead, we were minor celebrities. Passengers and crew approached us daily – although not too close, it must be said – eager to bestow blessings, congratulate us for resuming the upright position.

But not everyone was pleased to see us. For some, we were a blunt reminder of all they'd lost. The day of our release, one fellow survivor spent several hours with a bereaved husband, recounting his wife's final hours. I guarded my demeanour. Mustn't walk around beaming at my own good fortune with thirteen people dead. Or fourteen, in fact: that was the true death toll.

All clear, the doctors had promised us: that inhuman assassin zapped out of existence. But I remained on high alert, fighting a constant urge to re-wash my hands, re-san my cutlery. Alert to the threat, real or imagined, of all we could not see. Having played host to that microscopic invader, I sensed an unfamiliar presence: a hard knot of acrimony deep inside me, a wild spark of what could be hatred, ready to flare up if any proof was found.

Talk had intensified. Could another human being deliberately unleash such grief and suffering, leave all these families bereft? It was like trying to wrap your head around infinity, or the space–time continuum. The mind just baulked.

So strange to see everyone mingled in together, the crew's uniforms gone, the old pecking order dissolved. We'd clocked up forty days on the hospital ship, the traditional quarantine period decreed all those centuries ago when the Black Death rampaged across Europe. Tiny robots would remain floating in our blood, feeding data to distant medics. Ally had gone home to her kids and husband. My old flame had vanished back into the crew's quarters.

We'd all assumed we'd be sent back home, marked as soiled goods, a contaminated shipment, unfit for service – although the prospect of a long return voyage filled everyone with dread. Instead we found ourselves in limbo, no clue as to what lay ahead.

I knew I needed to occupy myself, turn my energy to constructive ends.

The children: there was no structure to their days, no safe haven available to them. Left to roam the ship, they risked witnessing scenes of grief and anger: adults weeping, scuffles breaking out as protest attempts were quashed; gaunt figures stalking the deck, weakened by self-imposed hunger. Tense armed soldiers, scanning the sky for airborne assaults.

One afternoon I saw a man teetering on the foredeck, holding a hand-lettered sign up to the empty sky: *RELEASE US*. One of the bereaved, his eyes dark holes, his lips a seeping tracery of rough-hewn stitches. A needle shoved repeatedly through living flesh, an outward demonstration of unspeakable pain. Soldiers hustled him away, but not before a group of kids had gathered to stare.

This incident sparked me into action: I couldn't leave them to languish. No longer on the payroll, I restarted school in an unofficial capacity. Lobbied the gov-liaise woman for art supplies, fresh vids, sports gear, games, sweets and chocolates for prizes. Excess sugar consumption was now the least of anyone's worries.

I'd never been so grateful to stand before a roomful of kids. It was like a reunion, a cadet squadron reconvening at the tail end of a war. Seeing all their faces – expectant, open, resigned, or already half-bored – I felt myself beaming like a loon.

Then my eyes landed on Lucy: she had a bewildered, unfocused look, still reeling from the blow of losing her mother. The sight of her brought me up short, cut off that sentimental overflow. A reminder that the war metaphor was horribly apt, that none of them would escape this experience unscathed. That for some, the damage would last a lifetime: Finn and Abbie. Shahid. Lucy and Cole.

Grief is such a dire thing. It seems monstrous that children can't be spared.

Each day we gathered in the schoolroom after lunch. I rested my bony rear on a desk. Cheered them on, cajoled them, tried to draw them out. Encouraged jokes and laughter, often at my own expense.

I vetted the clips for any distressing content. Chose games with no macabre undertones. Devised activities I hoped would not trigger bad memories. Tried not to san my hands too obviously or too often, kept my germophobia under wraps. Silently willed the children to hold on, to keep faith; to trust that they were now safe, that adults would protect them. That the future still held promise, and things would soon change for the better.

~

One afternoon I was parked in the shade, devising a word game for the kids, when there was a ruckus further down the deck.

'She's sick!' someone yelled. 'Get back!'

Adults rushed past me, kids in tow. As the crowd cleared I saw a woman slumped on the deck, her head between her knees, a circle of soldiers and grey uniforms surrounding her at a safe distance. Against my better judgement, I edged closer.

The woman was flushed, her pupils huge and black. On the deck before her, a puddle of vomit. Kneeling at her side was the head nurse, Billie, masked up, one gloved hand resting lightly on the woman's back. Speaking to her, the words inaudible.

A breeze touched my cheek, blowing from the direction of the sick woman. Holding my breath, not letting a single molecule of air enter my lungs, I beat a swift retreat, making straight for the showers.

An hour later I ran into Billie in the passageway, her face now bare.

'Your mask,' I said. 'That woman …'

'Heatstroke,' she replied. 'She stayed out in the sun too long, got burnt and dehydrated. Thank god. The captain's about to make an announcement.'

'They're sure? It's not the sickness back?'

'Positive,' said Billie. 'She's clean.' Relief was written plain across her face. 'Jesus, the sight of her. Almost gave me a heart attack.'

I pulled my mask off. But for us, the passageway was empty, the ship eerily hushed. People had retreated to their dorms. We were standing close, and suddenly I felt awkward: this woman had seen me naked, seen me empty myself into a bedpan, had wiped my arse for all I knew.

She asked after Cleary. Did he seem alright to me?

'Hard to say,' I answered. 'All the kids are shaken up. They cope in different ways. Why? Has something happened?'

She chewed her lip. 'His mum said there's been some weird stuff going on. He seems anxious, jumpy. Won't leave her side. You've not noticed?'

Trying not to sound defensive, I admitted I hadn't seen much of Cleary lately. He hadn't shown up to our schoolroom gatherings yet. A pity, it'd do him good.

She thought. 'Maybe it's some kind of delayed reaction. The shock of almost losing his mum.'

'Traumatic thing for any kid,' I said. 'And he's smart – he'd have known what was at stake.'

Abruptly Billie changed tack, asked if I was close to any of the crew. It seemed an odd question, but I just said a breezy no. She gave me a searching look, and I made some inane remark about things improving soon, once we were taken ashore.

She shook her head grimly. 'This country hates us.' The public was baying for blood, she said: calling us ship rats, dirty scabs, human trash. Toxic cargo, foreign invaders. And it wasn't just the howlers: the immigration minister had called us a walking death threat.

'I've been thinking,' she said. 'You remember what that sailor said? That young guy you know, back in the sick room. When he was off his head, delirious.'

Yes. I remembered.

'You didn't hear this from me,' said Billie. 'But I just got some news. Forensics found viral traces in one of the water tanks.'

'In the tanks?' *Devil water.*

'That sailor,' she said. 'He knows something. I think he knows who did this to us.'

~

In retrospect, my next move was reckless. Possessed by an urge to take action – to *do* something, however foolhardy or futile – I searched the ship for him. Came up against locked doors, crew-only sections. I didn't ask for him by name, just hunted doggedly.

I found him on a small balcony off the fore saloon, perched on a milk crate, staring out towards the open sea. No mistaking him: handsome, even from behind.

He didn't hear the door open behind him.

'Stewart.' My voice sounded oddly formal. 'I need to speak to you.'

He turned his head, startled. Saw something in me: a warning.

'Leave me alone,' he said. Cool, unperturbed. A quick recovery.

I held the door wide, projected my voice back into the saloon: 'You'd rather I said this in public? In front of everyone?'

Without a word he leant over and shoved the door shut. Then directed his stare back to the harbour. Trying for nonchalance, but less convincing by the minute.

Sunlight glanced off the sea in blinding flashes. In the distance yachts tacked back and forth. I felt a pang of self-pity, realised there was no comfort for me here.

I spoke. 'Do you remember being sick? Thrashing around, asking for a priest?'

Stewart didn't answer, gave no sign he'd heard me.

I pressed on. 'You were talking to yourself, rambling. Off your head. You don't remember?'

A twitch: a crack in his façade, a gap to push my words through.

'We're both lucky to be alive,' I went on. 'I was delirious too, for a while. But I remember what you said: *There's something in the water.*'

He sprang to his feet, fists clenched. Kicked at the milk crate, putting a feeble barrier between us. An effort so pathetic I almost laughed.

'So you know?' I said. 'You know who did this to us?'

He stood against the light, breathing hard, too thin in shorts and t-shirt, those remarkable looks chiselled down to gauntness. He hadn't gained an ounce of weight back.

'I've done nothing,' he said, voice cracking. 'Nothing, I swear.'

I knew he was lying. Any sympathy I'd felt for him was gone. Never had I been violent towards another person, but I was close now, and both of us knew it.

'Tell me what you know,' I said.

'Don't do this. You'll make it worse.'

'Tell me,' I said. 'Or I'll go to the police.'

He was sweating. 'It wasn't me,' he said, almost pleading. 'They offered me money – a lot of money. But I didn't take it, I swear. I said no.'

A putrid smell wafted up from below, rotting fish or kelp, some rancid marine stink. And all at once I caught his fear.

'Please,' he said, urgent now. 'They're watching. They'll come after you.'

I turned and left without another word. As the door slammed shut behind me I paused, still dazzled by the glare, my eyes adjusting to the gloom of the saloon.

Not two steps away from me stood a crewman, someone I vaguely recognised but could not name: tall and sloped, hard face, a black beard and deep-set eyes. He stared right at me, and there was something hostile in that look. Could he have overheard us?

I made for the exit, sought out the nearest wash cube, and scrubbed my hands, under my nails, between my fingers, until the skin was pink and raw. Then I headed to the schoolroom, locked the door behind me, necked three Calmex and lay trembling on the sofa, waiting for the drug to take effect, to wash away the terror.

~

Twelve hours later I woke to find the ship in chaos: crawling with soldiers, plastic barricades across the deck, police tape thrumming in the breeze. People clustered in small groups, casting anxious glances over shoulders, at each other, at the soldiers' guns.

'What's going on?' I asked a passing official, but he ignored me.

'Body in the water,' said a voice. I turned to see Delaney, my old truant officer, the one the kids called Santa.

'What?' Disoriented, my head still woolly from sleep. 'What body?'

'Young fella,' he said. 'One of the deckhands. Horrible. I can't believe it.'

An awful possibility stirred: an idea starting to form. 'What happened?'

Delaney looked shaken. 'Poor kid was floating face-down in the shallow water with his skull bashed in. Terrible business.'

I was afraid to ask, fearful of the answer. 'Who is it? What's his name?'

'Scottish lad,' said the old sailor. 'Nice boy. The one they called Scoot.'

13

CLEARY

From the doorway, he scanned the packed schoolroom: kids sitting on desks, crates, the floor. Popcorn scattered around, an air of cheerful chaos. In one corner a hologram mouse did stunts on a trapeze, while in the middle of the room a pile of Lego bricks was morphing into a lighthouse, children standing on chairs to click the next layer into place. Teach was assembling a cargo ship. He looked up smiling as Cleary and his ma came in.

At once Declan dragged him over to a table, pushed aside a pile of Christmas decorations and began commandeering an arsenal of coloured pens. A jar of glitter had spilt and stray sparkles glinted from the children's faces.

Laid out before Cleary was a tempting stack of creamy white paper. His friend was urging him to get to work, but he was watching his mother's mouth, trying to decipher what she and Teach were saying. He could only catch the odd word, not enough to make sense of.

Then his ma wove across the room, kissed his cheek and ruffled Declan's hair. *I'll be right there*, she signed. *Have fun, sweetheart. Enjoy yourself.*

She settled into a chair just outside the schoolroom, waved through the glass panel in the door and opened her magazine. Cleary watched her flick the pages. Then he chose a purple pen and ran a test line down the page. The inks were rich, but the paper held them fast, and he was soon lost in a world of shapes and colours: orchid, lawn-green, cornsilk, azure, thistledown, moccasin. Now and then he glanced up to check, saw her head bent over her magazine.

As he shaded the hull of a pirate ship, the girl opposite tapped his wrist and pointed to the door. His ma was waving through the glass: *Just going to the jacks*, she signed. *Back soon.*

Cleary unfurled a fresh sheet, but a prickling unease kept intruding on his thoughts. Declan scribbled demands for him to draw a rat, a triceratops, an astronaut, and he obliged with quick sketches, checking the door between pen strokes.

Why was she taking so long? The fear kept circling back to him, shark-like, until he couldn't bear it. As he stood up, ready to search the ship, she reappeared at the window. He sank into his seat and took a long breath, trying to soothe his pulse back into its regular rhythm.

~

Later that afternoon, soldiers ordered them to line up for a scan. The queue was long, the air dense and muggy, a rolling bank of cloud massing darkly out to sea. Gulls wheeled around the masts in nervous circles. Bad weather was coming.

A man crumpled to the deck in front of them. Cleary's ma knelt beside the fallen man and took his head in her lap. Grey-clad officials converged, scanners at the ready, but the man was already coming to; he waved them away, fanning himself, mimed struggling with the heat. Big of build but pared down now, with a rangy, sunken-cheeked appearance: one of the people who'd been sick. His face was familiar, but it took Cleary a moment to place it: the bald-headed man who'd harassed him at dinner all those months ago, upset his ma with nasty words. Now the man was weak and harmless, the sting gone out of him, giving his ma a grateful look, the two of them no longer enemies. The sickness had changed everything.

On the beach Cleary saw a pair of guard dogs romping across the sand, two German Shepherds tussling over a length of driftwood. The animals dashed and feinted, tails wagging, teeth snapping in mock ferocity. Glancing back, Cleary froze. His heart gave one solitary panicked thump. Looming over his ma was a tall bearded man with a stoop. The man was speaking to her, showing his teeth in a wolfish smile; she shaded her eyes and gazed up at him, listening.

The picture was so wrong, the shock of it so sharp, that at first Cleary did not register the vital detail.

Blackbeard was holding something in one hand: the shaft of a metal crowbar, black and heavy, the end hooked like a claw. He clasped he weapon aloft in a loose grip, pointing behind him, enacting this charade in plain sight. As if it was an innocent object, something you waved around to illustrate a point or indicate direction.

Nobody paying the slightest attention, except for one small child.

One swing of the man's arm and his ma would fall to the deck, bleeding and broken.

Still talking, the weapon held high, Blackbeard looked straight at Cleary for a long moment, then turned back to his mother's upturned face.

~

That night Cleary waited until his ma was fast asleep. He counted to five hundred in the dark, then touched her forehead lightly, checking for a response, any clue that she was not entirely under. Moving with great care, praying that the bed was not creaking, he slid out from beside her, wriggled into the narrow space beneath the opposite bed, and pulled the blanket down to form a curtain. Lay very still upon the dusty floor and tried to put his thoughts together.

What he'd seen today had forced him to think quickly. An ordinary weapon was no use against a man like that. Never mind that Cleary hadn't told a soul what he knew – that didn't seem to matter to the man. Blackbeard was getting closer, becoming bolder and more dangerous. It was only a matter of time before he carried out his threat: a finger drawn across a throat, a crowbar raised above his mother's head, a bird impaled on a spike.

There was one person who could help, one person he could trust. Billie would know what to do.

He couldn't put the danger into words. Could not risk spelling it out, an accusation he couldn't take back, sentences that could fall into the wrong hands and be used against him – against both of them.

Cleary propped the torch into position; waited to be sure his ma was still asleep, watching flecks of dust drift through the cone of light. Then he retrieved his pens and set out the colours he would need: *charcoal, navy, scarlet*. Smoothed the paper flat, shut his eyes, and brought the picture to mind. Once the image was clear, he began to draw.

BILLIE

The summons to gather on the main deck blared out over the PA.
Billie heard it from the nurses' cabin, where she was composing a
message home to Jamie and her parents, if only in her head.

Lackeys were setting out chairs on the main deck for the
gathering crowd. Last night's storm had scoured the ship clean, but
the heat was already building, the air humming with an uneasy
cocktail of anger, nerves and hope. Weeks of inertia and uncertainty
had fuelled talk of full-scale protests, and the hunger strikers were
weakening by the day.

By the rail she spotted Juliette, her back turned to the crowd,
pressing a wad of tissue to her reddened eyes.

In this charged atmosphere, word of the young crewman's death
had detonated a new wave of anxieties. Suicide was one popular
theory, but it held no weight with those who knew the gruesome
facts: severe blunt-force trauma was rarely self-inflicted.

Minus one more: Scoot now dead. After they'd fought so hard to
coax him through, to keep him alive. Gone, just like that. The life
smashed out of him.

No news on who might have carried out this brutal act. No
word from Mitch, the journalist, since his last message, those stark
words glowing on the screen: *forensics found viral traces in kiosk tank.*
Since its arrival, several days ago now, all her messages to him had
gone unanswered.

Once you got past the horror, it made sense. Just one tank
contaminated, then the kiosk swiftly sealed off, declared a crime
scene. All attention diverted to the dead man discovered lying in a

pool of his own blood. That first victim unplanned, an accidental witness to a split-second act; the tampering perhaps not obvious at first, but the culprit's presence at the scene enough to rouse suspicion in the aftermath, in the carnage that was to come. A retrospective clue, a chance the killer couldn't take. Davy Whelan and his memories swiftly dispatched. Meanwhile, the virus making its stealthy way from the water tank into the first human body, then leaping from person to person, unleashing havoc and destruction.

Now this: the young crewman from Aberdeen beaten to death and tossed away like garbage.

Robbie was waving her over, had saved her a seat: 'Big boss is here. Must be about our lad.'

Up on the foredeck the incident commander surveyed the crowd, half-moons of sweat blooming in the armpits of his shirt. Flanked by soldiers, he sat behind a row of trestle tables – barricades, Billie couldn't help thinking, in case this turned ugly. An expectant hush fell as the incident commander stood to speak.

'I'm here to share some positive news,' he began, his voice amped a touch too loud. 'You will all be transferred to a secure location in a matter of days.'

Whoops swept through the crowd. Jubilation dissolved into chatter, then shushing as the commander held up a hand. He'd allowed himself no more than a tight smile.

'The medical team has confirmed there is no further risk of infection. You're going to be taken ashore.' A murmur went up, hands were raised. The man patted the air, signalled for patience. 'I will take questions. But first I've been instructed to brief you.'

He spoke without emotion. They'd soon be transported to a new facility at an undisclosed location. This geographic vagueness was for their own protection: there was intense media and public interest surrounding this whole unfortunate affair, and the government had legitimate concerns about both privacy and safety.

'I must emphasise,' he said over the growing hum of disquiet, 'that we're dealing with a heightened security situation. But please be assured you have the full support of the Australian government. Protections will be put in place.'

As of now, they were all subject to a legally binding confidentiality writ: no speaking to anyone, in any jurisdiction, about events occurring on this ship. A silence both indefinite and legally enforceable: no anonymous comments, no private revelations to friends or relatives. Not now, not ever. Zero disclosure, for their own protection.

'Fucking gag order,' muttered Robbie. 'Can you believe this? Where's that bampot captain?'

The rumble swelled to noise. The commander pressed on. He spoke as if merely conveying information, as if he was a reluctant chess piece being moved by higher forces. There were several police investigations currently underway – into the viral outbreak, into the suspicious deaths of not one but two crew members. At this point none of the passengers or crew would be returning home. Nor would anyone commence work: their contracts were suspended until further notice. In the meantime, they'd all be housed at this secret location.

'Which will be a much more spacious facility than we've been able to provide here on the ship,' he added, raising his voice to be heard. He could not comment on the most recent death – that matter was now in the hands of local police – but could assure them that extra security personnel had been deployed. 'Your safety is paramount,' he said over the growing racket.

If not for the soldiers, Billie suspected a chair or two might be in danger of being hurled.

A passenger near the front rose to his feet. 'You're treating us like criminals,' the man yelled. 'I lost my sister on this fucking ship.' He turned to face the crowd, pointed at the officials. 'Look at these fucking arseholes up there! Treat us like scum, keep us in the dark. Why don't we get a say in what happens to us?'

Soldiers leapt forward to grab the man's arms and twisted them behind his back. He kept shouting as they manhandled him away, his face distorted by pain and indignation: 'Fuck you people! You brought us here. We're not criminals!'

Gov-reps ordered calm and threatened to close down the briefing. Further disruption would result in criminal action. That put a dampener on the noise, but the air remained charged. Question time, when it came, was limited to a few minutes. Answers were brief and scant on detail.

When the officials and soldiers left, the mood soon softened, conversation dropping to a hum. *The fight's gone out of them*, Billie thought. *They're tired.*

'At least we're escaping this death trap,' said Robbie. 'That's worth a drink, wouldn't you say?'

~

Billie stared into the dark, felt the cool wash of the fan skim back and forth across the hot cabin. Her aim had been to dip into the stream, fish out the necessary info and get out quickly, sidestep the hysteria. She'd always tended towards the dry side – avoided wallowing in that poisonous undertow of anger and opinion, the emotional runoff from millions of anonymous strangers.

But curiosity had won out: she'd seen the swirling fear and vitriol, the wild entanglement of fact and emotion. Unable to stop herself, scanning the accusations with a mounting sense of horror: the angry claims that lives had been lost because untrained people had taken on well-paid medical roles they were not qualified for. That those amateurs who'd profited so handsomely from suffering and death – those greedy frauds who'd been so cavalier with human lives, let loved ones die so pointlessly, stacked their bodies on ice down in some grubby cargo hold – now had blood on their hands. The sense of injustice was like a physical pain. She couldn't defend herself, was locked out of the conversation.

Her brain kept looping back to an anonymous piece by someone who'd lost a relative aboard the *Steadfast*. The tone was bereft, rather than aggrieved, but the item had attracted a sympathetic chorus of howlers, and the thread had swiftly taken a vindictive swerve. Become yet another rabid condemnation of the inept imposters who'd been paid big money to let twelve people die. Never mind that the thirteenth victim had died right here, in the care of local doctors.

That piece hadn't named the nurses, but the details were not difficult to dig up, her own name most prominent. They'd used an old work photo: Billie standing at a sink in a dirty set of scrubs, a scowl on her face. She looked like bad news – surly, guilty of something, unapologetic.

All those strangers – they didn't know her. Had no idea how hard she'd fought to keep the sick ones on this side of the void, stop death from claiming them. She felt tears pricking at her eyes, blinked them away. She was not a crier. Blubbing never helped.

She turned her pillow, seeking out a cool spot. Heard a rustle: felt something rigid beneath it, a foreign object. She shone her torch under the pillow. In the beam of light lay a large envelope, the flap stuck down. She turned it over.

The words were printed in a neat, familiar hand: *Private – Secret – Confidential. DO NOT TELL.* She smiled at the air of mystery, the childlike dedication to intrigue: the boy had snuck in here to leave this for her. He hadn't forgotten her.

Billie tore open the flap, and felt her smile fade. She recognised the first drawing at a glance, one of a set the interrogators had coaxed out of the boy. They'd photographed the whole series, as if it was important evidence, returning the originals to him in an envelope very much like this one.

The drawing had disturbed her at the time: a window framed by black-scribbled night. Goods stacked on shelves, water tanks set on a bench, a fire extinguisher bolted to the wall. Below all this, at the bottom of the picture, a pair of work boots attached to horizontal legs, and a floor awash with long streaks of bright red.

The second drawing was new, but there was no mistaking its subject. A stark portrait: fierce deep-set eyes, wild black beard, blue uniform shirt, the red star on the pocket. A strong likeness: the kid could draw. Smeared across the man's face, from cheek to temple, was a vivid slash of red. Marshall: the chief steward.

The torch beam hovered between the two images, alternating light and dark. Billie drew the torch back, the circle widening, so both drawings were caught in its bright gaze.

A dawning realisation: that she had been oblivious, had left the child to his own devices, missed the signs. That his fear, his vulnerability, ran much deeper than she'd cared to know.

Could there be another way to read this? Part of her mind rejected what lay in front of her, refused to join the dots, sought an alternative explanation.

Of course the boy could be mistaken, be imagining things, forming conclusions with no basis in fact. But this message was hardly ambiguous – it was a testimony of sorts.

Fragments of memory whirling and coalescing, the pieces now clicking into place: Davy Whelan, sprawled on the kiosk floor in a pool of his own blood, the open water tank on the bench above. Scoot's broken body, drifting with the tide. The boy's near-drowning, his injury, his constant watchfulness. A voice calling after them: *That kid's not right in the head*. One common denominator, a nauseous outline taking shape.

She recalled Marshall necking sly grog in the storeroom, singing along with her to 'Skye Boat Song'; standing guard that day the nurses were forced into service, his gaze sliding away from her. The man all but spitting in her face that time, accusing her of spreading the sickness. A glimpse of him in a passageway, sanning his hands with almost manic fervour. His recent disarray, his air of human wreckage. Talk of him weeping in public, passed out drunk, ranting nonsense. And his interest in the boy: there was a hostile edge to it. Whatever Cleary had seen, there was bad knowledge between the two of them.

Who could she trust? Not management: Marshall was one of them. She must tread carefully, for Cleary's sake. Handled rashly, this coded message could place the boy at grave risk.

By torchlight Billie retrieved the smuggled device from the lining of her luggage. In the dark of the kitchenette, shielding the screen's illicit glow, she sent a swift message: *Evan Marshall, on crew: look into him.*

~

Days passed with no response. No sign of Mitch since his last dispatch, the news about the poisoned water tank. Had the journalist left the ship? Been discovered?

Billie tried to focus on the child, to let him know she'd understood his message. To signal that she would do her best to protect him, to keep his mother safe. But Cleary refused to leave his ma's side, so Billie could not spell out these assurances too specifically: had to transmit them through gesture, eye contact, facial expressions; coded pledges. It wasn't enough.

Friends forever? she wrote in his notebook. *I'll come visit you in Dublin once we get home.*

Pinkie swear? Cleary put down the pen, held up his little finger.

They hooked their pinkies together and made a pact: come what may, they'd always stay in touch. Would always remain fast friends.

But her assurances felt flimsy, his hopeful glances almost painful. The boy looked thin and sleepless. His knee was healing, but wouldn't yet bear his full weight, the crutches still needed. The cabin he now shared with his mother was located near the stern, on the lower decks: relatively isolated, and not far from the crew's quarters.

How real was the danger? Kellahan had seen Scoot's body. Had described the injuries, cited the autopsy report: *Multiple fractures to the skull, patterned contusions indicating blunt force trauma. Abraded contusions and lacerations to the face. Chop injuries to the upper chest with underlying fracture of right clavicle.* If Marshall knew there was a witness to his crime, a possibility that he would be exposed, an undersized kid and his frail mother wouldn't stand a chance.

Another thought: it wasn't an easy task, beating a man to death. Had Marshall managed it alone, or did he have help? Who else might wish the child harm?

When a berth became free in the nurses' cabin, Billie pressed for Cleary and his ma to relocate and share the lower bunk. 'All those stairs are bad for his knee,' she argued. 'We're a quiet bunch. And this way I can watch him while you rest.'

Cate was reluctant, but the boy begged, and Kellahan helped secure clearance. Billie arranged new wristbands and tacked up a curtain so Cate could nap in her bed during the day. It wasn't enough, but it was something.

And then, at last, a reply. The message landed in the small hours of the morning: *Meet me 3 p.m. today. Same place.*

~

The saloon was busy, a gathering in progress, a group of passengers airing grievances and plotting insurrection, voices raised to unwise volumes. They'd soon attract attention. Billie slipped past and made for the concealed booth.

Mitch looked different. Unshaven and underslept, with an air of nervous brio, as if he'd overdone the coffee. The journo did not waste time on greetings.

'I've found something,' he announced. He seemed keyed up, eager to talk. But then he hedged. Asked why she'd singled Marshall out. What did she know about the chief steward?

Billie shook her head. 'Nothing you can use,' she said firmly. 'Just gossip.' She had to keep the boy out of this, not risk exposing him to further danger. 'I don't have long, so ...'

'There's this guy I work with,' said Mitch. 'Gun for hire, stream trawler.' This hacker pal had been awake for days – chasing digital trails, pulling in darkstream favours, cracking correspondence, digging into financial records.

'He's struck pay dirt,' said Mitch. 'The intel's not strictly legal, but we can feed it through a leak site.' He raised his eyebrows, seeking her reaction. A hint of arrogance, of self-congratulation, about him now.

Patience ebbing, Billie let the silence sit, refusing to buy into his performance.

'Evidence,' he said. 'Payments from one of the rival shippers, Orion. Three lump-sum transfers, made to a shadow account registered to a string of proxies.'

'Payments?' she echoed. He had her full attention now. 'To who?'

'The recipient's name is Evan Marshall – just like you thought.' The journo narrowed his eyes, gauging her reaction. 'A former Orion employee. The company's paid him a shitload of money, all covert, in instalments. The dates are interesting.' An initial payment made early last year, he said, just after Marshall joined Red Star. The second sum – triple the size, an obscene amount – landing soon after Davy Whelan was killed. The final chunk, like a dirty afterthought, deposited just two weeks ago.

'Billie?' said Mitch softly. 'Your tip helped. I think we've got him.'

Scenes of damage played in her head: open wounds, deep bruises; the mottled pallor of a fresh cadaver, the blistered sheen of autolysis.

'You're certain?' she asked. 'There's no doubt?'

'Positive. The payment trail leads back to Charon Group. A subsidiary of Orion.' He seemed pleased with himself. 'They were careless.'

There's something in the water … Devil water … Poison money.

Scoot: he'd known. She felt sick, her thoughts spinning. The picture coming into focus, despite her own raw sense of disbelief.

'What happens now?'

'Nobody else knows yet,' said Mitch. 'Can't risk a leak yet – it's not safe for me. I'll float the story in the next day or two. But first I need to somehow get myself out of here.' He swallowed, and Billie was struck by how young he looked. Doubt now flitting across those boyish features. 'There's been other breaches. Things are tightening up. They're running extra background checks.'

She couldn't take it in: the idea that all that horror, that brutal destruction of life, had been driven by something so banal. Money: a means of exchange. She felt a surge of revulsion. Understood, in that moment, the urge for retribution, the lure of violence. How you could hate someone enough to hurt them, badly.

'I owe you,' Mitch was saying. 'We'd have uncovered this eventually, no doubt, but you narrowed things down, pointed me in the right direction.' Conditional gratitude, then – a not-so-subtle bid to minimise any debt she might be owed in this exchange.

'What about us?' she asked. 'The nurses, the passengers, all of us – can you help get us out of here?'

Mitch tried for a smile, but it lacked the usual warmth. 'Once this story breaks I'll do my best – apply pressure, advocate for all of you to be released. Try to get some kind of resolution.' He rose abruptly. 'Gotta go. Hang in there.' And he was gone.

~

Staring out to sea, she let the images reel through her mind: Cate's unconscious form, her sunken cheeks and bloodless lips; the boy's dark eyes seeking out Billie in the dim of their shared cabin, all the hope and terror compressed into that small body. The hostile officials, the hologram judge and her sidekick, all seeking to lay blame wherever it might stick; the bluffing medicos, the silence from above. All those howlers, polluting the stream with their misdirected hatred.

And the dead: she recalled them all in detail, every single person who had died down there in that stinking room. Her own gloved hands, zipping the body bags shut.

What she'd give to confront Marshall herself, make him feel the full weight of her hatred, be diminished by it. What kind of inner deficit could bring someone to commit such an act?

No, it was too risky. He might trace it back to the boy.

Or could the opposite be true: what if she issued a covert warning, hinted that she had his measure? It might give Marshall pause, make him back off the kid.

~

Chance sprang an opportunity that afternoon.

In calm weather the crew unfurled the sails across the deck as shelter from the sun. Billie sat in the shade, watching Cleary play knucklebones with a group of kids, a circle of red sunhats bent over their game. Cate was stretched out nearby, dozing.

At the sight of Evan Marshall striding across the deck, Billie snapped to attention. The man came to a halt on the edge of the children's circle, observing the game's progress. Sensing his presence some of the kids squinted up, then turned back to their play.

But not Cleary: the boy did not raise his head. He crouched motionless, the knucklebones clenched in his fist. Billie watched as the other kids urged him to take his turn; she witnessed him fumbling the metal pieces, dropping them to the deck, forfeiting the game. Only then did Marshall move away.

Billie intercepted the man as he reached the hatchway. Blocked his path, met his eye.

'You're being watched,' she said. 'They know. There's evidence.'

Marshall glared back at her. Something crossed his face: a flicker of doubt, or apprehension. Then his expression hardened. He leant in close, as if sharing an endearment. 'Mind yourself, scab,' he said, spitting each word as if it was a curse. 'You don't know what you're dealing with.'

He turned and walked away.

Billie's legs felt boneless, and she was short of air. This was no longer a matter of dislike or contempt, or even disgust. No, it had gone beyond that. Now she was afraid of him too.

TOM

I was up on the main deck with the children, collecting stray knucklebones after a tournament, when an ungodly racket floated out across the water: a metallic clank and rattle, like a giant lawnmower firing up.

The *Nightingale* was drawing up her anchor chain.

The kids and I stood along the gunwale, watching the anchor's progress as it was winched up from the depths. Once it was flush with the hull, tugboats were manoeuvred into position, lines cast down. Then the hospital ship turned its back on us and began to edge away.

The children observed this procedure in near-silence.

As the *Nightingale* slunk past, its upper decks conspicuously empty, Mia turned to me. 'That means the bug's all gone,' the child declared. 'There's no more sickness.' She was scowling, as if defying me to disagree.

'That's right,' I said. 'We're safe now.'

Nearby I saw Billie, smoking discreetly, cigarette held low, exhaling out the corner of her mouth. In the shadow of the mast Cleary stood with his mother, bearing witness to the *Nightingale*'s slow retreat. I noticed the boy glance around, checking Billie's whereabouts. She smiled at him, and he turned back to watch the hospital ship inch away into the distance.

~

I was dead to the world when the alarm blared out, an urgent squalling that shattered any hope of sleep. Guards were stomping the aisles, rousing people, turfing stragglers out of bed. I heard the word *evacuate* and joined the queue of men shuffling from the room.

The upper decks were jammed with people in various states of undress – barefoot crewmen, passengers in pyjamas. Soldiers corralled us towards the stern. An acrid stink hung heavy in the air.

Fire! The ship's on fire!

We couldn't see the flames at first. A row of barricades hemmed us in behind the wheelhouse, and beyond it stood a line of soldiers. They came and went, craned their necks, keeping tabs on what was happening down the far end, out of sight.

Black smoke was drifting up through the rigging. A young boy had clambered up onto his dad's shoulders, the child's silhouette framed by an eerie flickering light.

A woman called out to the nearest soldier: 'How bad is it? Are we being evacuated?'

The soldier pretended not to hear, but the woman persevered, kept calling to him.

'We're waiting for instructions,' he yelled back, then turned away and busied himself with his radio. He looked no older than eighteen, and was clearly frightened.

A collective gasp: now we saw it – bright filaments of flame reaching up into the night, snatching at the air. The fire was towards the bow of the ship, the flames licking around the yardarm. Black smoke seeped across the moon and someone let out a sharp scream.

Fear swept through the crowd. People were leaning over the rails, calling for help. A group of men tried to shove the barricades aside, but the soldiers converged, weapons half raised, shouting at them to get back. A police boat ploughed into view, lights flashing, an official on deck wielding a loudhailer, his voice ringing out across the water: *Please remain calm. The fire is being contained. Please remain calm.*

Smoke roiled and billowed, the flames climbing higher now, the air rippling hot, the fire gathering force. I could feel the heat of it on my upturned face. Why weren't they evacuating us?

A passenger was braced against the rail, his young daughter held aloft, one arm wrapped firm around the girl's middle, holding her out like an offering. He was shouting to someone below, pleading: *Get the children off. Take the children!*

A fireboat chugged past and disappeared towards the *Steadfast*'s bow. Jets of water began shooting up the foremast, raining down through the rigging, but the flames persisted. Smoke drifted and belched overhead. People were clambering over the barricades now, making for the lifeboats. I saw the young soldier standing back, gripping his rifle, making no move to quell the crowd. His companions had melted away.

The crowd surged, lost to logic: one group tried in vain to launch a lifeboat, while crewmen scaled the rigging for a better view. Parents crowded the stern, as far as possible from the flames, holding their children out, shouting over the rail, appealing to those in the boats below.

The crew were handing out life jackets; through the smoke I heard shouting, coughing, intermittent sobs and screams. A chopper swooped low overhead, dropping a gutload of water on the fire. The air was rank with the stench of burnt plastic and singed wood.

Warning shots rang out and patrol boats circled, men bellowing across the water through loudhailers: *Step back from the rail. Remain calm. Do not attempt to leave the vessel.*

At last, as dawn began to leak into the sky, there was a lull. The flames subsided, the smoke dissipating. The fireboat chugged away, a solitary fireman raising his arm in farewell as they passed.

A fresh load of soldiers boarded the ship and swiftly took command: they assured us that the fire was out, that we'd never been in any real danger, that the situation was now resolved. We were ordered to return to our dorms and remain below decks until the breakfast siren sounded. Frightened and exhausted, we did as we were told.

~

The damage was a sobering sight: the foremast charred, the kiosk gutted, a gaping black hole in the foredeck. Melted plastic and scorched wood, the stink burnt into the very bones of the ship. People wandering around, their soot-smudged faces blank with shock.

Police were everywhere. There were more interrogations, and forensics teams sifting through the embers – *interference with a crime scene*, they were calling it. The looks they gave us left no doubt: we were all potential suspects or accomplices.

The fire had started in a storage space beneath the kiosk. A *lazarette*, old Delaney called it, or a *glory hole* – traditionally used to stow bodies, now a place to stash equipment. There was no word on how the fire had started, no clear reason why it would have burst into life of its own accord.

Billie told me the news at breakfast: a crewman had gone AWOL. Slipped away during the chaos of the fire, she said, or perhaps in its aftermath. Sliced open his own flesh with a razor blade, dug out his geotracker, and dropped the blood-stained pellet down the shower drain. Officials armed with wrenches tore the plumbing apart to retrieve it.

By the time his absence was noticed, Marshall was long gone.

Marshall. Images of him were soon posted all over the ship: printouts of his crew ID photo, appeals for information, taped to the walls like old-fashioned 'wanted' posters. The face leapt out at me like a slap. All hard lines and shadows: that dark beard, those deep-set eyes.

The ship was abuzz with anxious talk. Knots of people gathered, swapping theories in lowered voices. At first the arson was blamed on local vigilantes, attack drones dispatched by germophobes or migrant-hating nationalists. But once Marshall's disappearance became common knowledge, suspicion shifted to the absconder, his vanishing act read as an admission of guilt. A shadowy chain of events was now being traced back to one man: the first killing, then the unfolding devastation of the sickness; the second murder, followed swiftly by the fire.

Now I had some hope. If Marshall was indeed guilty – if he was captured, held for questioning, charged with breaching quarantine, or worse – then surely things would change for the rest of us. Blame would cease to be free-floating, would at last have a clear target. We would be taken ashore, as promised. The dominoes would stop tumbling. All this would soon be over.

LANDFALL

14

CLEARY

It was the motion of the ship that woke him. That rhythmic heave and sway, a sensation so familiar that at first he'd simply closed his eyes and almost drifted back to sleep. Then it hit him: after all those weeks at anchor, the *Steadfast* was moving again. They were back at sea.

Drawn to the glow of the kitchenette light, Cleary edged out of the bunk, careful not to wake his ma, grabbed his notebook and hobbled across the cabin. In the kitchen Billie was sitting up with some of the nurses, smoking a cigarette at the table, which was strictly against the rules. Her face was tight and the ashtray was piled high. At the sight of Cleary she crushed her smoke and tipped her wrist so he could check her watch: 2.10 a.m.

He gave her a quizzical look, slid his notebook across to her.

We're going ashore, she wrote. *A new place*. She pulled an excited face.

Cleary drank a mug of milk and watched the women talk. Their words seemed jumbled and anxious – *too weak to fight them*, Holly was saying, or perhaps it was *two weeks to find them* – but he didn't care where they were headed. Tomorrow was Christmas Day, and Blackbeard was gone. Billie had promised: the man was no longer on the ship. Cleary was safe.

But checking over your shoulder wasn't an easy habit to break.

Your body gets trained for danger, like a soldier – always alert, ready to run or fight. It forgets how to relax.

Laughing, Holly grabbed his foot and tied a loop of silver tinsel around his ankle.

So Santa can find you, she scribbled. *Better get back to sleep before he comes.*

~

The morning broke clear and warm. The *Steadfast* was slicing fast through choppy waves, and at first Cleary was puzzled to see her sails furled tight against the masts. Then he noticed the grey bulk of the warship forging ahead of them, and realised they were being towed.

The warship was vast, the size of an entire city block, its flanks dwarfing the *Steadfast* as she bobbed obediently in its wake. The cable that ran between them was as thick as Cleary's arm. Spray twanged off it as they churned through the swells.

They passed a sparsely populated island, then a more solid land mass began assembling in the distance. People squinted into the wind and sea-spray, trying to make out their destination. Crewmen wandered the deck, looking lost, their hands dangling loose – nothing to do, just passengers now.

Cleary saw a flinch pass through the crowd, and turned to see a soldier lowering his rifle as a wounded drone plunged into the waves.

His knee was still tender, but the crutches were not much use on a moving deck, so he was trying to work his limp into a kind of sailor's swagger. The kiosk had been demolished, the charred hole in the deck now boarded over. He peered up into the masts, but saw no birds.

This morning at breakfast the guards had handed each child a single present from a sack. Cleary had unwrapped the exact same gift as other kids: a miniature bear with clip-on paws, wearing a waistcoat and waving a flag: *Merry Xmas from Australia!* All over the ship identical koalas were clamped to the children's clothing, hanging on for dear life, like tiny jockeys.

Still, the other presents had made up for it: a stash of chocolate from Billie, and a magnetic chess set from his ma, carried secretly in her luggage all the way from Dublin. *Another present coming*, she'd scribbled in his notebook. *Just need to get to the shops!*

As the land drew closer Cleary joined his mother at the rail, binoculars aloft, seeking a glimpse of their new home. The screens in the saloon were black, no maps to plot this journey, but he sensed that they were heading south. Recalled seeing this land mass, a heart-shaped wedge below the mainland, surrounded by sea, but its name eluded him.

For hours they skirted a rocky coastline, past barren cliffs, steep hillsides thick with trees. Scant signs of human life: a lonely stand of wind turbines, a patch of razed forest, a cluster of buildings overlooking an empty beach. The wind tore through the rigging, and where land met sea white breakers shattered on the rocks in ragged lines.

They ploughed on. No city emerged from the landscape. The sun sank low and the wind grew colder, a new bite to the air.

As night fell the land slipped away behind them. Ahead loomed the pale mass of the warship, and beyond that a dark immensity of open sea.

~

Daylight revealed a bleak vista: a low slab of rock, treeless and scrub-flecked, its soil scoured away by a ceaseless wind. The island dropped steeply into the sea. Cleary trained his binoculars on a stony beach, a zigzag path climbing the rockface, a huddle of buildings perched atop cliffs.

All morning boats ferried their human cargo back and forth, the soldiers stacking luggage and passing out life jackets. It was almost noon when their turn finally came.

A strange feeling, to set your feet on dry land after all this time. Cleary and his ma stepped off the boat together, right foot first, for luck. But at the end of the pier the rich grass of his daydreams was replaced by splintered scree, the flinty smell of rock dust, gnarled shrubs clinging like bonsai to the cliffs. And a restless wind, pushing itself into every crevice.

The climb was steep, his knee shooting out warning pains; his ma lagged behind, pale and short of breath. A soldier grabbed Cleary and swung him onto his back like a rucksack, charging uphill as if the boy weighed nothing. At each hairpin turn Cleary tugged at the man's collar and pointed back, worried his ma would be left behind.

On a barren plain crouched a cinderblock building, enclosed by a razor-wire fence. They passed beneath an archway marked with faded letters: *Flint Island Processing Centre*.

Locked gates, a jerky turnstile. Unsmiling guards in khaki uniforms watched them file past. The building's interior was all pale green walls, brown linoleum, grey concrete. Their dorm felt oddly spacious after the confines of the ship. Rows of identical bunks, salt-crusted windows with a limitless view of nothing. A kip of a place.

Cleary's ma sank onto a bed and motioned for him to lie beside her, although he wasn't tired, was itching to explore. The bed was narrow, the mattress hard. She clasped him tight and stroked his hair, her eyes fixed on the ceiling, as families fussed around them, unpacking bags and peering into lockers, negotiating over beds. After a while she became so still he wondered if she'd fallen asleep, but each time he checked her eyes were open, and her hand recommenced its automatic petting motions, stroking his hair, as if she was in some kind of trance. *Don't worry*, she signed each time. *Don't worry.*

~

It was several days before Cleary realised they weren't alone on the island. He was outside with some of the kids, kicking a ball around the dusty concrete yard, when something caught his eye. Pausing at the boundary fence, he looked across the wide asphalt road that ran down the centre of the island.

Small and slight, the figure stood motionless behind a high fence encircling a cluster of run-down buildings. Black hair, brown skin, clothes the colour of dust; a shadow child, with thin dark limbs and indistinguishable features.

Cleary leant against his own fence. The child in the far compound raised its arm, and he waved back. He'd left his binoculars inside, and from this distance he couldn't tell if it was a boy or a girl.

One by one Declan and the other kids abandoned their game and drifted over to join him, peering into the wind at this dusty apparition. A second figure emerged from the far-off buildings, a taller version of the first kid, this one most likely a girl, with long dark hair that streamed out sideways in the wind. She did not wave, just watched them awhile, then took the smaller child's hand and led it back inside.

~

After that they saw the shadow children most days, wandering aimlessly along the razor wire or kicking a ball around the far compound. One day there'd be no sign of life beyond the wire, the next there'd be ten or fifteen kids ranged along the fence-line, staring back at them. Occasionally an adult would appear to distribute water or summon them inside, but for the most part they seemed to be unsupervised.

Cleary studied their faces through his binoculars: the children seemed solemn and dispirited, lacking in energy, as if the constant wind had worn them down. Reading their lips was impossible. When Declan clowned around for them – hung off the fence upside down, or did a silly dance – there was little response. The shadow children made Cleary uneasy, but he couldn't have said exactly why.

Meals at this new place were awful: bland and repetitive, worse than on the ship, and despite rationing attempts his Christmas chocolate was soon gone. The flickstream in the rec room was locked to one news channel, nothing worth watching. The soldiers had brought the toys and games across from the ship, the Lego and art supplies and storybooks, but Cleary found himself restless, fidgety. The island was pockmarked with scrub and rocky outcrops, its surface all dips and hollows – perfect for hide-and-seek. But they were not allowed out there. As far as he could tell there were no wolves or bears on the loose, and no way off the island. What was the point of the fence?

One afternoon, while his ma slept, he sat with Billie in the rec room, drawing pictures. There were birds living here, light-boned creatures that huddled on the plain or were tossed around the sky by the erratic winds. He drew the island, the rocky beach, the seabirds; the black dividing line, the two compounds on either side of it. Then he paused, unsure how to tackle all that empty space around them. He tapped Billie's arm, flicked open his notebook.

Where are we?

She sketched a rudimentary map: the solid wedge of Australia above them, slender New Zealand off to one side, and below them the great white expanse of Antarctica. He copied these land masses, then added penguins, whales, icebergs breaking off and floating north. He knew that people lived down there, on that icy continent – scientists, explorers. They were not the only humans at the bottom of the world. Billie took a pencil and drew cross-eyes on one of his seabirds. In retaliation he drew a hairy tarantula across the back of her hand, its fangs buried in her knuckles, while she squirmed and pulled terrified faces. Billie wasn't scared of much, but spiders put the heart crossways in her.

Days passed, one much like the next. A storm rolled through, no-one but them to witness it. A week or so into their stay Teach made an announcement: they were heading out, an expedition down to the beach. Cleary's knee was almost better, the limp all but gone, and he kept pace with the others as they navigated the steep track down to the shoreline, two bored guards bringing up the rear. Clouds tumbled across the sky and the briny scent of the ocean rose to meet them.

For hours the children combed the stony beach for treasure, collecting and comparing finds: broken shoes and frayed tufts of rope, skeins of kelp and sea-worn shells. A crab's claw, hooked like the beak of some strange parrot, a bird skeleton tangled in a web of fishing line. Dried starfish, sun-bleached bones, an old brick. Plastic bottles with the labels worn off, bearing a residue of silt and tiny shells. No messages inside: he checked them all.

So absorbed was he in beachcombing, so relieved to be roaming free of the camp, that it was some time before he noticed. Before he scanned the empty bay, the unbroken horizon, and realised that the *Steadfast* was gone.

BILLIE

The battery died three days after they came ashore. She had smuggled the device off the ship by tucking it inside her bra, worried the wardens would search her and seize it, charge her with some unspecified crime. But the guards showed no interest in searching their luggage, or their bodies. Nobody was going anywhere.

Her last few messages to Mitch remained unanswered: *Where are you? What's happening?* She'd sent him the name of this godforsaken island, but hadn't risked a photo: there were cameras all over the compound. Each day, conscious of the battery draining, she'd locked the bathroom door and checked the stream compulsively, sifting quickly through the flotsam, waiting for the story to break. Nothing: no new dispatches from Mitch. No word at all about Scoot's death. Not a single mention of Marshall or his disappearance, no hint that he'd been paid to set the sickness loose. The crewman seemed to have vanished from the world entirely.

Mitch had gone dark on her before, she reasoned. No doubt he was busy collecting evidence, firming up the story. But a voice kept niggling at her, saying she'd been a sucker to fall for his good looks and charm, a fool to trust that the journalist would follow through on what he'd promised, help get them released.

Had Mitch been genuine? She replayed their encounters, rehashing every conversation word for word. He'd been cocky, sure, and jumpy at times, perhaps out of his depth. But he hadn't struck her as a liar or a conman, someone out to take advantage. At gut level, he'd rung true.

But there was the catch: if he was truly a journalist – the one who'd argued so passionately in their favour in those articles – then Mitch was indeed a liar, and a skilful one. Had lied his way onto the ship using a fake name and identity, hungry for a story. Fooled the authorities, which was no easy task.

This silence – there must be a reason for it. Perhaps he'd simply got the facts wrong, or realised the evidence would not hold up. Dropped the story altogether, moved on to other topics. Abandoned them to this miserable windblown rock in some forgotten corner of the map.

'Can't get much further south than this,' said Robbie, surveying the wasteland beyond the razor wire. 'Last patch of ground before Antarctica.' You could feel it in the air: a chill edge, a proximity to ice.

Here the uniforms were khaki, and had a military look. The guards were not all bad, in Robbie's view, but they tended to clam up if you asked too many questions. He'd befriended one already, of course – Tucker, a sunburnt behemoth of a man, with forearms like smoked hams and a disconcertingly soft voice. Mona had reservations, said the crew apparently had reason to be wary of their new overseers, her husband should steer clear, but Robbie had waved this off, said there was no harm in having the guards onside.

'They don't like that other lot much,' he confided, jerking his thumb in the direction of the far compound. 'Dirt people, they call them.'

Billie had caught glimpses of the far camp's inhabitants: listless children rolling a ball back and forth, men lugging water barrels across the yard, a floppy figure being carted on a stretcher. They had the look of people in a news clip, ragged souls exiled from dusty deserts and far-flung war zones.

'How long have they been here?'

Robbie shook his head. 'No idea, hen. Afraid to ask.'

She knew what he meant. Bad thoughts could be contagious. In the dark hours nightmares rampaged through the dorms, unsettling all but the deepest sleepers, and most days you heard the sound of sobbing echo in the corridors. Several people, Owen included, now spent most days napping on their beds, medded up to the eyeballs. Two hunger strikers were confined to the medical clinic, drugged into submission and hooked up to IV drips, and there were rumours of force-feeding and self-harm. One of the bereaved children, a twelve-year-old girl, had stopped speaking, had to be coaxed to eat and drink. Seeing a child lose hope, shut down like that: it was disturbing. How long until others followed suit?

A group of people had begun gathering daily for a prayer service of sorts, a ritual of no particular denomination, led by the lapsed priest and one of the grieving wives. Passing by the room Billie had seen them sitting in a circle, heads bowed, united in some private rite to honour the dead. Had caught the odd word – heard them reciting the names of lost loved ones, offering tributes, snatches of remembered lives. People she'd known briefly; people she'd been unable to save. She'd ducked her head and hurried past.

Two nights ago at dinner, one of the women from this group, a fellow Scot, had approached Billie. Asked her to join the circle, sing for them, a hymn perhaps: 'Dark Island' or 'Amazing Grace'? Billie had declined as gently as she could. Doubted she could face them as a group, let alone sing in their midst.

Part of her envied those who could hold on to faith; whatever kept you afloat.

With Owen sunk into a silent depression and Captain Lewis' ineffectual presence now held in wide contempt, Kellahan was left to field the inmates' concerns and advocate for their medical needs. The doctor was doing his best to keep Billie occupied, had brokered an arrangement with the camp's medics: assigned her an informal triage role, checking on medication and helping with referrals to the onsite psych, a harried-looking woman who seemed short on sleep herself. It had helped to feel useful, but that impression was fading with alarming speed. Two weeks in, Billie could feel her own resolve slipping away. A dull hopelessness creeping in.

Day and night a screen flashed in a corner of the rec room, volume muted, captions only, and Billie found herself drifting on the periphery of those flickering images, watching for a signal that never came. The election Mitch had mentioned was now imminent: newsreaders served up opinion polls while local politicians flipped burgers, played cricket with schoolkids or thundered into microphones, hurling accusations at each other.

Further afield, bad news abounded: fatal floods in California, food riots in India, ominous rumblings between Beijing and Taipei. In Texas a bunker cult had declared itself a separate state, blown up all the surrounding roads. Back home the plague tolls rose in jagged increments. More than enough madness and pain in this world to keep the howlers occupied.

Parents had begged the guards to kill the screen, or switch it to a child-friendly channel, but the men just shrugged, said the thing was centrally controlled, they had no say in the matter.

Their own story seemed to be fading from view, reduced to the odd brief bulletin – shots of the damaged ship, men in lab coats saying reassuring things, condemnatory sound bites from the leader of the opposition, a five-second clip of an activist urging the government to have a heart. The problem of their presence being hustled offstage, the feeding frenzy shifting to other targets. *How quickly the crowd can turn*, she thought. *Or turn away.*

~

She was in the rec room, dispatching another dismal meal, when an image flashed onto the screen and stopped her dead, fork halfway to mouth.

A headshot: Mitch standing on a beach, handsome as ever, all white teeth and symmetrical features, grinning into the camera. Beneath the newsreader ran a brief caption: *Journalist found dead.*

Billie felt the blood drain from her face as the presenter read off her autocue: *Body discovered on suburban building site … covering human rights, fraud and corruption cases … police appealing for information.*

She picked up her plate and left the room.

~

The camp director stood before the crowd, khaki shirtsleeves rolled up, as if he was about to pitch in and help move some furniture. Three weeks here and this was their first sighting of the boss. A heavy-set man with a bronzed complexion and a broad gut, he had a genial air that seemed at odds with the grim setting.

This gathering was adults only, the children being supervised outside: a clue that unpleasant topics were on the agenda, emotions likely to run high. Billie scanned the crowd: anxious faces, but no open displays of anger. Since being towed here – dragged helpless behind that military ship, dumped in the middle of nowhere – the inmates had lost much of their bravado. Near the back sat Captain Lewis, his silver hair neatly combed, his expression unreadable. Dressed in civvies now, no gold buttons or brocade, all traces of authority gone. Reduced to a civilian with good posture.

'Thank you all for coming,' the camp director began, as if this was some dull party they'd all been kind enough to attend. 'It's important that we keep the lines of communication open.' He smiled, took a little stroll from side to side. There was no barricade or dais, no line of soldiers between him and the crowd. But ranged around the walls were close to forty khaki-clad guards, batons on hips. The man knew he was not in any danger.

'You've been through a distressing time,' the director went on. 'A terrible tragedy. My sympathy goes out to all of you.' His voice was smooth and confident, the man clearly a practised speaker.

'Wouldn't trust this lot as far as I could throw them,' Juliette muttered beside her. 'They'll do anyone's dirty work.'

It wasn't clear how long they'd be held here, said the director – unfortunately he wasn't privy to that information. National security, ongoing investigation, their own protection etcetera. The wheels turned slowly.

But there might be something they could do – a way to speed this process up.

'You will have heard the talk,' he went on. 'The rumours that a bioterrorist cell infiltrated your ship, caused the deaths of innocent people.' The claims that this disaster was the work of anti-migrant groups, vigilantes and extremists. Toxic orgs like StayPut, whose mission was to stop the free movement of people across borders – to prevent hard-working people like them from striving to make better lives for themselves, for their families. The director's expression darkened. 'I'm the child of immigrants myself. Believe me, I have no tolerance for those attitudes.' He paused, surveyed the crowd. The guy had a knack for sincerity, but Billie didn't find herself warming to him. However well he spoke, the man was still a jailer.

A gang of children drifted past the window, hair whipped by the wind, Cleary amongst them; a guard followed, trailing smoke, fist cupped around his cigarette. Remnants of old plastic bags flapped in the fence-line, and beyond the cliffs a slate-grey sea merged into an ashen sky.

'Rumours can be dangerous,' the director continued, 'and there may well be no truth in all this speculation. But if anyone here has information about events on that ship, I urge you to come forward – to speak to me privately, in confidence. You have my personal assurance that you will be protected.'

Mitch's smiling face flashed into her mind. Whoever had killed the journalist must be aligned with Marshall, was hell-bent on protecting the perpetrators of this horror by any means. There may well be others on the payroll, more dangerous men amongst the remaining crew members. Her association with the journo may well have drawn attention.

'Please,' said the director. 'If you have intel that might help advance the investigation, might help pinpoint the party responsible for these atrocities – share it. Help bring this terrible affair to an end. If you can shed any light, do the right thing. My door is open.'

He smiled again and held his hands out in a gesture of welcome. Then his expression changed.

'The truth,' he added, 'is that the cause of this disaster cannot remain a mystery. The authorities have made that clear. Unless information is forthcoming, you may be held here indefinitely.'

The room was strangely quiet. Billie felt the desperation of her fellow inmates, the sense of anger fast sinking into despair. This was no place for children. It was no place for human beings.

She mustn't give in to the idea that they were helpless. Better to stay angry. She would find a way to speak to the camp director – make him listen.

~

Billie waited until the afternoon lull, the lethargy that settled over the camp in the slow hours after lunch – kids playing a desultory game of ping-pong on a scarred table; the adults staring at the TV screen, playing cards or napping.

There was no fuss. A quiet word with one of the guards, and she was escorted through a set of doors and down an empty corridor.

The camp director's office was smaller than expected, the room dominated by a window that overlooked the pier, the distant cliffs, the waves battering the rocky headlands. A sparse room: filing cabinets, a framed picture of a racehorse, a row of neglected cacti on the sill.

As she entered he rose to shake her hand. 'Ray Harker.' His grip firm but not forceful.

'Billie,' she replied, as if her full name was any kind of secret. As if he didn't have it at his fingertips, perhaps already knew it. The director dismissed the guard and waved her into a chair, waited for her to speak.

She laid it out simply, bare details only, as she'd planned: said the missing crewman, Evan Marshall, had been paid to contaminate the ship's drinking water. When Davy Whelan caught him tampering with the tanks, Marshall had slit the man's throat.

'What happened to us wasn't bioterrorism,' she said. 'This was commercial sabotage. Marshall was paid to do this. We need to get the police involved.'

The director held up his hands. 'This is a lot to take in. Can I ask where this information has come from?'

She hesitated. 'It came from someone who's no longer with us.'

He looked surprised. 'One of the deceased?'

She nodded. 'We need the police. I'll tell them everything I know. Can you make contact?'

'Of course,' said the director. 'I'm in close contact with senior federal police. We're helping facilitate the investigation, setting up remote interviews with camp residents.'

'When?' said Billie. 'Can I speak to them today?'

'Let's slow down a bit,' he said. 'We can certainly arrange a link. But first I'd like to clarify what you're telling me. You say this crewman, this Marshall, was paid to do what – to deliberately contaminate the drinking water on the vessel?'

'Yes. The police need to look into his finances. Track the money trail. There are records of the payments.' Three dirty sums, deposited discreetly. But not quite discreetly enough.

The director frowned. 'Records? You've seen these records?'

'Not me. One of the people who died. He found proof.'

'Proof of what? Payments?'

'Yes,' said Billie. 'From a rival shipper.'

'Really?' He sat back, clasped his hands across his belly. 'Does anyone else in the camp know about these allegations?'

What did that matter? Was this guy slow on the uptake? 'I'm not sure. But it's not just allegations. You know another crewman was killed, just before we got towed out here? Scoot – Stewart Armstrong. I think he knew full well who was responsible. I think Marshall killed him too.'

The director shifted in his chair. 'I'm sure the police will be keen to speak to you, but I'll need to brief them. I'm trying to get my head around what you're saying. You were one of the nurses, correct?'

Of course: he knew she wasn't just a random passenger.

'I've read the reports,' he said. 'My impression is that your presence was a godsend. Without you the death toll would have been much higher.'

So, he didn't side with the howlers. Reassuring, but this wasn't the time for compliments.

'Are you hearing me?' she said. 'All those deaths – I'm saying it was deliberate.'

'You're aware that police are looking into alternative theories – you know about the encounter with the Spanish ship?'

Not this again. 'Yes. And the floating-corpse theory. Neither one stacks up.' She waited. 'This wasn't an accident. There's evidence.'

'Alright,' he said, suddenly decisive. 'I'll put a brief together and send it through this afternoon. Let them know you're serious, request a linkup. Just one more thing. This rogue company. Do you know its name?'

'It's a shipping firm,' she said. 'It's called Orion. This can't wait. Can I make a statement today?'

The camp director sat back. 'Ah,' he said with a slow smile. 'Now, this is a little awkward.' He opened a drawer, dug around. Then, watching her closely, he slid a card across the desk.

Billie skimmed his name, his job title. Then her eyes fell on the logo: a thick black O, sliced through with a lightning bolt. Below it, the full company name spelt out, five letters.

A sudden weight of dread. A falling sensation.

'We're a large corporation,' he was saying, genial as ever. 'International in scope. Fingers in many pies, diverse interests across multiple territories – security, transport, logistics. Oversight of mobile workforces. And certain other groups, of course.' Scanning her face, he feigned surprise. 'You didn't know? Not to worry. I'm sure this sensitive information will be handled with great care.'

A sick lurch in her chest: the realisation that there was no way to reverse this.

'Thanks for hearing me out,' she said, keeping her voice steady. She made to rise, but the camp director waved her back into her seat.

'No rush. I have a few more questions, if you don't mind.'

'I'd rather wait and speak to the police. I'd like to leave now.'

He leant forward to press a button on his desk. 'Not yet,' he said. 'Not just yet.'

TOM

That ceaseless wind. Shrieking and moaning, a creature possessed by demons, hurling itself across the barren landscape, thrashing against the cinderblock walls and battering the windows. Rattling the glass in its frames, trying to get in. All night I listened to it howl around the building like a lunatic.

Madness manifest, insanity impersonating weather. A mindless force that drained your energy, made it difficult to put two thoughts together.

The children had stopped asking when we'd leave this place. They sensed when they were being lied to, or fed platitudes. Had soon learned which questions made the adults uneasy.

Our lessons had resumed – a bid to keep them occupied, distract them from the bleakness of our surroundings. Myself too, I'll admit. We made do with an ink-stained whiteboard, loose sheets of paper, the art supplies and games brought from the ship, and an ancient and incomplete set of encyclopaedias one of the guards had unearthed from some musty storeroom. *What keeps the sun alight? What causes chilblains? What is the ether?*

Their drawings had taken a disturbing turn: fences, razor wire, birds in cages. Rain clouds and burning ships, dotted lines of tears streaming down unhappy faces.

I had no training for this.

'Who can tell us the order of the colours in a rainbow?' I asked brightly. 'Does anyone know what's inside a camel's hump?' Grinning at them like some kind of simpleton. 'Who remembers the name of the first woman on Mars? What's the difference between a stalagmite and a stalactite? Who can guess what a seahorse eats?'

I knew Cleary was missing his friend. Apparently he'd woken one morning to find Billie's bed empty, her belongings gone. There'd been no sign of her since. Doctor Kellahan made enquiries, asked the guards where she was, and eventually got an answer of sorts: it seemed she may have been shipped back to the mainland to assist with the police investigation. They couldn't say for sure.

One morning, as I walked a circuit of the prison grounds, battling the wind, I found some of my students gathered at the fence. Across the asphalt, in the opposite compound, a group of ragged figures waved from a rooftop. A platoon of guards or soldiers stood below, their rifles trained upon the men on the roof.

The scene unsettled me, and I hustled the kids inside. As the door slammed shut I heard the crack of gunshots carry on the wind. I tried to go back out, see what was happening, but the guards blocked my way.

'Who are they?' I asked one of the men. 'Those other people?'

'Nobody,' he said. 'Get back inside.'

Flint Island: a barren rock at the arse-end of the globe. Dumped in that nowhere place like spoilt goods, we languished in a kind of half-life. Morale sank lower daily and our jailers confined themselves to the most rudimentary of responses: more soap could be obtained from the dispensary. Group outings to the beach were limited to children and must be signed off by the director. Outbound communications were not permitted. Variations to the menu were not possible. The windows in the dorm rooms did not open.

Leaking taps, broken locks, a layer of windborne grit coating everything. Mould in the bathrooms, black blotches creeping out from damp corners. Drifting spores, tiny toxins … the thought made me shudder.

We were cast adrift from the world – unreachable, all ties severed.

Time stretched blank to the horizon, day after day, no endpoint in sight, like a map devoid of landmarks.

Hold yourself together, Garnett: I spoke sternly to myself. Falling apart was not an option. Nor was chemical obliteration, although that urge had reasserted itself, a constant sullen undercurrent. But meds were limited and the children needed me.

One night I saw a news report, a brief reference to our presence here: the leader of the opposition, fired up in electioneering mode, saying we should have been sent home, should never have been brought to this godforsaken outpost. A disgrace, she said. A shameful waste of taxpayers' money, a bad choice made by a gutless party who were not fit to govern this fine country. Then a seamless shift to promises of tax breaks, infrastructure projects, hospitals and nursing homes and high-speed trains.

She delivered it with passion, but her accusation was hazy: was it inhumane to send us here, or just improvident? The answer left open to interpretation.

We were cut off in more ways than one. Flint Island had been excised from Australia's migration zone. There was no recourse to the mainland from this place.

~

One morning, our weekly trip down to the shore was curtailed by an unexpected visitor. A group of kids were squinting up into the sky, taking turns with Cleary's binoculars. I assumed they were birdwatching, but a guard followed their line of sight and snapped sharply to attention.

A drone hovered overhead, directly above the children.

'Get them out of here,' said Tucker, a great bear of a guard with enormous arms. 'Back up the path, quick.' He unclipped his handgun from its holster.

'It's not one of yours?' I asked.

He shook his head. 'Must be media. Get the kids back inside.'

The second we were off the beach he started shooting – shot after shot rang out, none hitting their target. The drone zipped away, a black dot shrinking into the pale sky.

My fear was that this incident would spell the end of our outings. Kellahan and I had lobbied hard for these small glimpses of freedom, submitted our carefully worded rationale in writing, the page sprinkled liberally with references to mental health, emotional wellbeing, the need to mitigate trauma. I couldn't face the prospect of telling the kids there'd be no more excursions. That their world could shrink still further.

Those other children, the ones confined to the far side of the airstrip: I asked the beefy guard, Tucker, about them. Did they ever leave their compound? Could we arrange a joint outing, get all the kids together? He looked away. 'No chance,' he said.

~

Night was falling as I joined a small group gathered at the rec-room window. Two guards were approaching from the direction of the sea, picking their way across the rough ground towards an outbuilding beyond the perimeter fence, their khaki uniforms merging with the scrubby landscape. The light was fading, but the detail was discernible enough to send a chill through me: the men were carrying a stretcher. On it was a black shape that bore a strong resemblance to a body bag.

We watched the guards until they disappeared behind the outbuilding. Shortly they reappeared, just visible in the gloom, now minus their load. One of them clicked on a torch and we watched in silence as the beam wobbled along the boundary fence, around the corner, out of sight.

Later I found Tucker, the big guard, alone in the rec room, mopping the floor. I posed the question with no lead-in, gave him no time to prevaricate: what happened out there?

'Body on the rocks,' he answered. 'Looks like one of yours.' Then he set his mouth in a tight line, ignored my further questions, and left the room.

~

A week or so later, we awoke to fresh news: there had been a change of government. The screen was full of cheering crowds and breathless pundits gesturing at graphs. The new prime minister beamed and waved, thanked her family and supporters, addressed journalists by their first names. Promised a new era.

Victory was spelt out in colour-coded maps, the country daubed bright red with smaller patches of defeated blue. None of the maps depicted a dismal rock in the southern reaches of the Pacific. Out of sight, out of mind.

Halfway through the broadcast, as the incoming prime minister was delivering her victory speech, the screen went dead. And stayed that way: a black rectangle, a void in the wall.

The guards shrugged. No explanation was offered.

The place fell silent, save for the howling wind.

~

We heard it before we saw it: the drawn-out roar of its approach, the growling whistle of descent, like a bomb plummeting home; the engine growing louder, louder, then fading out as the machine lumbered to a stop down the far end of the wide road that divided the island.

Everyone rushed over to the window, the children jostling to see. A plane squatted on the asphalt. It was a sizeable craft, white with a long blue stripe, no company name or logo in evidence. We gaped at our strange visitor; this luxurious machine, great guzzler of precious jet fuel. Then the room broke into excited chatter.

Nothing was announced. The guards remained tight-lipped, the screen a void. But we stole glances at each other, the air between us buzzing with new hope: there could be only one explanation for an aircraft of that size to land in this remote location.

A new era.

It had come for us. We were leaving this godforsaken place.

CLEARY

Cleary gripped his mother's hand as the aircraft gathered speed, his back pressing into the seat as they hurtled down the runway, the plane trembling with the force of its own momentum, the thrum of the engines vibrating through the soles of his feet.

A skip, an almost imperceptible lift – the cord snapped, gravity's hold broken. An odd floating sensation in the pit of his stomach. Flying at last.

Face to the glass he watched the ground drop away beneath them; objects shrinking, the camera zooming out, the landscape transforming into a map.

The plane banked, turning as it climbed. Sliced down the middle by the black stripe of the runway, the island now resembled a photograph: no sign of life in either compound, the buildings static, nothing moving. He craned his neck, seeking one last glimpse of the shadow children, but the place looked deserted, no-one in sight.

Soon all they could see was empty sky and the distant sea below, sunlight winking and shattering on its surface. Kids undid their seatbelts to roam the aisles or crowd the windows, open-mouthed with wonder, drinking in this impossible perspective. Mia and Captain Lewis were huddled together at a window seat, pointing at the towering clouds. Cleary was transfixed by the dark mouths of the jet engines perched below each wing; by the air-vents, the tray tables, the call button. The sheer power and expense of this rare craft, sent just for them. Declan, who had already announced plans to become a pilot, was now wrangling snacks from the cabin crew, messing with the call button and testing the stewards' patience.

Soon they began passing over land, the interlocking grids and highways of a city, a horizontal honeycomb of suburbs; then a stretch of patchwork fields, eventually followed by a wide span of rusty red dirt, broken by mountain ranges and strange rock formations. A destination they'd never reached, a country they had not set foot in. No close encounters with kangaroos or koalas, like his granda had promised. No tropical fruit or golden beaches.

But Cleary didn't mind. You could see it on everyone's faces – the sense of hope rekindled, of sheer relief or quiet jubilation. They were going home: that was all that mattered.

Going home: those words were like a sweet ache. Like arms held wide, or the smell of your own pillow.

He was doing his best not to dwell on the other thing. He wasn't angry with Billie, not really. But it had hurt, the way she'd left so suddenly – no farewell hug, no send-off. His ma had offered an explanation: said Billie was helping the police figure things out, teaching them about the sickness, explaining what had happened on the ship. *She had to leave in a big hurry*, his ma said. *She didn't have time to say goodbye.* But surely she could have left a note?

His ma had pulled him close, said not to worry. His birthday was coming up soon. Gran and Granda would be over the moon to have him back. Did he have any ideas for presents? What about a cake?

Deep down he knew Billie wouldn't break her word. Once she'd finished her work – whatever she was busy with down there, in that unknown country – she would seek him out, get back in touch. Come visit him, like she had promised. After all, they'd made a pact: thick or thin, near or far, sea monsters or tornadoes, their friendship would not fade. Nothing would ever separate the two of them.

Cleary settled back and closed his eyes, let the thrum of the engines lull him towards sleep. Before long he was airborne himself, skimming high above the clouds, his wings spread wide and feathers shining, flying effortless and free through an infinite expanse of blue.

Book club notes are available at www.uqp.com.au

ACKNOWLEDGEMENTS

My heartfelt thanks to the following people: Andi Pekarek, for his steady encouragement, vital moral and practical support, and astute advice on drafts. Thanks to my literary agent, Martin Shaw, for unswerving guidance, advocacy and friendship; my publisher Aviva Tuffield for being such a gun editor and collaborator, and for patiently continuing to back me; my talented and ever-sunny editor Vanessa Pellatt, plus Jean Smith, Kylie Rathborne, Sally Wilson, Kate McCormack, Emily Knight and the whole lovely UQP team; Ian 'Eagle Eye' See for his top-notch proofreading; designer Christa Moffitt for the gorgeous cover; Tony Birch, for a fantastically unprintable quote; Anna Krien, Graeme Simsion, Jane Rawson, Favel Parrett and Jed Mercurio for their generous endorsements; Bob Carey-Grieve and Jon Bauer for crucial imaginative insights; Toni Jordan for being an enabling force of nature; and Joanne Manariti, photographer extraordinaire.

Thanks to Pip Smith, Eliza Watters and Alana Horsham for sharing their knowledge of tall ships and emergency medicine; beta reader Tessa Kum for invaluable input and enthusiasm; Jessica White for sharing the wisdom of her lived experience to help me realise Cleary's world more fully; Robert Lukins for kindly passing on secret background bizzo; Sara Knox for her compassionate steerage; and Damien Wilkins and Hazel Smith for their thoughtful responses. Thanks also to Billie, Helmut and Ursula Pekarek for helping me free up writing time; Lex Hirst and Catherine Lewis for their support; Varuna, the National Writers' House for a Second Book Fellowship; Mary Kruithof, author of *Fever Beach*, for telling the story of the *Ticonderoga*; and Clare Forster for the years we shared. Last, but never least, thanks to Pam, Dave and Niamh Mundell for their encouragement, advice and steadfast belief in the value of creative obsessions.